LOW TIDE

LOW TIDE

A Rarity Cove Novel

Leslie Tentler

Low Tide

Published by Left Field Press

Publisher's Note: This is a work of fiction. Names, characters, places, and incidents are a product of the author's imagination. Locales and public names are sometimes used for atmospheric purposes. Any resemblance to actual people, living or dead, or to businesses, companies, events, institutions, or locales is completely coincidental.

ISBN 978-0-9906390-6-0

The wheel of life takes one up and down by turn.

—Kalidasa

CHAPTER ONE

Los Angeles, California

"It was a good night." Bianca Rossi looked up at Carter St. Clair, a smile on her lips. Tall, with the willowy body of a supermodel, her sleek, raven hair fell around her shoulders. Her words were spiked with an Italian accent. "At least it was for me. I know how you claim to hate those kinds of things."

"They're pretentious and exhausting." Carter gave a resigned sigh. "Rich, over-privileged people preening and grabbing up swag, all in the name of charity."

"You're talking about your own kind, Carter. And it *was* for a good cause." Her manicured nails toyed with the covered buttons on his tuxedo shirt. "People go to events like that in hopes of mingling with someone like *you*. It's why they buy tickets and write those big checks in the first place."

When he merely shrugged, she ran her fingers through his thick, dark blond hair. "You've been distracted all night, gorgeous. What can I do to change that?"

Arms sliding around his neck, she pressed her mouth to his. As they kissed under the mansion's porte cochere, Bianca ran her hands over his chest. She got frisky when she drank, and she'd had plenty of the two-hundred-dollar-a-bottle champagne the gala had served. She had been caressing and fondling him as he drove them back to his home located in the hills high above Los Angeles. Pulling away from her, Carter punched the key fob he held, locking the Aston Martin from which they had emerged. Then he unlocked the home's front door.

"The security system's not on," Bianca commented.

Carter had noted the absence of the high-pitched shrill, too. "Housekeeping was here today. They've left it off before."

As they entered, Bianca's high heels tapped over the marble floor in the dramatic, two-story foyer. Carter tossed his keys onto the table that sat under a crystal chandelier, then turned to find Bianca in front of him. She slid his undone tie from his shirt collar. He'd left the black tuxedo jacket in the car, having escaped from it at his first opportunity.

"I feel *dirty*," she said in a silky voice, her espresso-brown eyes mischievous. "I'm going to take a shower. Join me?"

"I'll be up soon. I need to check my voice mail."

A faint petulance flickered over her features, but she kissed his jaw. "Don't make me wait too long. I might have to start without you."

He watched as she traveled up the staircase. To her credit, she wobbled only slightly from the champagne, her long, shapely legs displayed in a short haute couture cocktail dress. Once Bianca had disappeared onto the second-floor landing, Carter dug his cell phone from his pocket. He'd felt its repeated vibration as they posed for the cameras at the high-profile fundraiser. There were indeed several messages, including a rather tense one from Elliott Kaplan, his agent, another from his publicist and one from the producer of his most recent film, pressing him to attend a party he was having that weekend. His heart lifted as he played the final one—from Emily, his eight-year-old niece.

"Daddy said I could call to say hi," she said on the recording. Excitement in her voice, she updated him on an upcoming school field trip to the South Carolina Aquarium. Then, "Are you coming home for Nana's birthday?"

By *home*, she meant Rarity Cove, the seaside town near Charleston where Carter had grown up. Where all of his family still lived, with the exception of his younger sister, Mercer, who resided in Atlanta. In the recording's background, he could hear the happy chatter of his three-year-old nephew, Ethan. Emily rambled on until Carter's brother, Mark, confiscated the phone.

"Hope you're doing well, little brother," Mark said. At thirty-six, he was two years older than Carter and ran the historic St. Clair hotel that had been the family business for generations. "We *are* throwing a party for Mom's birthday—her sixty-fifth. If you can make it in, it'd be a real treat for her. Maybe you could extend your stay through Thanksgiving, since it's only a week later? We haven't seen you in a while, but we know how busy you are. Give us a call when you can. Samantha sends her love."

Carter had also heard Mark's wife, Samantha, in the background with Ethan. Tiredly clasping the back of his neck, he checked his wristwatch. With the time difference, it was far too late to return Mark's call. He wouldn't be able to attend his mother's birthday party, he knew, wishing the situation were different. Filming on his next movie—an action adventure—started in two weeks in Perth, Australia.

Despite the woman waiting for him upstairs, Carter wandered into the immense kitchen with granite counters and Mexican-tile floor, opened the Sub-Zero, stainless-steel refrigerator and took out a beer. He hadn't been anywhere close to keeping up with Bianca's alcohol intake and, in fact, had kept his wits about him so he could drive them back afterward. He needed some quiet to decompress. Bottle in hand, he walked out onto the large rear terrace and closed the glass doors behind him. The outdoor space featured an infinity edge pool and a dazzling view of the twinkling lights of Universal City and the San Fernando Valley below. It was a warm night for early November, and Carter settled into stillness as he sipped his beverage, watching coyotes as they traveled down the chaparral- and lupine-covered hillside, the animals visible in the strong moonlight.

Over the past three years, there had been little time for reflection. From television to a string of hit movies to press junkets, appearances, interviews and photo shoots, his life had been moving at the speed of a freight train. He loved filmmaking, but he also felt a growing weariness. Carter made a point of savoring the cool, yeasty taste of the beer, as well as the surrounding solitude. Then, a short time later, he left the empty bottle on the ledge and returned inside. He suspected Bianca was still waiting for him, probably in his walk-in rain shower. Bianca was young—in her early twenties—and a rising star on a new network television show. The two had begun seeing each other only a month ago, making them a hot topic for the celebrity news columns. After the gala, three cars of paparazzi had tailed them through the city and to the base of the canyon, until Carter had opened up the powerful sports car and left them in its dust.

As he took the stairs to the second level, he noticed the hallway appeared dark. Traveling toward the master suite, he heard no running water coming from its adjoining bathroom. With the amount of champagne she'd drunk, maybe Bianca had ended up facedown in his bed, asleep. But the suite's double doors stood open, revealing the king-size bed to still be made up and empty. Carter entered.

"Bianca?" Her dress lay crumpled on the floor, high-heeled designer shoes, bra and panties dropped a little farther away like a trail of seductive breadcrumbs. Moving closer to the closed bathroom door, he could see light seeping around its edges.

He knocked. "Bianca, you in there?"

No response. He tried the door handle, but it was locked from the inside. Faint alarm flickered through him. Had she had more to drink than he'd realized and passed out? Carter knocked on the door again and called her name louder. Something was wrong. He hesitated for a second before slamming his shoulder against the door. When it didn't budge, he remembered the key and rushed to the nightstand, where he opened the top drawer. Finding the key, he returned and quickly slid it into the lock, then turned the knob and pushed the door open. Carter's heart clenched. Bianca lay sprawled on her side, nude and turned away from him. Blood splattered the marble tile floor.

"Bianca! God!"

Racing inside, he fell to his knees beside her. Carefully rolling her onto her back, panic made him lightheaded. Blood slicked Bianca's skin—her neck, collarbone, breasts. Carter stared in disbelief at the gruesome wound to her throat.

But Bianca was looking at him, dazed. *Still alive.* Her body trembled, and little bubbles formed in the blood seeping from the ugly gash as she gasped for air.

Adrenaline sent him into action. He grabbed a towel from the vanity above him and pressed the cloth to her throat. She wheezed as the thick cotton began to soak with her blood.

"Stay with me," he pleaded. He had to call for help. God. He'd left his cell phone downstairs. Carter stood, slipping on the blood before getting his feet under him and stumbling into the bedroom. He grabbed the wireless handset on the nightstand and ran back. On his knees beside Bianca again, he dialed 911 with shaking fingers.

"I'm at 1211 Lone Oak Canyon Road," he rasped to the answering operator. "I need help, now!"

"What's your emergency, sir?"

He drew in a ragged breath. "There's a woman—she has a bad wound to her throat!"

"She's breathing?"

Anxiety knotted his belly as he looked at Bianca. Her lashes had fluttered closed, but he could still see the fast, shallow rise of her chest and hear her wet gasping. His throat convulsed. Carter's voice broke. "Yes. We need someone now! Please!"

"I'm sending police and an ambulance, sir. Stay on the line with me, all right?"

As the operator began giving instructions on what to do, Bianca's eyes slowly fluttered open again. They grew wider, focusing on a spot behind him. She kicked feebly and made a gurgling sound.

Carter's skin prickled in sudden awareness. He'd been so shell-shocked, so frantic to help Bianca…

Whoever had done this was still here.

Before he could turn, a stabbing force hit his right shoulder. *Jesus!* Agony hurdled through him. Carter managed to twist halfway onto his back, falling on top of Bianca as a strangled cry tore from his throat. His vision swam, his heartbeat roaring in his ears as he used his forearm to try to defend himself against whatever plunged into him again, this time between his ribs. Everything exploded into red.

Can't breathe.

More vicious strikes sliced through his chest, the pain nearly ripping his soul from his body. His lungs, his arm, were on fire. Unable to move, Carter heard his own strained gasps growing farther away.

He fell into darkness.

***

Mark St. Clair paced the corridor of Cedars-Sinai Medical Center, a short distance away from the ICU waiting area where he had left his mother, Olivia. Despite the vibrant mid-morning sky visible through the windows, he felt an all-consuming grayness. He paused as two LAPD detectives, based on the holstered weapons and gold shields at their waists, exited the elevator. Mark had been told they were on their way, and he wanted to speak with them out of Olivia's hearing.

"Is there any change in your brother's condition?" one of them, a heavyset, African-American male who looked to be in his fifties, asked somberly once they approached and introduced themselves.

"He made it through surgery. He's in the ICU." Mark dragged a hand through his hair, unable to suppress the tremor in his voice. "The surgical team said it's touch and go. The next twenty-four hours are critical."

They nodded their understanding. Detective Warren, the one who asked about Carter's condition, indicated a row of upholstered chairs. "You have our sympathy, Mr. St. Clair. Would you like to sit down or go to a private room? We know you just got off a plane from the East Coast."

The hallway was actually quiet, with police watching the floor and making sure no one got near the closed-off portion of the ICU without authorization. Mark was aware they were on the lookout for paparazzi hoping to get a photo of his brother. It sickened him.

"I'd rather stand." He'd been awakened by the ringing phone in the middle of the night. Carter's agent, Elliott Kaplan, had shakily relayed what had happened, at least as much as he'd known at the time. Mark and Olivia had caught the first flight out of the Charleston airport, while Samantha stayed behind with the children. Mercer's flight from Atlanta had landed a short while ago, and she was en route to the hospital.

"Where is she?" Mark asked tightly, referring to Carter's attacker.

"Kelsey Dobbins is in custody at the downtown precinct," the second detective, a tall Latino named Ortega, assured him. "She's being transferred later today for a psych evaluation. She has a documented history of paranoid schizophrenia. Hallucinations, hearing voices—"

Mark's jaw ached. He felt no sympathy. "I don't give a damn if she is mentally disturbed. I want her in prison."

Ortega nodded. "We'll do everything we can."

Since his arrival at the hospital, Mark had witnessed the nonstop news coverage on the waiting room's mounted television—video of police cars surrounding Carter's gated home, yellow crime scene tape cordoning off its front entrance. Since the media didn't know who they were, Mark had been able to get Olivia past the photographers and fans gathered on the street in front of the hospital. Kaplan was sitting with her now, appearing anxious and disheveled himself, doing his best to console her.

This didn't seem real. The more salacious news programs were describing the attack on Carter and Bianca Rossi as a slaughter. Rumors were circulating online that both were dead. At least for now, that was the case for only one of them. Rossi had been declared dead at the scene. Overwhelmed, Mark drew in a breath and rubbed his burning eyes.

"Are you all right, Mr. St. Clair?" Ortega asked. "As a family member, we have some questions for you, but we can wait if—"

He shook his head. "No. Let's do this now."

"Did your brother mention having a stalker?" Warren settled his hands on the belt at his thick waist, one of them just above his holstered gun.

"He's had a few of them. It comes with the territory," Mark said as a nurse went past.

"Did he mention Dobbins specifically?"

"He said she'd sent letters. A lot of them." He recalled Carter having described them as sad and a little disturbing. "He never mentioned her trying to make physical contact, though."

"It's possible he didn't know," Ortega said. "We talked to his studio. Six weeks ago, Dobbins was intercepted by security, attempting to get onto one of the lots where he was shooting scenes. A woman who works for the maid service your brother uses at his residence also recognized her from a photo."

Mark's stomach fluttered. "In what context?"

"Dobbins rang the bell at the front door—must've climbed the fence to get onto the property. She kept loitering even after being told Mr. St. Clair wasn't home. She left only when the maid threatened to call police."

"When was this?"

"Last week."

Regret spiraled through him. Carter should have had better security. But he had insisted he didn't want to be one of those people who went around with bodyguards or an entourage. Mark believed Carter had never been fully prepared for the level of stardom he had reached, and so quickly. After leaving the soap opera he had been on for over six years, he had appeared on a hit television show, eventually getting out of his contract so he could work full time in movies. Last year, he was an Academy Award nominee. Mark might be biased, but he believed Carter had lost only because the recognition went to another actor *posthumously*. An ache filled him. He didn't want that word ever being used in connection with his brother. "Have you spoken with Elliott Kaplan about this woman?"

"We did," Warren acknowledged. "Mr. Kaplan said he knew about Dobbins but had written her off as just another overzealous fan."

They asked Mark a few more questions, then Ortega gave him his business card and encouraged him to call if he thought of anything important.

"We'll be in touch," he added as both men shook Mark's hand again. "We're praying for your brother. You and he look a little alike, you know."

As they began to walk away, Mark halted them. He couldn't help it. He wanted to know if this woman—this psychopath—felt any remorse. "Detectives. Has Dobbins said anything? Can I ask that?"

Warren finally spoke. "She's saying she didn't do it."

Shocked by the statement, anger flushed through Mark's body. He already knew police had captured Dobbins in the house when they arrived after Carter's 911 call. She was in the home's palatial master bathroom with Carter and Bianca Rossi, in fact, her hands and clothing covered in their blood.

"She's a delusional schizophrenic," Ortega reminded. "Her prints are on the shears used in the attack. It's basically an open-and-shut case."

As the elevator doors closed behind the two detectives, a second set opened inside the bay. Mercer emerged. When she saw Mark, her reddened eyes flooded with tears.

"Oh, God," she murmured, going into his embrace. He held her, letting her cry against his chest before gently setting her away from him.

She sniffled. They'd spoken for only a short time once her plane had landed at LAX. "Has anything changed?"

"No. Come on. I'll take you to Mom. She needs you."

Sometime later, they were given permission to see Carter. Mark stood at his brother's bedside with a heavy heart. Only two visitors were allowed into the ICU at a time, and he'd gone in first with Olivia, while Mercer waited with Kaplan outside.

Carter lay comatose, pale, IV lines and tubes running in and out of his body. A heart monitor in the room's corner beeped, accompanied by the mechanical whooshing sound of the ventilator breathing for him. Life support. Fear clawed at

Mark's gut. Surgical dressing covered the wounds to Carter's chest and right shoulder. His lungs had been punctured in multiple places, the chief surgeon had told them in the private consultation room. Worst, Carter's heart had been lacerated. There had been no choice—they'd had to crack open his sternum in the ER. Cardiac damage and the hypovolemic shock resulting from the severe blood loss remained the largest concerns.

Mark stood by, helpless, as Olivia wept. She sat in a chair on the left side of Carter's bed, clasping his still fingers.

"My darling boy," she said softly.

His right hand and forearm were bandaged, as well. He had tried to defend himself against the large, pointed-end shears Dobbins had plunged repeatedly into him, wielding them like a knife. Mark tried to swallow, but couldn't.

Carter had flatlined twice—once in the ambulance and a second time before the surgical team could get him onto a bypass machine. In Olivia's absence, the chief surgeon had confided to Mark the survival rate for such trauma wasn't good. He winced inwardly, aware the surgeon had been trying to prepare him.

Once Olivia left the room, Mark moved closer to the bed. Throat tight, he stroked a comforting hand through Carter's hair. He hoped that, somehow, his brother could sense his presence. That he was in no pain.

"You're a *fighter*, Carter," he urged, emotion thickening his voice. "*Fight.* Don't leave us like this."

He'd had to be strong in front of his mother. But now, tears blurring his vision, Mark said a silent, fervent prayer.

CHAPTER TWO

Rarity Cove, South Carolina
Ten Weeks Later

"If you wanted an ocean view, you could've had that in *Malibu*," Elliott Kaplan pointed out tensely.

Carter stood with him on the deck of the rented beach house, staring onto the rough waters of the Atlantic.

"I needed to be out of LA," he said, his voice so low it was nearly carried away by the wind. It was a gray, chilly mid-January afternoon—cold enough even in South Carolina that he wore a heavy sweater to block the ocean breeze. Carter shivered. His body reacted poorly to the cold these days, as it did most things.

Elliott started to say something, but stopped when the glass door opened and Mercer emerged.

"It's time for your meds," she said as her long, honey-blond hair whipped around her face. Her expression was apologetic for having interrupted them. Coming forward, she carried a small paper cup that contained a number of pills, as well as a glass of water. Repressing a sigh, Carter took them.

"Thanks, Merce."

She laid a hand on his arm. "Wouldn't you rather talk in-side? I'll go upstairs if you need privacy."

He shook his head, avoiding the concern in her eyes. "We'll be in soon. I just need some air."

Once she returned indoors, Elliott moved closer. More than a decade older than Carter, he had become a friend but remained first and foremost his agent. Their three-year relationship had begun when Carter relocated from New York City to the West Coast, parting ways with his former representation. Gently bracing his hands on Carter's upper arms, Elliott studied him. "Damn, but it's good to see you up and getting around under your own steam."

The statement was barely true. Carter found himself fatigued by just the walk from the home's interior. He wore sweatpants and slip-on loafers, and he relied on a cane when traveling more than a few dozen feet.

"You look good—"

"I look like hell."

"No one expected you to come back from this. Give yourself a break," Elliott countered in a soft voice. He asked carefully, "How're you progressing?"

Carter glanced down at his right hand and one of the scars clothing couldn't hide. It marred his palm, limiting dexterity in two of his fingers. He thought of the other mutilations on his body. Even now, his chest ached, and his right arm was in a sling. He'd had a second surgery to repair the partially lacerated tendon in his right shoulder once the doctors had deemed his heart strong enough. Carter had been hospitalized for seven weeks at Cedars-Sinai, three of them spent in the ICU. After finally being released, he had slipped out of Los Angeles, with Mark's help, by private plane.

"I'm improving," he replied quietly.

Elliott narrowed his eyes at him. "I heard you fired another physical therapist."

So he had been talking to Mark. Perhaps it was what had spurred his visit here. But Carter didn't want to discuss it, and he figured Elliott already knew the specifics.

"Look, just because the one guy was a jerk doesn't mean they're all bad," Elliott reasoned. "Your brother said you barely gave this last one a chance."

"We're looking for someone new. We have recommendations from the hospital."

"I have a few excellent PTs to recommend myself. And they're all back on the *West* Coast." When Carter didn't respond, Elliott continued. "So you came back here to be in the bosom of family. After all that's happened, I get that. But you need to come back to LA where we can get you the kind of leading-edge care—"

"I *can't* be in LA right now. Try to understand that." Carter was aware of his curtness. Elliott had only been here an hour, and already he felt his strength and patience waning. "And I have everything I need here. This isn't Mayberry."

Elliott let out a hollow laugh. "I drove through town on the way from the airport. Could've fooled me."

"I'm talking about *Charleston*. The doctors there are as good as anywhere." Carter walked slowly to the deck's railing, wincing slightly as the crisp breeze cut through him. Mercer was right—he should go back inside, but after what had seemed like endless confinement to a hospital bed, he craved the freedom of being outdoors. Hearing the screech of seagulls that flew overhead, he peered at the waves crashing onto the shore below. The house was set on a bluff, rare to the lowcountry, on a stretch of private beach. Still, Carter had seen beachcombers walking through from time to time. He wondered how long he would have before his presence was discovered, whether he would need to hire security to keep photographers with high-powered lenses out of the area.

"I'm pushing, I know that," Elliott conceded, coming to stand beside him. "But you can't blame me for wanting you back where you belong. Where you can get into a first-class therapy regimen. All you need is to get back your strength and start hitting the gym—"

"*That's all*," Carter murmured, his tone cynical.

"How bad is the scarring?"

His stomach hardened at Elliott's directness. Absently, Carter's fingers rose to touch the center of his chest. He couldn't detect the grim, vertical scar from the open-heart surgery through the wool of his sweater, but he knew it was there. His body, like his face, was his Hollywood currency.

"Bad enough," he rasped.

Pain registered in Elliott's eyes. "So they'll use body makeup or a stand-in. Or we can choose the right parts that don't require skin. Hell, these days they can CGI-out anything. You're an in-demand *star*, Carter," he emphasized, his voice lowering. "Now more than ever. You stared into the abyss and *lived*."

You lived.

Thinking of Bianca, a recurring blackness washed over him. Kelsey Dobbins was *his* stalker. If Bianca hadn't been with him that night, she would still be alive. Carter closed his eyes briefly, shaking off the despondency that seemed to always be just under his surface. In a slightly breathless voice, he said, "You've never told me why you're here, Elliott. Why you flew all the way across—"

"You didn't give me a choice. You weren't taking my

phone calls."

"Not when you call three times a day."

Elliott shoved his fingers through his salt-and-pepper hair, a sign of his rising frustration. His voice roughened. "Maybe I just needed to see you with my own eyes. Have you thought I'm here because I *care* about you?"

But despite their friendship, Carter also understood it was Elliott's business to evaluate his progress. He needed to see how well he was doing, whether he looked even remotely strong enough to start considering work again. Carter also knew he was the biggest-name actor on Elliott's client roster. He wanted a plan for his return. But at the thought of going back to the West Coast, he felt himself shutting down.

"They recast your role in *Game Town.* It hasn't hit the trades yet, but it went to Chris Hemsworth."

Carter had no response.

"Look, I'm not going to claim I don't have a dog in this hunt. You've made us *both* a lot of money—something I hope continues. But you mean more to me than that." Elliott swallowed. "You're *special* to me, Carter. I hope you know that. I…don't want to see this tragedy beat you."

He stared at him so emotionally Carter had to look away.

"I just want you to know I'm so goddamn sorry for what happened to you."

He stayed for the remainder of the day, keeping Carter occupied with Hollywood gossip, including who was sleeping with whom and the latest greenlit movie projects. They shared an early dinner, the food courtesy of Samantha, Mark's wife who owned, but no longer managed, the popular Café Bella just off the town square. Then Elliott embraced him and said good-bye, but not without a final plea for him to work harder at his recuperation. He'd departed in his rental car—a top-of-the-line BMW—headed to Charleston to catch an evening flight out, due back in LA for a meeting the next day. Carter had watched as the property's automated gates closed behind him.

"Are you all right?" Mercer asked a short time later as she came up behind him, laying a hand on his shoulder. Brooding, he sat on the sofa and stared into the flames of a gas-fueled, stacked-stone fireplace. Several movie scripts that Elliott had delivered, hoping Carter would read them, were stacked on the coffee table. He felt exhausted, despite the fact he had excused himself temporarily from Elliott's company to take a nap, fatigued by the conversation, the persistent pain and the hurdles he knew he must eventually cross. He looked up as Mercer came around the sofa and sat beside him.

"You hardly touched dinner. You're hurting, aren't you?"

"I'm okay," he lied.

"Is your agent always like that? He reminds me of an overcaffeinated squirrel trying to cross the interstate."

Carter forced a faint smile, knowing Mercer was trying to lighten his mood. For a time, they sat in silence, until she said, "I can't believe I'm going back home in a few days. I could call and extend my leave."

He shook his head. "You've been here for weeks, Merce. You have a life of your own to get back to."

"I don't want to leave you." She bit her lip worriedly. "All alone in this big house."

"I'm hardly *alone.* Mark and Samantha are ten minutes away and check in constantly, not to mention Mom, and Jolene's here, too," he reminded, referring to the motherly but slightly bossy head of housekeeping who had worked at the

St. Clair for as long as Carter could remember. Mark was lending her out to him for housework a couple of times a week since she could be trusted with discretion.

"I still don't understand why you won't take one of the bungalows at the resort."

"I've explained why."

"Why not stay with Mom, then? The Big House has plenty of room," Mercer persisted, referring to the white-columned estate home on the edge of the St. Clair property. It was where they had grown up.

"So she can fuss over me like I'm a toddler?" He recoiled in feigned horror. "No, thanks. She does enough of that here. Besides, now that she has a *gentleman friend*, as she calls it, I don't want to cramp her love life. Dad's been gone a long time, and she's finally met someone. She's getting older and doesn't need her invalid son to look after."

Mercer frowned. "You're hardly an invalid. It takes you a little effort, but you can take care of yourself for the most part. And Mom would *love* to have you. I think her feelings are hurt you aren't staying with her."

His guilt flared. But even if he'd wanted to stay with their mother, the home's high staircase would be too much. Carter sighed. "I just need some independence after being confined for so long. And *you're* needed back in Atlanta."

He didn't have to provide further rationalization. Mercer had a career she loved there, as well as a husband who had recently been diagnosed with prostate cancer. Dr. Jonathan Leighton was a professor of English literature at a private women's college in the city. He was also nearly twenty years older than Mercer. At one time, she had been one of his students. It all sounded a bit scandalous, but the entire family had grown fond of Jonathan, and despite their substantial age difference, he and Mercer seemed happy. The cancer was caught early, and Jonathan was young for such a prognosis, but the diagnosis was relatively recent. He needed her with him for moral support.

"You should be with your husband." Carter reached over and briefly squeezed her fingers. "Besides, this isn't the first time you've had to give up your life for a family crisis. I won't have you doing it again because of me."

They talked awhile longer, until Mercer doled out his evening medication and said she was going up to her room to call Jonathan. After a kiss on his stubbled cheek, she checked the security system's console and departed.

Carter remained on the couch, alone in the quiet of the well-furnished beach home. Of the lowcountry tidewater style, the six-thousand-square-foot, five-bedroom structure featured multiple sets of French doors for accessing the wide, wraparound, covered porch. The home had multiple fireplaces, a gourmet kitchen and a sweeping solarium overlooking the ocean. There was also a bottom-level workout room and a heated, saltwater pool, currently covered for the winter. While still in LA, Carter had checked on its availability and leased the house under an alias. It suited his needs: furnished, private, secure and with an elevator—installed by a former, elderly owner—so he wouldn't be forced to climb stairs.

He *had* considered taking up residence in one of the seaside bungalows on the St. Clair property, as Mark had suggested. But he also knew once the paparazzi discovered he was no longer in LA, his family's hotel would be the first place they would look. He didn't want to interfere with the St. Clair's business or wish that level of insanity on anyone.

He *would* miss Mercer, he admitted to himself. Getting along without her worried him some. Carter adjusted the sling supporting his right arm, the pain in his shoulder nearly making his breath catch. He didn't have to wear the sling all the time, but it helped. At least he was left-handed.

A short time later, he used the remote control to cut off the gas inside the hearth. Reaching for the cane he'd leaned against the sofa arm, he rose to go upstairs. He exited the elevator on the house's top floor, where pearlescent light spilled from the large master suite that included a king-size bed and separate sitting room. The suite's oceanfront wall was made almost entirely of glass and provided a stunning view on moonlit nights. Entering the space, Carter looked out, white-capped waves visible as they crashed onto the shore below. In the wall's glass, he could almost make out his shaggy hair and frail reflection.

Even with the elevator, the trip to his bedroom had left him shaky and slightly breathless, his body weak from the damage that had been done.

After struggling in the bathroom to remove the sling, brush his teeth and undress himself, he lay down in bed, waiting for the pain medication to kick in. He couldn't help it. Carter thought of Kelsey Dobbins, the woman who had hunted him down. He traced the surgical mutilation on his bare chest, flinching inwardly at it and the other raised, puffy scars from the large pair of shears she had plunged repeatedly into him. Five times, to be exact. She had taken them from the desk in his upstairs study, according to the police and forensics reports. His eyelids hot and gummy, Carter stared blindly at the high ceiling. He recalled the dozens of letters Dobbins had sent him. In them, she had referred to herself as his *number-one fan* and professed her undying love. Those rambling letters were now in police custody.

Before leaving, Elliott had carefully asked again whether any of his memory had returned.

Once Carter had been weaned from the ventilator and was able to talk, the detectives had shown him Dobbins's mug-shot. She was tall and heavyset for a woman, with dark eyes and black hair. He hadn't recognized her. He could recall nothing of the attack, in fact, the black spots in his memory too large. As he thought of Bianca, guilt cut through him.

With the extent of his trauma, the specialists had said memory loss surrounding the attack wasn't uncommon. There was a slight possibility he might eventually remember some things, but more than likely, he never would.

Maybe it was a blessing.

Mark had attended Dobbins's hearing on his behalf. She had been remanded into the custody of the state of California and, ultimately, declared unfit to stand trial. She was confined to a mental institution. Her face was now nearly as famous as his. The media had gotten photos of her, had plastered them in magazines, on the Internet, on television.

Carter drifted into an uneasy sleep, until a dream brought him awake again. Breathless, he swallowed heavily in the darkness, feeling the too-hard beat of his heart.

In the dream, he had been on the red carpet when he saw Kelsey Dobbins staring back at him from a cordoned-off crowd of fans. He'd stood, paralyzed, as she had broken through the barricade, threading past the others until her icy fingers clenched his arm. Her words echoed inside him.

I love you more.

CHAPTER THREE

It was the dog's barking that pulled Quinn Reese from her meditation. She sat in *Padmasana*, facing the ocean and wearing an old Stanford University sweat jacket, her wavy auburn hair wound into a loose knot from which tendrils escaped in the strong breeze. Having completed her yoga practice, she had been focused on mindful breathing when Doug's excited barking pulled her back to the cawing seagulls and snap of cold, briny sea air. Opening her eyes, she shielded her face from the anemic slant of sunlight that had temporarily broken through the clouds. Surprise filtered through her as she recognized the approaching man Doug now trotted alongside. Quinn stood and brushed off her yoga pants, knocking away grains of sand her bare feet and the wind had scattered onto her mat.

As he came closer, a smile of recognition on his even features, Quinn felt a tug of bittersweet emotion.

"Mark," she said as her former brother-in-law reached her. Taking her hands briefly in his, he then embraced her. Quinn closed her eyes against his chest. In the time since her sister's passing, she'd seen Mark only on occasion, whenever she was in town for a visit and wanted to see her niece. The last time had been over three years ago, something she regretted.

"I hope you don't mind. I went by the house." Mark wore khakis, loafers and a windbreaker, giving her the impression he wasn't working at the St. Clair that day. "Nora gave me your new cell number, but you didn't answer. She told me where I could probably find you."

Quinn thought of her phone buried inside her yoga bag, aware she had purposely been keeping it on mute.

"You were looking for me?" Wobbling a bit, she slid her feet into the shoes she had removed earlier, ignoring the sand still stuck between her toes. "How'd you know I was here? In town, I mean. I've only been home a few days."

"It's a small town. Word gets around."

Quinn felt a flush creep onto her cheeks at the concern in his eyes, wondering just how many people here knew her business. She shoved her hair back from her face in the soughing breeze. "I was…planning to call once I got settled in. I've been hoping to see Emily. I know it's been a long time. Too long."

Mark nodded.

A pang inside her, she shook her head and forced a smile. "She probably won't even remember me."

"Of course she does. She gets a kick out of your gifts."

Quinn thought of the last thing she mailed to Emily, an oriental fan and child-size kimono she had purchased in San Francisco's Chinatown. That was last summer. "I was going to ask if you could bring her by Mom's for a visit. I wasn't sure about coming to your house since—"

"You're Emily's *aunt*. You're welcome anytime. Nora, too," Mark assured her. "Samantha and I want Emily to stay connected to her mother's side of the family."

Nora had given Quinn a distinctly different impression of Samantha St. Clair. But she also knew her mother was less than accepting of Mark's new marital status. Five years had gone by since the car accident that killed Quinn's older sister, Shelley. Mark had remarried some two years later. But it was as if her mother expected him to live out the rest of his life as a widower, continuing to mourn her daughter just as she still did. Shelley had always been the apple of Nora's eye. Quinn suspected she had taken Mark's remarriage as a betrayal.

"Congratulations on getting married again." Her heart squeezed as she added, "And on your little boy. Ethan."

Mark thanked her. His features appeared pained as he studied her. "I…heard about the miscarriage, Quinn. And about the separation. I'm sorry."

She simply nodded, watching as Doug ran along the shore, harassing seagulls fishing in the tide. She was sure Mark had questions, but to his credit, he didn't push.

"Who's your friend?" he asked as the dog bounded back to them a few seconds later, shaking off his wet fur and sending cold saltwater flying. Shaggy-haired and underweight, he appeared to be a combination of several breeds, most predominantly a wheaten terrier. Mark bent to pet him.

"That's Doug," she said.

He squinted up at her. "Doug the dog?"

She shrugged. "It's a placeholder until I can think of something better. Or until someone claims him. I found him on the beach the first day I was here, and he followed me home. I've put up fliers, but no one's called about a lost dog. I took him to the vet to see if he'd been microchipped, but no luck. They said he's already been neutered, but I got vaccinations for him, just in case. Nora hates him with a passion. She claims he's bringing fleas into her B&B."

Mark chuckled.

Quinn pulled her sweat jacket more tightly around herself, trying to ward off the chill, which had grown sharper without the distraction of her yoga practice. Carefully, she asked the question that was on her mind. "Mark…how is Carter? There hasn't been much on the news about him lately."

Her own personal tragedy had been a mere footnote on the televised sports programs, focused solely on Jake Medero's loss, not hers. But what happened to Carter had been a headline story for weeks. No matter what feelings she had about Mark's brother, the brutal stalker attack had shocked and disturbed her.

"That's what I wanted to talk to you about, actually. I was wondering if I could buy you a cup of coffee? The boardwalk's closed, but my car's here. We could go into the square. Nora said you walked here."

"I've got Doug."

"We'll sit outside, then. At least we'll be off the water where it's warmer."

Curiosity nudged her.

"All right," she said hesitantly. "But make mine green tea."

***

"You're between jobs right now. It makes perfect sense."

Clasping her teacup, Quinn faintly shook her head. They sat on the bricked patio of the Coffee Cabana, which had the benefit of an outdoor heater.

"I'm licensed for PT in *California*," she reasoned. "You need someone now, and it could take several weeks for me to get instated here."

And that was if she even made the decision to stay.

"I've already spoken about you to Carter's cardiac physician in Charleston," Mark told her. "He's researched your credentials and knows your relationship to our family. He said your CSCS certification could help us get around the rules and let you start working with him before your license comes through here."

In addition to her doctorate in physical therapy, Quinn was also a certified strength and conditioning specialist. She'd worked with professional athletes to improve their performance. It was how she had met Jake, in fact.

She sighed. "I don't know…"

"We're in need of someone *good*, Quinn, and that's you. Everyone I've talked to says Brookhaven is the top sports medicine and rehabilitation center on the West Coast."

Quinn felt the teacup's fading warmth against her palms. *Where she'd worked. Past tense.* Following her separation from Jake, she had tried to get her former position back. Quinn had been readily offered the job, only to have it yanked away from her at the last minute. She'd also found herself blackballed at two other large rehab centers in the Bay Area. It wasn't a mystery to her as to why. Attempting to ease her thoughts, she peered out over the town square with its tiered fountain and ancient live oaks that provided a canopy for the hibernating green space. Nostalgia filtered through her as she remembered summer festivals and picnics here as a child.

"Carter hasn't responded well to physical therapy so far," Mark confided. "He needs to build up his strength and endurance. He has fatigue and some occasional breathlessness. His sternal precautions ended a couple of weeks ago, and his doctors are adamant he needs to do more."

He placed his coffee mug on the table, his forehead creasing. "He's unmotivated and sleeping too much. I worry he's leaning on pain pills to get him through the day."

Quinn frowned at Mark's confession. She was aware of Carter's open-heart surgery, one of the many grim details that had made the news. Her voice gentled. "Depression *is* common with cardiac patients."

"Don't ask. He won't see a mental health professional. He gets angry if you even suggest it." He shook his head in obvious frustration.

"He sounds like a handful," she said, forcing a smile.

She tried to process the situation, still surprised that *Carter St. Clair* was here in Rarity Cove. Beneath the table, Doug released a sigh. He'd lapped up the water the shop's waitress had brought to him in a plastic bowl and now lay on his side, napping, his leash looped around one of the table legs.

"There's outpatient therapy at the medical center in Charleston, but with Carter's celebrity, it hasn't proven to be the most practical idea," Mark said. "We're trying to keep his presence here under the radar."

"But I still don't understand, why me?" she asked, puzzled. "There must be scores of properly licensed PTs in Charleston who can do private, at-home sessions."

"I need to be completely honest with you, Quinn." Mark hesitated. "Carter's been through three therapists already. Although, the first one wasn't his fault."

Anger reflected on his features. "The guy had excellent references and came highly recommended, but the greed got to him. Carter found a hidden camera he'd planted. He was in negotiation to sell photos to *Starglazer* magazine."

Quinn stiffened. "I hope you reported him."

"To the hospital and to the APTA. He won't be working anywhere else anytime soon."

"What about the other two therapists?"

"I don't have a similar excuse. Carter clashed with both of them. He let the most recent one go last week."

"And you think things would be different with me?"

"Maybe. You have a history with us, Quinn. He'd be less likely to dismiss you so easily. You've also been trained to be part of a more *holistic* approach, and I think that's something Carter needs. That might be standard in California, but it's still somewhat uncommon here. We need more than just someone who'll run him through the exercises, which he currently isn't doing, anyway. I don't know, maybe you could work with him on meditation or yoga to relieve stress and try to improve his outlook? He's under a lot of pressure—the studios want him back to fulfill commitments."

"I *do* incorporate therapeutic yoga and meditation with my patients who are willing," Quinn explained. "But Carter would have to be open to it, and from what I'm hearing..."

"I'm just looking for something that might help." Mark rubbed a hand over his mouth, his concern visible. "I'm worried about him, Quinn. He won't talk much about it, but he's been thrown hard by all this—his own near-death experience and compromised health, Bianca Rossi's murder."

Quinn thought of the up-and-coming young actress. Images of her with Carter had been aired nonstop in the weeks following the attack. "Did you know her?"

He shook his head. "No, we never met."

With a tense release of breath, Quinn became aware of the winter sun finally beginning to burn off the clouds that had been hovering since she had arrived in town. Farther down the square, the bell tower on the centuries-old, Methodist church chimed. Where Mark and Shelley were married.

"My family *trusts* you, Quinn. And you already know Carter. The last two therapists treated him with kid gloves because of who he is, and he used it to deflect their efforts. You wouldn't be so intimidated by his fame."

She understood the implication. Pensively, she toyed with the teabag that sat on the edge of her saucer. Quinn had been married for ten months to Jake Medero, a high-profile running back for the San Francisco Breakers—technically, she still was. The state of California required a six-month waiting period before finalizing a divorce, and there were still four months remaining. As she thought of the situation she had fled, Quinn's stomach soured. It was another reason why she wanted nothing to do with someone else considered to be a god by the rest of the country. Not to mention, she had her own clandestine, awkward history with Carter. But the desperation in Mark's voice tugged at her.

"Carter's changed since you knew him. Despite his fame, he's grown up. He's not the guy you knew in high school."

Quinn doubted it. If anything, wealth and fame only brought out the worst traits in people, she'd learned. "I don't know, Mark. How long do I have to consider this?"

"We'd like a decision soon. Mercer's been staying with him for the past few weeks, but she's going back to Atlanta."

"Wait. It's a full-time, live-in position?" She bit her lip. That was something she hadn't expected.

"Not necessarily. We have other help, and Carter doesn't require constant supervision. He's ambulatory and able to handle the basics. I'm not expecting you to be his caretaker. You could come and go as you please." Pausing, Mark stared briefly into his coffee mug. "Mercer's been a big help, and losing her is going to be an adjustment, but Carter and I agree we don't want her delaying her life again for family."

Quinn nodded, understanding that, too. After Shelley's death, Mercer had come back to Rarity Cove to help Mark care for Emily. They all owed her. It was a role Nora should have fit into, but she had been far too devastated by Shelley's death. Her constant crying and hysterics wouldn't have been healthy for a child Emily's age, who'd been suffering from emotional trauma herself. And Quinn had been completing her residency at the UC San Francisco Medical Center, not that it was a bulletproof excuse. Guilt nagged at her. She had intentionally disappeared from Rarity Cove. Even her sister's death had brought her home only temporarily.

"Does Carter know about this?"

"I wanted to talk to you first."

She peered out again across the town square. An image of Shelley as high school homecoming queen—blond and luminous, waving as she rode atop a float traveling down Main Street—appeared in Quinn's mind. She had loved her sister, she missed her, but she'd always taken a backseat to her.

It was disconcerting to be back here. Quinn was painfully aware that, at the age of thirty-two, she had little funds and not really anywhere else to go. She'd left California and gone to the other side of the country to escape her problems.

Mark used a pen to write on the back of one of the Coffee Cabana's paper napkins, then slid it toward her. "Just think about it, all right? We'd pay you well for your time."

Quinn looked at the napkin. The amount he'd written on it was startling.

CHAPTER FOUR

They sat in Mark's Volvo as it idled outside Quinn's childhood home, a large, revival-style brick colonial. The carved-wood sign in front proclaimed it The Reese House Bed & Breakfast.

"I'm happy for you, Mark. I want you to know that," Quinn said sincerely. "I believe Shelley would've wanted you to move on with your life."

Mark peered at the house. "She blames me, you know."

Quinn laid a hand on his arm. "There was *nothing* you could've done. You were hit head on by a drunk driver and were injured yourself. Deep down, Mom knows you're not responsible and that you still have a life to lead."

He appeared doubtful, but after a moment, he changed topics. "You'll come on Saturday, then?"

The family dinner Mark had invited her to would give her a chance to see Emily…as well as meet Mark's new wife and son. But Quinn also understood the real reason for the invitation. It would let her evaluate whether she might be able to work with Carter, at least from a personality standpoint. She couldn't control the small flutter in her stomach. Despite the fact they'd been in-laws, her exposure to Carter had been minimal during Mark and Shelley's marriage. He'd been in New York, and she had been on the West Coast. The few times when they *had* crossed paths at the occasional family gathering, things had been polite but impersonal. She and Carter hadn't been in the same room since Shelley's funeral more than five years ago, in fact. At that time, he'd been a soap opera actor, on the cusp of superstardom. And she had been too grief-stricken to dwell on what had happened between them when they'd basically both been just kids. Quinn had never told anyone about it. Based on Mark's apparent unawareness, neither had Carter, she guessed. She'd always figured it had been so meaningless to him that he'd simply shrugged off the entire incident.

Quinn thought of the substantial hourly rate Mark had written on the napkin. If she could set teenage hurts aside, it would provide her with some needed income while she tried to figure out her next steps in life.

"I'll be there at six," she confirmed, releasing a tight breath as she exited the Volvo. She opened the rear door so Doug could bound out and retrieved her yoga bag from the backseat. It also now contained a copy of Carter's medical history. "Thanks for the ride."

"Remind Nora to let us know any time she'd like to see Emily. She calls, but not often. You look good, Quinn."

Lifting her hand in a small wave, she watched as Mark's vehicle disappeared down the residential street that was six blocks from the Rarity Cove public beach. The B&B sat on a roomy cul-de-sac, a little farther back from the other properties. As she went up the sidewalk, she noticed the crepe myrtles on the property's edge that had recently been pruned back to promote growth in the spring, as well as the trellis against the house's front that in summer hung heavy with confederate jasmine. A sunroom on the home's east side, tucked under the outspread limbs of an ancient live oak, made for an inviting spot for guests to relax. The B&B was in no way competition for the large and elegant St. Clair, but was instead patronized by an older, more budget-conscious clientele who preferred the quieter atmosphere and didn't mind the lack of a pool or distance from the shoreline. However, since it was a weekday in the off season, there were currently no guests. Nora claimed she had turned the four-bedroom home into a B&B as a hobby, but Quinn guessed it was also for the income and to assuage her loneliness. For not the first time, she wondered at Nora's seeming impassiveness toward her granddaughter, whom she should be doting on. But Quinn knew her mother. If Emily had grown to love Mark's new wife, Nora was most likely hurt by it.

As she opened the front door and entered the well-maintained living room, she heard her mother's voice from the kitchen.

"Quinn? Is that you?"

"Yeah, Mom." She entered the kitchen, seeing Nora at the oven, sliding in a casserole to take to a church social that night. Her mother's blond hair had faded and was streaked faintly with gray, but she was still prideful about it and wore it long and tied back in a ponytail.

"I guess he found you since he dropped you off." Quinn didn't doubt that her mother had been watching from the window. "What did he want?"

She wasn't sure what to say since she'd been tasked with discretion regarding Carter's presence in town. "He...had a lead for me about a possible job."

Wiping her hands on a dishtowel, Nora turned to face her. She looked with disapproval at Doug, who trotted past her and went farther into the kitchen, probably to inspect his food bowl. "A job? What kind of job?"

"PT. Someone he knows is looking for some private help."

Nora frowned. "Does that mean you're planning to stay here?"

Quinn knew it wasn't that her mother didn't want her. It was more that she thought she should be back in San Francisco, trying to work things out with Jake. Quinn couldn't fault her since she'd never been able to give Nora the full truth.

"I don't know, Mom," she said with a small shrug. "The work would only be for a couple of months, and it pays really well. I told Mark I'd at least talk to the guy."

Nora moved closer. Concern lined her face. "Losing a baby is one of the hardest things that can happen in a marriage, Quinn. Especially in a marriage that's so new. You and Jake need to work through this *together*. You can't do that if you just up and run off."

"It's about a lot more than the miscarriage, Mom," Quinn said quietly, looking away. "I've told you, we were having problems before that."

"Jake called again this morning, right after you left. He said you weren't answering your phone."

Quinn felt a sinking sensation in her stomach. She'd changed cells, but it hadn't taken long for Jake to get her new number. She suspected Nora had given it to him, although she wouldn't admit it.

"Can't you at least talk to him, honey?"

Quinn wished once again that she could open up to Nora. Lean on her. Tell her what had really gone on inside her marriage. But in her heart she knew it wasn't possible. There were things she just couldn't talk about, especially not with her mother. Humiliating things that embarrassed Quinn deeply and that she knew would upset Nora's delicate sensibilities. Quinn feared she would look at her differently, or even think there was something wrong with her. She hated that Jake was calling here, manipulating her mother.

"I know he still loves you," Nora said hopefully. "We talked for a long time. *He wants you back*, sweetheart. It's not too late to drop the divorce proceedings, or at least put a hold on things."

Laying a hand on Quinn's shoulder, she released a sigh. "I know better than anyone that men cheat, if that's what this is all about. They're genetically pre-wired for it, and Jake's a wealthy, professional athlete. There're bound to be beautiful women throwing themselves at him, and he's off traveling with the team so much of the time. You married someone *famous*, Quinn. They're held to different standards."

Quinn tried to ignore her warped rationalization. It wasn't the first time her mother had speculated on adultery being at the crux of her impending divorce. Quinn's father—a prominent Rarity Cove physician—had left Nora for a much younger woman when their daughters had still been in high school. She recalled Nora making a spectacle of herself, confronting the other woman in public and trying to hold on to her husband by any means possible, including a halfhearted suicide attempt. The stunt had brought her father back only temporarily. George Reese now lived in Mobile, Alabama, and was raising a new family. His oldest was probably close to being out of high school herself by now. Quinn saw him even less than she did Nora.

"Just call him back, all right? He sounded so blue."

She gave a faint nod, although she had no intention of returning Jake's call. Pretending to acquiesce gave her an opportunity for escape, though.

"I'm going upstairs," she said, then called for Doug, who came skidding around the corner. She picked up the yoga bag she'd dropped on the floor.

"If you're insisting on keeping that thing, it needs to be tied up in the backyard."

"I'll keep an eye on him."

Quinn headed back through the living room toward the stairs with Doug on her heels. She heard her mother calling after her, frustration ratcheting up her voice. "You could come to church with me tonight. There's a potluck dinner. You could talk to Reverend Cutshaw about things."

At the top of the stairs, instead of going to her bedroom, Quinn entered the room that had once been her father's study. It had a large window and built-in bookcases along the walls. It now served as a den for Nora—somewhere she could relax in privacy, other than her bedroom, when the B&B had guests.

The medical tomes that had once lined the shelves were gone, replaced by her mother's knickknacks, including her Hummel figurine collection and souvenirs she had collected during her travels. A miniature replica of the Golden Gate Bridge from one of her visits to see Quinn was there, along with an actual San Francisco Breakers game ball that Jake had had the entire team sign for his new mother-in-law. It held a place of honor, prominently displayed on the center shelf. Looking at it in the glass box that contained it, Quinn felt a heaviness inside her. She tried to have sympathy for Nora, who had already lost so much.

The den had also become something of a memorial to her sister, with framed photos of Shelley everywhere. Shelley had been classically beautiful—blond, with sky-blue eyes and a model's tall, slender build. Comparisons had been made to Princess Grace. There were photos from Shelley's time in school, as a cheerleader and as the lead in a musical, and photos of her playing piano with the Charleston Symphony Orchestra. In a few of the images, Shelley posed with Emily as an infant and toddler. But Quinn noticed none of the displayed images included Mark. No wedding photos, either. Those had been banished.

Admittedly, there were some photos of *her*, too. Quinn picked up the closest one. She was in her gown, hood and cap after completing her doctorate at Stanford. Quinn looked nothing like Shelley. She instead took after her paternal grandmother, Fiona, who had been petite and Irish. It was where Quinn's wavy russet locks had come from, as well as her gray-green eyes. *Quinn* had been her grandmother's maiden name, in fact.

While there were also several candid photos of her with Jake, taken during Nora's visit to San Francisco, there were no wedding photos, since none existed. They'd eloped after an intense, whirlwind courtship, going off to Las Vegas.

Briefly closing her eyes, Quinn swallowed down the hard reality. Her mother thought she had won the proverbial lottery when Jake Medero chose her.

Quinn had once believed that, too.

At first, it had all been rather *Fifty Shades* and, truthfully, a little dangerous and exciting. But after their marriage, Jake's sexual demands had grown baser and more disturbing. Quinn had also learned his dominant, controlling nature in the bedroom extended to other aspects of her life, as well. All the while, he'd continued to do what he wanted and when.

A bitter taste in her mouth, Quinn thought of the wild, drug-fueled parties he threw, the countless nights with his teammates partying in their home until dawn. He'd had *friends* there the night she fled the house and miscarried in a hotel room, alone.

Miscarriages were common in the first trimester. Jake hadn't even known she was pregnant, nor had he wanted a child. But he'd put on a different face in front of the media, revealing the loss to garner sympathy in a post-game interview. Quinn's throat tightened with anger and grief. It should have been a private thing, something the world didn't ever need to know.

There was no prenup, and Quinn hadn't asked for even temporary support as part of the separation—she wanted nothing from Jake except her freedom. She deeply regretted that, at his insistence, she had quit her job at Brookhaven so soon after marrying him. She had a small amount of money she'd set aside in a savings account prior to their marriage, which was what she was living on now. It made Mark's offer even harder to turn down. Quinn sagged onto the couch. Doug pushed his nose into the yoga bag that sat nearby, looking for the treats he knew she had stashed there. Leaning forward to dig into the bag, she handed him one and watched as, tail wagging, he sank onto the rug to devour it.

Quinn pulled out Carter's medical records next, as well as

her cell phone.

For a long moment, she stared at the phone's screen, wishing she could recapture the inner calm she had maintained during her yoga practice. Then, with a tense sigh, she checked her voice mail.

Five messages had been left since morning. One was from Mark, but the rest were from Jake. Apprehension created a knot inside her as she listened to the first one.

"Quinn, I need to talk to you." Jake's voice was a low, repentant rumble. "I know you don't trust me anymore, and with good reason. But I miss you like crazy, baby. I know I let things get out of control, but I want you to come back home. Everything will change, I promise. Call me back, all right?"

Quinn swallowed, her mouth dry, as she listened to his next message. It was mostly a repeat of the first one, although his tone had hardened somewhat. By the third message, he was demanding to know what she was out doing—who she was with—that she was too busy to pick up her phone.

Her throat dry, she listened to the last message, left just minutes ago.

"You were *nothing*, Quinn, but I chose you. You can keep pretending like you're some good little girl, but we both know the truth."

His next comments became increasingly vile and degrading. Things she had heard in their bedroom before. Quinn sat through as much of it as she could take. But she didn't delete the messages.

Limbs weak, she saved them.

CHAPTER FIVE

"Why am I just now finding out about this?" Blindsided, Carter stood with Mark in the beach home's vast living area.

"Because I didn't want to give you time to come up with a reason to say no. You've always been a little standoffish where Quinn's concerned."

"That should've been your first clue to how I'd feel about this," he countered tensely. "Not to mention, this is *supposed* to be a going-away dinner for Mercer. Just family."

"Quinn *is* family." Mark looked pointedly at Emily, who sat cross-legged on the floor nearby as she hunched over a board game with Mercer. His sister was keeping the children occupied while Samantha prepared dinner. Carter watched as Mercer grabbed Ethan around the waist, keeping him harnessed to her so he didn't knock over the game pieces as he wandered about, a bright yellow Tonka truck in his grasp.

"Regardless, I get the final say, and it's not a good idea."

Mark frowned, clearly going into older-brother mode. "Give me one reason why not. And by reason, I mean a *sane* one. We're looking for a top-notch physical therapist.

Quinn's available, and she's open to it."

Carter didn't respond. Even if Quinn Reese was willing to let what happened in the past stay there, it didn't mean the situation wouldn't be damn awkward.

"Quinn's who we've been looking for," Mark pressed. "And we can trust her completely."

Carter thought of the photos the first physical therapist had planned to sell.

"We'd be doing Quinn a favor, too." Mark paused as Ethan managed to roll the toy truck onto the game board, sending pieces flying. As Emily voiced her dismay, Mercer pried one of the game pieces from the toddler's grasp so he couldn't put it into his mouth.

"Quinn's had a tough go of things lately," Mark confided. "She's at loose ends and could use the job."

Carter recalled what Mercer had told him a few days earlier. She'd heard through the town grapevine that Quinn was back home, staying at her mother's. She was in the midst of a divorce, and there had been a recent miscarriage, as well. He knew Quinn had married a pro football player not long ago—Jake Medero of the San Francisco Breakers. An aggressive player on the field, Medero was equally renowned for his hard-partying ways and seemed an odd match for Quinn, Carter had thought at the time. But he also knew through Mark that she'd worked at a top sports medicine and rehabilitation center in the Bay Area, which he guessed was where they met. The marriage had been remarkably short, even by Hollywood standards.

"I gave Quinn a copy of your medical records so she'd have a more thorough history."

Carter bristled. "Of course you did. Screw HIPAA and my

opinion on any of this."

He felt contrite for his sharp comment. Even with a young family and a hotel to run, Mark had stepped into so many aspects of Carter's life following the attack. While hospitalized, he'd needed Mark to oversee his considerable assets and then later help him make the transition from LA to here, including, admittedly, finding a suitable care team. Staring down at the white pine floor, he released a breath.

"Look," he began uncertainly, "I appreciate the trouble you went to. Talking to Quinn on my behalf. I'm sure she's good at what she does, and I know she holds a special place in your heart." He wavered, his voice losing power. "But I just don't want another witness to all this. Especially not someone I know. I'm…not in a good place."

Mark said quietly, "I *know* that. Which is why you need Quinn. Why we all need her."

Carter fell silent. The wall console buzzed, indicating someone was at the gate, requesting entrance. He hoped it was Olivia and Anders Bauer—their mother's *gentleman friend*—who were arriving, but they had the passcode.

"She's here. I told her to park in back." Mark's voice held a plea. "Be nice. Just see how this feels. That's all I'm asking."

As Mark went to the console to electronically open the gates, Carter took the television remote from the coffee table, flipping the channel to the closed-circuit-camera view of the driveway. On the screen, an older-model Buick rolled through the entrance, then parked at the bottom of the rear driveway near the line of palmettos.

"I'll go meet her." Mark headed out.

Carter saw Mercer looking up at him from the floor.

"Did you know about this?" he asked.

She pulled Ethan down onto her lap and shrugged. "I think it's a good idea."

Carter felt a nerve jump along his already tightened jaw. His entire family had been in on this. He had some physical impairments, but his brain was still fucking intact. He should have been consulted before they approached Quinn Reese.

Calm down. He tried to rein in his frustration. He knew the anger inside him wasn't about Mark or even Quinn. It was directed at his own weakness. He understood Mark had his best interests at heart. Carter looked at his cane, which leaned against the sofa arm. His strength was waning. He knew he should sit but remained standing.

Carter was also convinced Mark knew nothing about what occurred between Quinn and him back in high school. Considering Mark's old-fashioned sense of propriety, if he *had* known, it would have most likely ended in twenty paces with derringers under the St. Clair's centuries-old live oaks.

On the television screen, a woman emerged from the vehicle. Quinn. Carter's stomach gave a funny little flip of recognition. The bookish glasses from her teenage years were gone, but the fit, slightly busty figure was definitely hers, as was the tumbling auburn hair the ocean breeze whipped around her face, partially concealing her features. She wore jeans, boots and a sweater and carried some type of duffel bag. Unexpectedly, a shaggy-looking, wheat-colored dog leaped from the car's back when she opened the rear door. The dog trotted over to greet Mark as he appeared within the camera's range. Carter watched as Quinn and Mark talked. Then he pointed her toward the ground-level elevator bay, and they disappeared off-screen. A short time later, they entered the living area. The dog was no longer with them, and

Carter figured they must have left it in the solarium.

"She's here," Mark announced to Emily, who looked up from her spot on the floor.

"Aunt Quinn!" Scrambling up, Emily ran to her. Laughing, Quinn knelt to wrap her in a tight hug. Placing Ethan on his feet, Mercer hurriedly put away the game pieces and rose to greet Quinn warmly, as well.

Shelley had been the sunny, tall blonde with looks that could have quite possibly gotten her a modeling contract, if she hadn't preferred a life here with Mark. But Carter noted that Quinn had grown into her own subtle beauty, something he hadn't noticed at Shelley's funeral five years ago. He did remember embracing her, telling her how sorry he was. Carter swallowed at the memory. Shelley's death had devastated both families.

Quinn's cool, gray-green eyes turned to him.

"Carter, you remember Quinn," Mark said.

Carter's mind jumped to Quinn at fifteen. How he'd coaxed her out of her bathing suit and lain on top of her on the cool, white sand. He had taken her virginity that spring night. And all the while, he had been thinking about her older sister. He wasn't proud of what he'd done, or the way he treated her afterward. He had been a seventeen-year-old asshole, uncaring of Quinn's feelings and stupidly in love with his brother's girlfriend.

His shoulder ached. Carter gave a small nod.

***

Nora had been right about Mark's new wife being exceptionally pretty. But Samantha had also been welcoming toward Quinn—nothing at all like her mother had implied. Quinn was in the kitchen with Samantha, having offered to help with the dinner clean up so the others could spend more time with Mercer, who would be returning to Atlanta the next day.

"I can't believe Mark didn't mention you were vegetarian." Samantha's long, dark hair fell over her shoulders as she washed one of the china plates in the sink before handing it to Quinn. "I really am sorry."

"It's fine," Quinn assured her. She dried the plate with a dishtowel, then placed it in one of the gourmet kitchen's glass-fronted cabinets. "I'm used to eating around things, and I wouldn't want you preparing something special for me. The salad and roasted vegetables were delicious. And I went vegetarian just a few years ago. Mark probably didn't even know."

The dinner had been casual, filled with family conversation taking place over heaping platters of fried oysters and soft-shell crab. Quinn had sat between Mark and a talkative Emily and across the table from Carter, who had been polite but quiet, even detached from the discussion going on around him. Quinn couldn't blame him. The medical documents she had reviewed were a grim reminder of what he had been through, as well as the discomfort he was no doubt still in. She'd noticed he had lost weight from his already lean frame, and he kept his weakened right shoulder immobilized in a sling. There were other changes in his physical appearance, as well. His thick hair, normally lowlighted and cropped close for the cameras, had darkened and was unruly and longish. Facial scruff masked his famous features. But each time Quinn had lifted her gaze to find him looking curiously back at her, those piercing, midnight-blue eyes were unmistakable.

His scrutiny had created a wary tingling in her stomach.

"Quinn, I have to say again it's wonderful to have you here," Olivia enthused a short time later as she entered the kitchen. She had brought in a serving tray that held coffee cups and the remains of a beautiful chocolate torte Samantha had prepared for dessert. Olivia placed the tray on the wide, granite island. She had aged some since the last time Quinn had seen her, but she was still stylishly dressed, a string of pearls around her throat and her trademark silver bob perfectly maintained. A small ache inside her, Quinn recalled how fond Shelley had been of her mother-in-law.

"It's been far too long since you've been home." Olivia's clear blue eyes shone with hope, and she took Quinn's hands in hers. "I just know you're going to be able to help our Carter get back to himself."

Before Quinn could respond, Anders appeared at the kitchen's arched entrance. He was a big, jovial man, with a full head of gray hair. Quinn had already connected the name to one of Charleston's oldest investment firms.

"You ready to go, Olivia, dear?" he asked.

"I am. I've already said my good-bye to Mercer." Releasing Quinn's fingers and giving Samantha a quick embrace, she accepted the arm Anders extended to her.

"That was a crackerjack dinner, Samantha. Good night, ladies," Anders said.

"They're quite a couple," Quinn commented once the two had disappeared around the corner. "How long have they been together?"

"About seven months." Samantha took the china cups from the tray and began rinsing them in the sink. "Anders gave her a huge sapphire for Christmas, but Olivia swears it's not an engagement ring."

Quinn covered the remainder of the chocolate torte with foil, then placed it in the stainless-steel refrigerator. Turning, she ran her hands uncertainly over the thighs of her dark jeans, focusing for a moment on the row of vintage copper lighting fixtures that hung over the island before speaking. "Samantha…I want to thank you for being such a good stepmother to Emily. I haven't been here, and my mother…"

"I love Emily as if she were my own," Samantha assured her, her soft-brown eyes sincere. She added gently, "And I know Nora's had a hard time with all this."

Quinn gave a faint nod, unable to say anything that would defend or explain her mother's behavior.

Samantha walked around the island to where Quinn stood. "We really *are* glad you're here, Quinn. Mark has a lot of faith in you—the whole family does. You probably already know we've been through a string of physical therapists."

"I don't know if I'm taking the job," Quinn admitted with a tense sigh. "Or if Carter even wants my help. He hasn't had much to say to me tonight."

"Don't take it personally. Olivia's right—he isn't himself. He's hurting, and the studios are starting to pressure him. He has a film releasing in the spring, and they have expectations he'll do publicity for it. He's contractually obligated."

"He isn't ready for that," Quinn acknowledged.

"Maybe you could go try and talk to him now? I can finish up in here."

She couldn't put it off any longer. Leaving the kitchen, Quinn wandered back toward the main living area of the massive, beautifully furnished beach home. Decorated in creamy whites and neutrals, it seemed typical of a place where one of the *rich and famous* might live. She thought of Jake's Mediterranean-style villa in San Francisco. It wasn't as large as this house, but it had a view of the bay and was nearly as luxurious. In the beginning, she'd been enchanted with it.

Now, the thought of ever going back there sickened her.

Quinn stopped outside the living area with its high, vaulted ceiling and exposed, reclaimed-wood beams. Mercer and Emily were curled together on an overstuffed couch, watching an animated movie on a large-screen television. Nearby, Mark paced slowly in front of a stacked-stone hearth with flames dancing inside it. He held a sleeping Ethan, the toddler's cheek resting on his shoulder. Quinn's heart pinched as she took in the family scene unnoticed.

Carter wasn't with them.

It was possible he had retreated to the home's upper level. If so, Quinn didn't feel comfortable looking for him there. Instead, she backed from the living area and headed to the solarium to check on Doug. He'd been whining earlier, but had since quieted down. Reaching glass doors that opened onto the sweeping enclosed space, she felt her heart skip a small beat. Carter sat on a slip-covered sofa that was part of a larger seating arrangement, leaning forward as Doug trotted to him with his favorite ball in his mouth. She watched as he rubbed the dog's chest, speaking lulling words to him in that faintly honeyed drawl that was nearly as famous as his face. After a short time, Doug relinquished the ball, dropping it into Carter's left hand so he could toss it again.

"Mark said I could bring him. I hope you don't mind," Quinn said a bit nervously, making her presence known. Carter looked up at her as she stood between the open doors. "I brought some of his things to occupy him. I didn't want to leave him at my mother's—she isn't very dog-friendly. I'm sorry about the whining."

"He just got lonely in here." Doug returned to him, and

Carter rubbed the dog's ears. "The kids were in here earlier. I came in to supervise, mostly to make sure the dog survived."

Tentatively, Quinn entered the room as he and Doug played tug-of-war with the ball. She had thought herself immune, but Carter's profile in the subdued lighting caused her breath to stall momentarily inside her chest. For the longest time, she had stubbornly avoided seeing anything he was in, until her curiosity had finally won out. Since then, she had seen him on television and in movies. He *was* a good actor, more than a sex symbol, she conceded. He had the ability to connect with his characters, disappear inside them so completely she would momentarily forget who she was watching and that they shared a past.

A memory of that night on the beach came to her without warning. Quinn shook it away.

"I know you know why I'm here," she said, breaking the room's quiet. "I'm sorry for what happened to you, Carter." Thinking of Bianca Rossi, she added, "And for your loss."

He bowed his head before finally speaking.

"Mark believes you're some kind of miracle worker." He didn't look at her as he tossed the ball and Doug went scrambling after it again. This time, however, the dog settled onto the seagrass area rug with it, nudging the orb back and forth with his nose.

"I've had patients who would say *slave driver* is a more apt description," Quinn said, trying to keep things light as she moved closer. "But there's really no miracle to it. What's most important to a patient's recuperation is his attitude and motivation." With honesty, she added, "I've been warned neither of yours is very good at the moment."

Carter's lips pressed together in silent acknowledgment.

Quinn stumbled for something to fill the void. "Mark gave me a quick tour of the workout room on the bottom floor when I got here. You have everything you need—as good as at any rehab facility. Whoever equipped it was thorough."

He frowned into the glass he had picked up from the coffee table, taking a sip before placing it back down. Quinn had noticed Carter hadn't had wine with the little dinner he'd eaten, but she suspected he had gone off to be by himself afterward to have a drink without being criticized.

"You're right—he *was* thorough," he grumbled. "He even equipped it with a hidden camera."

"I…heard about that," Quinn admitted. She eased down onto the sofa beside him. "Carter, I've gone over your case files. I know the extent of your injuries and the surgeries. I understand what kind of pain you must be in."

He ran lean, masculine fingers through his shaggy hair, his jaw tense.

"You should know I've worked with people who are just as frustrated as you. Just as angry about their situation. And I know what you most likely think about physical therapy."

He looked at her then, his eyes like dark blue velvet. Quinn noticed again the hollows underneath them.

"You think it's going to hurt and progress will be slow." She drew in a breath. "Both are likely true—"

"And you'll make it harder by insisting I'm off pain medication."

She shook her head. "Not if you need it. I'd rather you be able to participate in therapy, not retreat from it because you're hurting. If we work together, after we've made some strides and you're seeing benefits, we could try tapering down the meds to evaluate how bad the pain still is."

She indicated the crystal tumbler he had picked up again.

"Carter…you should be careful about mixing prescription meds with alcohol," she reprimanded gently.

His smile was tight-lipped. "It's just one drink. And I can see why Mark's so big on you. You and he are reading from the same script."

She wasn't deterred. Quinn lowered her voice. "That's because he *cares* about you. You're lucky to have so many people who love you—your family as well as your fans." She thought of the explosion in social media after the attack, as well as the makeshift monument fans had created in front of Cedars-Sinai during those first days of his hospitalization, when his survival had been so uncertain. "After…what happened, I've never seen such an outpouring of love. People who didn't even know you were praying for—"

"What's your point, Quinn?" he asked tiredly, rubbing his brow. "That I should be working harder for everyone?"

"No. You have to want this for *yourself*." She thought for a moment, trying to find some incentive that might attract his interest. "Is there something you'd like to get back to? Something we could work toward?"

Despite his closed expression, he finally said, "The beach."

She had expected him to say something related to his career—to get back to the top physical condition he'd obviously been in, to be well enough to take part in promotions for his next movie. Carter stared at the floor. "I'd like to go down the goddamn steps to the beach and take a walk without losing my breath…" He swallowed heavily. "Or being afraid I might not make it back up them."

Quinn had noticed the rather steep wood stairs that led

down to the sand when she'd arrived.

"It's a good goal," she said quietly. "Anxiety *is* normal after cardiac surgery. And I know it doesn't feel like it, but the damage to your heart and lungs has been repaired. It just takes some time to recover and get back your strength and lung capacity. I'd be monitoring your heart rate and oxygen levels closely. Making certain you're not overtaxing yourself."

He sat very still. Quinn rose from the sofa to give him time to think about what she had said. Looking around the room that she imagined was painted with light during the day, she noticed that, like the rest of the house, it had a coastal aesthetic, with seashells in glass jars and groupings of driftwood among the artwork and expensive-looking accents. A cushioned window seat ran the length of the room, and above it, tall windows revealed the whitecaps of crashing ocean waves that were in contrast to the black night. Focused on the view, Quinn failed to realize Carter had risen from the couch, too. When she turned, he stood closely in front of her. At the dearth of space between them, she felt her heart beat harder. He'd removed the sling earlier, and he held his injured shoulder carefully, his left hand lightly cupping his right elbow. The cane she'd seen him using remained against the sofa's arm. Carter was tall like Mark, and she had to look up at him.

"I appreciate your coming here, but this isn't going to work, Quinn."

Her face grew hot. She felt the same reasoning deep inside her, but some part of her wanted to hear him say it. "Why not?"

A look of discomfort crossed his gaunt yet still-handsome face, deepening the lines of tension bracketing his mouth. He paced a few halting steps from her and then returned. At some point, Carter had pushed up the sleeves of the soft-looking sweater he wore with jeans, and her eyes fell to the shiny, raised red scars on the inside of his right forearm.

Defense wounds. The violent details of the stabbing reported by the media flashed through her mind.

"Do I have to spell it out?"

His terse words drew her eyes back to his. Carter's eyebrows had drawn together in a hard frown. He spoke in a slightly breathless tone, as if he had overexcerted himself. "It's what we've been dancing around for years at every family event. That night on the beach. You were just fifteen, and I *used* you. You've never forgiven me."

His words quivered inside her, like an arrow that had hit its mark. Still, Quinn raised her chin fractionally. "You're wrong, Carter. That was a long time ago. We're both adults now."

She added in a rush of words, "But whether you choose me or not, you need to start working with someone. You need to start getting serious about your recuperation. If you fall much further behind, you may never recover from this. I'm offering you my services, Carter. You can take them or leave them."

For several seconds, his sapphire gaze remained on her, his squared jaw set. Then with a dismissive air, he turned and walked stiffly from the room, the cane forgotten. Doug trailed him to the glass doors, where he sat expectantly, tail wagging, as if he might return.

Quinn's breath burned inside her throat. Irked and embarrassed by his curtness, she grabbed her duffel from the floor and began blindly packing up the dog's things.

CHAPTER SIX

"Carter...we're leaving soon."

Samantha's soft voice caused Carter to open his eyes. He realized he had fallen asleep, upright on the sofa in the master suite's sitting room where he had sequestered himself. Lifting his head from where it had fallen back against the cushions, he sat up straighter. Samantha held Ethan on her hip. The sleepy-eyed toddler sucked his thumb.

"Ethan isn't the only one who's tired," Samantha noted as she stood over him, concern in her eyes. "You should try to go to bed soon."

"Yeah," he rasped, scrubbing a hand over his face. He reached up to toy with Ethan's small, sneakered foot. "You want to give me some of that thumb, bro?"

Ethan shook his head, grinning. To Samantha, Carter said, "Thanks for everything. Good night."

Exiting the room, she brushed shoulders with Mark, who stood in the doorway.

"I'll be down in a minute," he told her, touching her arm. "Mercer's getting the kids' things together."

Once Samantha was gone, Carter dropped his head, avoiding Mark's discerning gaze as he entered and used the remote to mute the television.

"I didn't get to speak with Quinn. She rushed out a while ago," he said pointedly. "Since she'd barely make eye contact and you'd disappeared, I take it things didn't go well."

Carter sighed. "Mark, I'm sorry, all right?"

He appeared disappointed, but not angry. "It was worth a shot. All I asked was for you to see how it felt, and you did. I can't say I'm surprised, since—"

"I slept with her."

It felt strange to finally say it aloud. Mark stared at him, a look of befuddlement on his face.

"Jesus, Mark." Carter shook his head. "Not *tonight.* I couldn't if I wanted to. It…happened a long time ago."

Mark's eyes narrowed. "When?"

He didn't want to dredge up that painful period in both their lives, when they had been at each other's throats, fighting over the same girl. The girl Mark had eventually married. Even now, Carter felt guilt cut through him. It didn't matter that he'd been hung up on Shelley for most of his teen years. She had belonged to Mark, and Carter had stepped between them. It wasn't something brothers did to each other.

A thickness in his throat, he answered Mark's question. "In high school, not long after Shelley dumped me. I was on the beach with some friends, and Quinn was there with hers. I…sort of broke her off from the herd, and we ended up taking a walk alone."

He swallowed his remorse. "We shared a few beers I'd smuggled from the St. Clair bar. One thing led to another…"

"Why have I never heard about this?" Mark asked tightly.

He rubbed his brow. "Because I knew you'd kill me."

"Quinn was what? Sixteen?"

"Fifteen," Carter corrected, his face hot.

Eyebrows slanted downward, Mark sat in a chair opposite the sofa. "So you two were dating behind everyone's backs?"

"No." Blood began to pound in Carter's temples. "I...she was a virgin, and afterward, I gave her the cold shoulder. A month later, I graduated and left for New York."

Mark's features held disbelief. "*Why* would you do that? Considering the whole screwed-up triangle between you, Shelley and me, why'd you feel the need to bring Quinn into it, too? You know how shy and awkward she was as a teenager. And she was too damn young for sex *or* alcohol."

Carter nearly flinched at Mark's stern tone. "I *know* that. I was seventeen, horny and stupid. And I don't know why I did it. Shelley had broken things off with me, and I was hurting." Self-recrimination tightened his voice. "Maybe I just wanted to hurt someone back, and Shelley's little sister seemed like a good choice. Another trademark jackass move, right?"

"I won't argue that." Mark regarded him. "Now I finally understand why things have always been weird between you two. Did you and Quinn talk about this tonight?"

"I brought it up as the reason this thing wouldn't work."

"What'd she say?"

"She said it didn't matter." Carter stared at his hands. "That it happened a long time ago, and we're both adults now."

"Maybe you should listen to her."

He said nothing. After a moment, Mark sighed in resignation and rose from the chair. "We can start looking again at recommendations from the hospital tomorrow. Do you need any help before I go?"

Carter thought of his sling as well as his cane, both of

which he'd left behind in the solarium. Even with the elevator, he had barely made the trip from there to the upstairs, but he'd been too proud to let Quinn see his slow, labored return for them. He would ask Mercer to get them later. He shook his head. "No."

"Good night." Mark began to walk out.

"Mark." As his brother turned around, Carter absently rubbed his chest. "I haven't said it near enough, but thank you for all you've done. I know I've put a lot on you."

"It's okay, Carter," Mark replied quietly. "Family's everything. I know you'd do the same for me."

As he disappeared into the hall, Carter closed his eyes. His mind turned back to Quinn, with her delicate features and those gray-green eyes that brimmed with intelligence and empathy. It occurred to him that he hadn't asked about *her* problems, hadn't expressed any sorrow or concern for the unfortunate turn of events in her life. He had also done it again, he realized heavily. She had offered her help, and he had turned his back on her, just as he had all those years ago. Whether it had been due to his shame over his past actions or his male ego, unwilling to let her see him in this vulnerable state, he didn't know.

Whether you choose me or not, you need to start working with someone, start getting serious about your recuperation. If you fall much further behind, you may never recover from this.

***

Driving Nora's Buick, Quinn traveled south on the two-lane highway that ran alongside the beach, headed back into the Rarity Cove township. She had said a quick good-bye to the others, promised Emily she would see her again soon and made her escape. Carter had been nowhere around.

She turned on the radio, leaving it on the easy listening station her mother had it set to. She needed something—anything—to redirect her thoughts.

Carter's arrogance was maddening. Still, despite his wealth, his looks, his fame, she realized she felt sorry for him.

His defense wounds were proof he had fought to live. But it seemed now that, for whatever reason, the fight had gone out of him. His ambivalence, even hostility, toward his rehabilitation vexed her. Carter had the world at his feet. He should be doing everything he could to reclaim the life he'd had. But a rational inner voice cut through her pondering.

If you're not going to be working with him, it's not your problem.

I used you.

It hadn't been so much an apology, but an admission, after so many years.

It surprised her when, a short time later, the turnoff to her childhood home appeared ahead. Quinn had been so lost in thought she barely remembered driving past the Rarity Cove welcome sign or through its quaint downtown. Doug had been snoozing in the backseat but sat up, alert, as she slowed the car and turned onto the circular, crushed-shell driveway in front of the B&B. There were a couple of unfamiliar cars parked there, and Quinn recalled her mother had said guests would be arriving. She'd mentioned an older couple who had stayed with her in the off-season before. Parking behind the two vehicles—a white, compact economy sedan and a maroon Lincoln Navigator with a rental decal on its bumper—she cut off the Buick's engine and let Doug out from the backseat. Carrying her shoulder bag and the duffel that held the dog's things, Quinn walked onto the porch and entered the warmly lit interior. Sure enough, a gray-haired man and woman were there, watching television in the living room while they nibbled on a cheese platter Nora had put together that afternoon. Quinn politely introduced herself and, after taking Doug into the kitchen to feed him, she went upstairs in search of her mother.

Shock brought her to a halt at the den's entrance. Quinn felt the blood drain from her face. She now knew to whom the rented SUV belonged. Jake sat with Nora on the couch. They'd been in conversation, but upon seeing Quinn, he rose, unfolding his tall, rock-hard frame as he stood. His powerful shoulders strained against the fabric of his sports shirt.

"What's he doing here?" Quinn demanded as her gaze swung to her mother.

"Quinn." Nora's tone was scolding. "That's no way to talk after Jake flew all the way here to—"

"It's all right, Nora," Jake said calmly, then spoke to Quinn. "Before you jump her, she didn't know I was coming. Hell, I didn't know myself until this morning. You haven't been returning my calls. I had to see you."

"You need to leave. Now."

"Quinn, don't be so rude!" Her mother had risen to her feet. "This is a B&B. I have enough bedrooms. I'll put Jake at the other end of the hallway. But you two need to talk."

"Fine. Then I'll go." Quinn fled down the stairs, her throat dry and pulse racing. Passing the living room, she noticed Doug, his tail wagging as the two houseguests lavished attention on him. Closing the front door behind her, she'd gotten halfway to Nora's Buick when she realized she had left the car keys on the kitchen counter, along with her cell phone and purse. She cursed softly under her breath. Then she would have to walk. Arms hugged around herself, she set off in the direction of the beach.

"Quinn!"

She looked over her shoulder. Jake called to her from the porch, then strode after her. A chill fell over her that had nothing to do with the night air. Quinn picked up her pace, then stopped, common sense overriding her panic. She was here on a residential street, with people in houses all around her. Far safer here than on an uninhabited beach at night. Steeling herself, she waited for him to catch up to her.

"I kept your voice mails. They're enough to get a restraining order this time," she said tightly when he reached her.

Jake's raven eyebrows crashed downward. "We're in the playoffs, and I still came all the way here just to talk to you. Is that too much to ask? Look, I know those messages got out of control, but you're making me crazy. You're *still* my wife."

For four more months. And then I'll be free. But Quinn kept the words inside her, instead digging her nails into her palms.

"We took it *too far*, babe, is all. I let things get out of hand, and that's on me," he said, a desperation in his low, placating tone. His dark head bent closer to hers as he towered over her. "Come back home with me. We'll start over. You'll be *safe*. I'll be more respectful of your limits—"

Quinn shook her head hard. "No. This is over."

A muscle jumped along his squared jaw. "You've made your point, you won. It's time to come home."

He attempted to touch her, but she backed away as if he were a poisonous snake. Jake sighed with exasperation. "How many times do I have to say it? *I fucked up*. You don't want Mike around anymore, he's gone—I've already told you that."

At the mention of Mike Buczek, Jake's close friend and teammate, Quinn's stomach clenched. Despite the weakness in her knees, she kept her control. "I'm not changing my mind about the divorce. We were a *mistake*, Jake. All of it was. You have to let me go."

His body stilled. Then he clamped his hand on her arm possessively, a thread of warning in his voice. "Get in the SUV. We're going somewhere private to talk this out."

"No!" Quinn struggled against the fingers that bit into her. "Let go of me, or I'll scream!"

Her lungs squeezed. For a moment, she thought he might pick her up bodily and force her into the vehicle. But instead, he released her. A shadow darkened his face. He no longer touched her, but his big, powerful form was still too close. "Be careful how you treat me, Quinn."

He squinted back at the house, a calculating calm to his voice. "Nora's a fragile thing. Wonder how she'd like knowing what her little girl is really into."

Anger and humiliation swept through her.

"I have the phone messages, and they're bad," Quinn threatened again. She had begun to shake. "If you don't leave right now—leave my mother and me alone—I'll give them to the Rarity Cove Police."

Jake's rugged features turned to stone. His dark eyes imprisoned hers for several heartbeats. Finally, he pointed a finger. "You belong to me, Quinn. That hasn't changed."

She stood rigid as he stalked around to the driver's side of the SUV, got in and started the engine. Tires screeching, he pulled from the drive and raced down the street.

Adrenaline made it hard to catch her breath. She wondered if Jake was headed to the airport, or if his retreat was only for the night. Even if the Breakers were off the schedule tomorrow, he had to be back for team practice, didn't he?

Quinn shivered from the chill and fatigue. How had she been so blind, unable to see that Jake was a functioning sociopath? He actually *believed* she was his possession, like his home or his cars. *I own you.* It was something he'd said to her often enough in their bedroom. Quinn had initially taken it as part of their role-playing, part of his dominant fetish. But she had learned he wasn't playing a game. She hated herself for ever believing she loved him, for ever letting him think she shared his dark desires. She would use the messages to keep him away if she had to.

There was nothing left to do but go back inside. As she entered the foyer, Doug whined and rose from the spot on the floor where he waited. The houseguests appeared to have retired for the night. Nora stood in the living room, her face creased with distress. Quinn figured she had seen their confrontation from the window, even if she couldn't hear it.

"I'm going to bed, Mom," she said wearily, avoiding eye contact as she went past.

"He flew across the country, Quinn. That should mean something to you." An ache filled Nora's voice. "If only your father had cared *half* as much for me."

Quinn halted, a pang inside her at her mother's words. It hurt that after so long, Nora was still so bitter and unhappy. With an inward sigh, she turned and went back to her. Taking her mother's hands in hers, she drew in a breath before speaking. "There are things you don't know, Mom...about Jake and me. About our marriage. Bad things I can't and don't want to tell you." She swallowed dryly. It was as close as she could come to a confession. "But you have to trust me when I say it's for the best that we split up. Jake...he isn't who you think. He can't come back here, okay?" Her voice trembled. "And I could *really* use your support right now."

Her mother peered at her sadly. Quinn hugged her, said a subdued good night and then went upstairs to her bedroom with the dog following.

Jake isn't who you think.

I'm not who you think, either, Mom. Her mother took pride in having *raised her girls right.* The idea of disappointing her…Quinn died a little at the prospect.

Determined to keep some normalcy in her life, she readied herself for bed before dutifully beginning her nighttime yoga practice. She went to the floor and into *Balasana,* also known as child's pose, which she held for some time. After moving into several more poses on the floor, Quinn stood and went into a wide-legged, deep forward bend with her arms straight and hands clasped together behind her. Eyes closed and breathing deeply, she tried to imagine the stress pouring out of her in this inverted position. But not even the poses that typically calmed body and mind could suppress her jitters over Jake's appearance. Quinn stood upright and ran shaky fingers over her forehead, still in disbelief that he'd actually come here. She prayed her threat had worked and that he was headed back on the next flight out of the Charleston airport.

We took it too far, babe, is all. I let things get out of hand, and that's on me.

How could he possibly think she would ever forgive him? That it had merely been a simple case of letting things go too far? Even now, a cold sickness pooled inside her.

Mike Buczek had nearly raped her that night, with Jake's approval.

CHAPTER SEVEN

Her breath rasped out as her silk blouse tore open like paper under his hands. With the speed of a puma, Mike had shoved her back, using his bulking body to pin her against the wall of the villa's second-floor landing. Quinn's cry was swallowed up in the raucous laughter and loud, hip-hop beat coming from the media room down the hall. Mike clapped a hand over her mouth, grinding into her despite her squirming.

"C'mon, baby. I know how you like it." His hot breath fanned her face, his other hand squeezing her breast, then pinching her nipple hard through her exposed lace bra. Revulsion shot through Quinn, tears flooding her vision. As he yanked her bra strap down her shoulder, she sank her teeth hard into the meaty palm covering her mouth. With a roared curse, Mike jerked his hand away, his weight off her long enough for her to slide out from between him and the wall. She broke into a run.

"Quinn."

Jake stood outside the media room's doorway, a beer bottle dangling from the fingers of one hand.

"Jesus, Jake! Your little bitch bit me!"

In that moment, she knew. She nearly vomited. Quinn stumbled down the stairs to the first floor with Jake following and calling her name.

Unable to sleep, Quinn lay in the bed that had been hers as a child, reliving what had been the final breaking point in her already dysfunctional marriage. She had never liked Mike Buczek and the leering, knowing way he stared at her. But that night, he'd actually come after her. Quinn's stomach churned at the memory.

Jake had blamed the incident on their both being high and had begged for her forgiveness. An ache inside her, Quinn turned onto her side and curled into a ball under the covers.

It hurt to think about just how far Jake had planned to let Mike go. How long he had been standing there, watching. His gaze had been filled with lust. Had he planned to join in at some point, or simply be a voyeur to it all?

It had finally proven to her just how dangerous, how unbalanced, he was.

Quinn stared blindly at the bedroom wall where a *Backstreet Boys* poster had resided in her adolescence. She wondered how she had gotten so far from the awkward young girl she had once been. How she had married a man who degraded her, and she had willingly allowed it.

Before that horrible night, Quinn had been mustering the courage to talk to Jake, to tell him that, despite precautions, she had somehow gotten pregnant. She had held her secret inside her for nearly nine weeks, trying to come to terms with it herself, trying to figure out if a child was a reason to stay in an otherwise ill-fated marriage. Some naïve part of her had actually hoped her news might be a turning point in their relationship, that it might be the thing that tempered Jake's wild, dark side. With a baby on the way, he might begin to look at her as a wife and mother, not as a possession or an object for his domination and sexual use.

After breaking free from Mike, Quinn had fled the house, crying, nearly hysterical. She had driven around the Bay Area before finally checking into a hotel. The cramping, then bleeding, had begun during the night.

She could have filed sexual assault charges against Mike. Quinn thought about it often. But the media frenzy that would surround such an accusation against a San Francisco Breaker—made by the wife of another player—was more than Quinn believed she could bear. Not to mention, if Jake thought he could punish her for not returning to him, there was no telling what he might say about her in a courtroom.

Nora's a fragile thing. I wonder how she'd like knowing what her little girl is really into.

Sitting up in bed, Quinn wrapped her arms around her shins and hung her head. The sexual things she had done, the kinks she'd agreed to, had been done to please Jake, private things between a husband and wife. And now Jake was taunting her for the very thing he had inducted her into. She thought of her gradual descent into bondage and submission—the spanking, the humiliation and use of sex toys that melded pain with pleasure. None of it had been enough for him. Jake had planned to *share* her, as if she were a *thing.*

Quinn startled as her cell phone rang inside her handbag, which lay next to the cushioned dog bed on the floor. At the sound, Doug lifted his head and tilted it inquisitively. Quinn had taken the phone off mute on the drive back from the beach house in case Mark called—she had anticipated he would to apologize for things not working out. Fearing the caller was Jake, she climbed from the bed to check the cell's screen. It showed only a number, not a name, but she recognized the area code as Los Angeles, not San Francisco.

Uncertain of what to do, she answered.

"Quinn…it's Carter." At his low, hesitant voice, her pulse kicked up. "Mark gave me your cell number, and I…" She heard his release of breath. "God. I'm being thoughtless again, calling so late."

The clock on the nightstand indicated it was nearly midnight.

"It's all right. I wasn't sleeping," she said, although her tone was cool.

"Look..." he stammered. "I'm sorry about tonight. For walking out on you. And for my harshness. I'm not excusing myself, but the pain meds obliterate my internal filter."

Quinn held the phone against her ear, waiting for whatever else he planned to say.

"I haven't been the most level-headed person lately, so I hope you'll forgive me. I've also been thinking about it since you left. If you're still willing to work with me, it'll be weird, but maybe we should give it a try, at least. I know Mark's already discussed a rate for your services. I'd self-pay, so we wouldn't be dealing with insurers."

Quinn was dumbfounded by his change of heart. After Jake's surprise appearance, she had been considering packing up and leaving Rarity Cove, moving somewhere else where it would be harder for him to find her. She had been too easy to track to her mother's. The only problem was, she didn't yet know where *somewhere else* would be. Despite her renewed reservations about working with Carter, her practical side thought again of the income and how useful it would be.

"You were pretty adamantly against this," she said as she walked back to the bed and sank down on its edge. "What changed your mind?"

"Your willingness to let the past stay there, I guess." The airwaves stretched out between them, until he rasped, "I know I was a jerk to you back then. I was a self-centered, immature idiot who couldn't think past his own..." He stopped himself, clearing his throat. "If you can set that aside, I suppose I should be able to, too."

Quinn thought for a time, running a hand through her bed-mussed hair. "If we do this, we'd need to get started as soon as possible. No more lost time. You can't afford it. And no *diva* behavior, either, Carter. I won't put up with it."

He gave a strangled laugh. "It sounds like you're planning to live up to your slave-driver reputation. Should I be afraid?"

"You should be prepared to work. I won't put you through anything you aren't ready for, but some of it won't be easy. You'll have to trust me."

"So how do we start?" he asked seriously.

"I'll need to confer with your care team. We'll also talk about the level of pain you're experiencing. And I'll have to put you through some endurance and muscle testing in order to get a baseline."

"I'll get a meeting set up for you in Charleston for Monday morning. I sort of have VIP status with the doctors." He hesitated again. "I've also been thinking, Quinn. Since we'd already be working together, I could use your help with some other things. Mercer's leaving tomorrow, and I've been leaning on her pretty hard. I don't want to be a burden to my family any more than I've already been. Mark's got his hands full with the St. Clair, and Mom—"

Quinn stirred uneasily. "What kinds of other things?"

"Driving me to doctor appointments, running errands, whatever I need. You could sort of be on call to me."

"You want me to be your personal assistant?"

"It wouldn't go that far. I know what I'm asking is way below your credentials, but I'd pay you the same hourly rate as I would for therapy." He must have taken her silence as indecision, because he added, "I can find someone else, but like Mark said, we trust you, and you're family."

Carter's sternal precautions had ended after eight weeks, but Quinn knew his injured shoulder didn't have the strength or range of motion for driving. Not to mention the pain medication he was taking. She felt a tightness in her muscles, thinking that if she accepted, it would mean spending even more time with him than she'd anticipated. But it would also mean additional pay.

"Mark said the car you were driving tonight is Nora's."

"Transportation won't be an issue. I can rent something." Quinn had flown here from San Francisco and, even there, her Lexus coupe—a gift from Jake for her birthday—was in his name. She had returned the car, leaving it in his driveway when he had been on the road with the team. Since their separation, she'd been relying on the Bay Area's cable cars, mass transit and Uber to get around. "The only reason I haven't leased something here yet is because I wasn't sure how long I was staying."

"I'll arrange a car for you."

"That isn't necessary—"

"Consider it a job perk. I'll provide you with a credit card for expenses, as well."

Quinn rubbed a hand over her eyes, not completely sure of the wisdom of what she was getting into.

"All right," she agreed finally. "But I'll have to bring Doug with me for our sessions."

"Not a problem."

Feeling as if she'd just taken a blind leap off a cliff, Quinn sheathed her inner anxiety. "I'll wait to hear from you about the meeting on Monday."

"Good. It's, uh, settled, then." He sounded nervous, too. "I'll leave a message with the hospital's answering service and have someone call you with a time." A long beat of silence passed between them, until he spoke her name. "I'm sorry about your marriage not working out…and other things. I should've said that tonight."

It didn't surprise her that he knew. After all, Mark knew. Quinn thought of the small-town gossip that was rampant here, as well as Jake's televised interview that had brought her miscarriage to the forefront. She had already moved out of his home, but Jake had acted in front of the cameras as if they were still together, a couple heartbroken over a baby that would never be. His emotional discussion of it had been shown in clips on the sports news shows. Quinn regretted ever telling him, but despite everything, she'd thought he had a right to know.

"It's okay," she said softly.

"We have something in common, Quinn." The cadence of his famous voice washed over her, as familiar as a pair of broken-in jeans. "Growing up, neither of us could wait to get the hell out of Rarity Cove. I hightailed it to New York after graduation. You took off to San Francisco…"

"And now we've both come home to lick our wounds." As she finished his observation, a small ache filled her. She said good night, although she sat with her cell phone still in her hand long after she had disconnected.

CHAPTER EIGHT

"You *can't* pass this up. Diane loves you, and she's hot for your comeback interview."

Using his left hand, Carter clasped the back of his neck, tension radiating through him as he sat on a teakwood barstool at the kitchen island, his cell phone in front of him and Elliott on speaker. He stared blindly at the closed plantation shutters blocking out the late morning sunlight.

"You won't even have to fly here—her team will come to you. They want to film it this week and air it during February sweeps."

Carter's breath sawed silently out of him. He fidgeted with an olivewood salt box that had been left on the counter. "No," he said quietly.

"I won't accept that—"

"You'll have to." Carter knew what Diane would want from him. To open up for the cameras. To tear himself apart as they talked about what happened. About Bianca. He swallowed heavily, not wanting his emotions on display.

Through the airwaves, he heard the rattle of ice cubes, as if they were being dropped into a glass. It gave him a bad sense of déjà vu. Agents weren't immune to the pressures of Hollywood, and Elliott had done a brief stint at a Malibu rehab center a little over a year ago to get in front of a problem. Carter knew he was in no place to be lecturing anyone. Still, he asked carefully, "What time is it there, Elliott? Before eight? Tell me you aren't drinking on a Monday morning—"

"If I am, it's because you've driven me to it," Elliott half snapped before backpedaling with a tight laugh. "Relax, it's just a Bloody Mary. I had a tough night. I can handle it."

Carter had been the one to drive Elliott to New Beginnings. His voice lowered in concern. "What about the coke? Are you handling that again, too?"

"God, no. And don't change the subject. Let me give you some advice, Carter. You may not be back to your former eye-candy self, but it's better to let the public see you through a medium we can control—a little makeup, the right lighting, some shrewd editing. We don't need another *Starglazer* situation bent on showing you at your worst."

Carter closed his eyes, wishing Elliott would stop talking. The scent of praline pecan rolls, something Samantha had brought over from the café that morning, hung in the air. They sat under a glass dome, untouched.

"Can I appeal to your business sense, at least? They're offering *two million freaking dollars* for a one-hour exclusive. That's fifty thousand a minute, in case you're wondering—"

"I don't care about the money."

"That's why you pay *me* to care about it for you."

Carter squeezed the bridge of his nose. "Tell them no."

Elliott cursed softly. "I love you, Carter. How can I not love a star whose last movie netted over three hundred mill worldwide? But you're killing me, you know that?" He paused as if to bring himself under control. "You've got to understand. I just want you *back*. We all do. You're an industry. And I'm sorry, but you won't be refusing interviews at the press junket in March. Those you'll be doing *for free* under the terms of your contract. I talked to the studio, like you asked. Short of another hospitalization, they're holding you to it."

Once the call ended, Carter dragged a hand through his hair. His chest hurt. On impulse, he shoved the phone away. It sailed over the island's edge and landed on the tile floor.

"*Carter*!"

The reprimand had come from Jolene, who stood inside the kitchen's arched entryway. Even with the slosh of the dishwasher behind him, Carter had nearly forgotten her presence. The St. Clair's head of housekeeping, Jolene was in her fifties and had been with the family business since before Carter was born. She had started coming by on Monday and Thursday mornings to take care of household chores before heading to the hotel to oversee staff. Hands planted on her ample hips, she eyed him critically from beneath short dreadlocks, muttering in lowcountry Gullah before returning to English. "I swear you haven't changed since you were knee-high to a grasshopper. Only now you're tossin' around expensive cell phones instead of toys."

"Sorry, Jo," he mumbled and looked away, embarrassed she'd witnessed his outburst.

"Let me tell you, this pretty child could throw some tantrums in his day. All that drama—even then, I knew he was going to be a star."

Jolene was talking to Quinn, Carter realized, heat sweeping over his skin. Not a good start to her *no diva behavior* mandate. Dressed in leggings and a hip-length sweater, she must have been in the hallway and had entered a few seconds behind the other woman. The straps of her duffel and purse hung over one slender shoulder. Doug had trotted into the room, as well. He headed to where Carter sat.

"Quinn Reese is here," Jolene announced.

"Thanks for the heads-up," he replied dryly, absently rubbing his chest as Quinn stared back at him, no doubt another observer to his meltdown. He figured Jolene had let her in through the security gate while he'd been on the phone.

"It's good to see you, Quinn, honey. You grew up real good." Jolene gave Quinn's arm an affectionate squeeze before departing to another part of the house to return to her work.

"You okay?" Quinn asked.

He gave a faint nod. Putting down her things, she went to retrieve the phone from the floor.

"Well, it's not broken," she said after a brief examination of the device.

Carter rose stiffly to face her, his right arm in its sling. Quinn's wavy, auburn hair hung over one shoulder in a loose, heavy braid, wisps left curling around her oval face. He did what he could to improve his frame of mind. He hadn't slept well last night, but he was glad he'd gotten up early enough to manage a shower and dress himself, although he wore jeans and an untucked, button-front shirt. He had expected Quinn to come by after her morning meeting in Charleston with his care team. Based on Doug's presence, she had gone back to her mother's afterward to pick him up.

"Hollywood calling?" she guessed, handing him the phone.

"A reminder I have a press junket coming up this spring.

With photo-calls." His frown deepened. "Attendance is mandatory."

"Well, it *does* give us something to work toward," she said, although her eyes held empathy.

He changed the subject. "How'd your meeting go?"

"Good," she said, although she appeared somewhat ill at ease. "We discussed the therapy regimen I've planned. It got their approval."

"And the car?"

"Delivered early this morning." She brushed a loose strand of hair from her face, her delicately arched eyebrows drawing in a bit as she regarded him. "You really didn't have to get me something so nice."

The car was a top-of-the-line Mercedes with satellite radio and tinted windows. He shrugged as best he could. "I'm going to be riding around in it, too, you know."

Doug had been roaming around the kitchen, investigating his new surroundings, but he returned to Carter and placed his front paws insistently on his thigh, seeking attention.

"Doug, down!"

"It's all right." He stroked Doug's head, his mood lifting a fraction as the dog rewarded him with an openmouthed smile and thumped his tail against the island's leg. Carter liked dogs. He would have one himself if his travel schedule permitted. He looked up in time to see Quinn move to the windows, opening the shutters wide. January sunlight flooded the room, bringing the aqua-glass tiled backsplash and ivory walls, the high-end stainless-steel appliances, into sharp focus. He squinted against the invasion of light as she consulted her sports wristwatch.

"Well, there's no time like the present." He noticed again

the nervous edge to her voice, and he wondered if she was dreading the session as much as he.

"Can we go downstairs?" she asked. "I noticed a massage table there, which I can use for my evaluation. I need to do some muscle testing and see how well you're healing. I've also talked to Mark about using the hotel ballroom this afternoon."

"For what?"

"A six-minute walk test. We need a large area with a flat, hard surface. It'll help me gauge your endurance level and give us a benchmark for improvement."

Carter's throat dried. "Six minutes?"

"It's self-paced. You can stop to rest as much as you need, and you can use your assistive device."

She looked at the cane that lay across the seat of one of the counter stools. Carter reached for it, intending to use it for the trip downstairs, but he accidentally bumped it with his hand, knocking it off and almost losing his balance as he made an unsuccessful grab for it. Quinn steadied him, then knelt to pick up the cane from the floor. As she handed it to him, he nearly winced at the concern in her eyes.

"I used to spend two hours a day with a personal trainer. Now I can't walk thirty feet without losing my breath…or without this damn thing." He placed the cane's tip on the floor, his face hot.

"That's what we're going to work on," she said softly.

***

The ground-level floor featured a view of the covered pool and beyond it, the powder-blue winter sky and lapis ocean. As Quinn had noted before, the space had been well-equipped for physical therapy, with a treadmill and upper-body ergometer for arm pedaling, free weights and a mounted pulley system. Carter sat on the padded massage table as Quinn had instructed while she stood in front of him, helping remove the sling that held his right shoulder.

"Were you given specific instructions about wearing this?" Made self-conscious by their closeness, she kept her hands busy folding the sling several times before laying it on the table beside him. "I've seen you without it—"

"I warned you this was going to be weird, Quinn. You and me."

She met his dark blue, knowing gaze. Quinn wished he hadn't so easily picked up on her nerves. It was unlike her to be uncomfortable around a patient, even a famous one. But the truth was, she'd spent the remainder of the weekend second-guessing her decision to work with him—that, and keeping an eye out for Jake. At least it appeared Jake had taken her threat about the phone messages seriously. She hadn't seen or heard from him since the rental SUV had roared from the B&B's driveway on Saturday night.

"I guess I am a little on edge," she admitted. "I was hoping it wasn't obvious."

"We can still call this off, no harm, no foul."

"I'm afraid you'd like that too much," she joked weakly. "Besides, it's not just you. I mean…us."

His eyebrows lifted as he waited for her to continue.

"Coming back here, this unexpected job and getting back into the swing of work—it's made me a bit off-kilter," she tried to explain. Quinn forced determination into her voice. "But *this* is going to work. Things are awkward right now, but we'll power through it and get used to one another."

Carter peered at her before answering her question. "The

doc in LA left it up to me about the sling. He said to wear it if I need it. It keeps me from jostling my shoulder. The one here hasn't said much about it."

Drawing in a breath, Quinn stepped closer and gently manipulated his shoulder, touching him as she would any other patient. She felt his slight flinch as she guided his arm movement. "Is the shoulder pain only at the surgery site?"

"It's everywhere," he said, his voice strained. He tensed as she moved his arm into another evaluating position. "That and stiffness."

"Can you hold your arm in that position for me? How's your pain tolerance with the meds?"

"I have a feeling I'm going to find out," he deadpanned under his breath.

Quinn guided him through several more arm movements, using her hand to create resistance for him to push against. Then, lips pressed together thoughtfully, she typed notes regarding his strength level and range of motion into her iPad that she had placed on a nearby credenza. "We have your orthopedics appointment Thursday. We'll talk to your specialist, but if he agrees, I'd like to try to go without the sling."

Carter shifted uneasily on the table. "Is that a good idea?"

"Maybe. When one part of the body becomes atrophied from disuse, it can sometimes affect connected parts. The immobilization may be making things worse—causing what's called a frozen shoulder." Quinn forced herself to be direct. "Do you need help taking off your shirt? I...need to see how well you're healing."

At her request, his jaw clenched.

"I got myself dressed this morning like a big boy. I can reverse the process."

Slowly, he began undoing the buttons on his shirt using mostly his left hand. Quinn looked away, aware she had already known he was left-handed, just as she knew his birth date and middle name. Ashton. Things a teenage girl made a point of knowing about a boy. It bothered her that her mind had stored such trivia. She provided aid only when Carter struggled to disentangle his right arm from the garment. As the shirt pooled around his hips, he didn't look at her, his somber gaze instead focused on a spot outside the window. A weighted feeling inside her, Quinn kept her face impassive as she took in the scarring on his torso, his pectorals and abs still somewhat defined despite the weeks of inactivity.

The long, ribbon-like scar—reddened and puffy, the result of his emergency room open-heart surgery—ran vertically down his chest, nestled in the light matting of chest hair. More elevated, angry tissue marked other healed wounds. Compassion tightened her throat. Quinn thought of the steamy love scenes in his films that had showcased his toned body. Letting her see him like this couldn't be easy.

"Souvenirs from a night I don't remember," he said without inflection, the unemotional comment clearly a smoke screen.

Quinn stepped close to examine the scars on his chest, as well as the smaller one on the side of his neck, which she had noticed before.

"That one's on me," he said as she gently turned his jaw to the side so she could get a better look. "ICU psychosis is a real thing, apparently. I ripped out my catheter and created one hell of a mess, I was told."

At his words, Quinn briefly laid her fingers against his collarbone in a comforting gesture, then moved behind the table to evaluate the scar on the back of his right shoulder. The tendon attaching the posterior deltoid had been partially lacerated in the attack, requiring a separate surgery. "Your color's good. You seem to be healing well. Do any of the scars give you pain?"

"Some." Carter tensed again as she lightly stretched the puckered scar tissue on his shoulder. He paused as Doug rose from his spot on the floor and turned in circles several times before curling back down. "I get numbness and tingling. Especially in my hand."

"That's good. That means the nerves are regenerating." Returning to stand in front of him, Quinn reached carefully for Carter's right hand, tamping down the involuntary flutter in her belly as she cradled it, palm upward, within her own, smaller one. She examined the scarring on the fleshy pad. There had been a separate surgery there, as well. At one point, his fingers had most likely been badly swollen, but they now appeared normal, long and lean like his body, the nails well cared for. Mercer, she guessed.

"How's your dexterity?"

"It could be better."

"We'll work on that, too. Massage breaks down the scar tissue, which helps build collagen and lets the tendons glide more easily." Quinn took a bottle of oil from her duffel, depositing a small amount onto his palm. Then, using her thumb, she applied pressure over the scar in a circular motion to show him what he could expect during their sessions. He scowled faintly, but didn't complain at the discomfort she knew her action created.

"I mentioned some of this might be a little intense," she said with a small, sympathetic smile. "Everyone's pain tolerance is different, so you'll need to tell me how much you can handle. In addition to your shoulder exercises and cardio work, we'll massage twice daily. We'll focus on your palm and shoulder, where the scarring is tight."

"Do you want to talk about it?" he asked a short time later.

Quinn had been concentrating on her task, continuing the massage on his palm, but she looked up at him.

"About the things making you off-kilter," he clarified in his low rasp. "You didn't mention it, but I'm guessing your separation from Jake Medero is one of them."

They stood close, Quinn between his long, jeans-clad legs that dangled from the massage table. She felt her traitorous stomach flutter again. Even in his current condition, even with the bluish hollows forged under his eyes, he remained a remarkably beautiful man—even features and wide, sensual mouth, straight white teeth, his complexion flawless beneath his facial scruff. For a surreal second, she felt like the ingénue in one of his movies, playing caregiver to his wounded hero. But this was Carter. The now-famous version. She had no intention of letting her guard down.

"Thank you," she said, breaking eye contact. "But no."

Releasing his hand, she lightly cleared her throat and took a deliberate step away.

"We'll start your regular cardio work tomorrow, after we've completed the walk test this afternoon. You've lost weight and some muscle mass, but the excellent physical condition you were in prior to the accident will make our—"

"It wasn't an accident."

"Of…course not." He had managed to fluster her. "I'm sorry. It was a slip of words." Quinn heard the start of a car engine outside, then glimpsed Jolene's Honda Civic pulling from the rear driveway. "You can put your shirt back on."

She went to the window to give him privacy, looking out at the covered pool and lovely landscaped terrace.

"According to ZMZ, my home's the number-one stop on the Hollywood Death and Mayhem Tour." His softly bitter tone broke the silence. "It beat out Cielo Drive."

Quinn turned to him again, surprised by the comment.

"My punishment for web surfing last night. It popped up in front of me." He shook his head, a grim twist to his mouth. "People can be ghouls."

She recognized the Cielo Drive location—where the first Manson family murders had occurred in the late sixties. Absently, Quinn ran her hands over her upper arms.

"Have you been back?" she asked carefully.

"To my house in LA? No." Carter struggled with the remaining buttons on his shirt. "Mark went while I was hospitalized, once the medical examiner's office and police released the scene. He packed some of my things and hired the cleanup crew, then closed the place up."

Quinn's lips parted in confusion. "I thought the police took care of—"

"It's the responsibility of the property owner."

Her stomach twisted at the thought of Mark witnessing the bloodied bathroom where Bianca Rossi had been murdered, his brother nearly killed.

Carter grimaced as he put the sling back on, declining Quinn's offer of help. Then he rose stiffly from the table and reached for his cane. "Speaking of Mark, we'll be seeing him soon enough. I'm tired. I'm going upstairs to rest before we go to the hotel."

Quinn had more testing to take him through, as well as a pain questionnaire she needed him to complete, but she agreed he should rest before that afternoon. After such a long period of inactivity, the walk test would be a challenge.

"Samantha called as I was driving over," she mentioned, halting his departure. "She said she came by earlier and left lunch for both of us in the fridge." Her voice gentled. "You really should *eat*, Carter."

He gave a pained smile. "You just want to fortify me for this six-minute torture test you're planning."

"I can make you a protein shake, if you prefer. I noticed a Vitamix on the counter—"

"No, I'll eat something."

Carter had initiated the subject, but uncertainty made Quinn hesitate. "Your medical files indicated retrograde amnesia. You really don't remember anything at all?"

He fell silent, and she feared the question had been too invasive. Finally, though, he answered.

"It's funny you ask. I…had a dream last night. I can't stop thinking about it, actually." He leaned on the cane, his gaze inward. "I was at my home in LA, trying to break down the bathroom door. It was locked from the inside. I kept calling to Bianca, trying to get her to open it."

He frowned. "I've been dreaming a lot. Mostly crazy stuff, but this one seemed so real. I'll see you upstairs," he said quietly, then made a slow retreat from the room.

Dreams *were* a common side effect of the pain medication. But as Quinn collected her things, she couldn't help but think about the other unsettling possibility.

She wondered if some of Carter's memory might be returning.

CHAPTER NINE

"How'd he do?" Mark asked in a hushed voice. He had slipped into the St. Clair ballroom and now stood with Quinn, who was using one of the hotel podiums as a makeshift desk, typing notes into her iPad following her evaluation of Carter's post-test heart and respiratory rates. A pulse oximeter and mechanical lap counter she had purchased that morning in Charleston lay on the podium's top, as well.

"It's not really a pass-fail situation," she explained. "The walk test evaluates aerobic ability and endurance. It gives us a starting point to improve on."

Carter rested in a chair on the other side of the ballroom, near a line of soaring French windows hung with heavy velvet drapes. Olivia and Ethan were with him, keeping him occupied. Her small grandson in tow, Olivia had stopped by the hotel after learning of Carter's presence, although Quinn had requested they wait in the hall until testing was completed.

"He has a way to go," she said, knowing she hadn't given Mark the answer he was looking for. "We'll be working daily on rebuilding his stamina and lung capacity."

Carter had been instructed to cover as much ground in the

six minutes as he could, using the thirty-meter lap course Quinn had marked with orange pylons borrowed from the hotel's valet service. Chairs had been placed at intervals to be used for breaks, as needed.

"Emily had an after-school program today," Mark said. "She'll be sorry she missed you."

"I have a dinner date with her on Friday, actually. I talked to Samantha this morning, and she said it'd be all right."

He nodded. "Of course. Did you get inside okay? I was tied up when you arrived."

"Richard was very helpful." The hotel's assistant manager had led them in by way of the kitchen, which had a service door to the high-ceilinged ballroom with its tiered chandelier and inlaid-wood flooring. The route had limited Carter's exposure to staff and the lighter number of guests during the winter season.

Mark peered again at Carter. "He looks beat, so I guess he's actually cooperating."

Quinn noticed Ethan had taken possession of Carter's cane. The dark-haired child bounced about with it, wielding it like a sword. Despite their distance away, she could hear Olivia talking about a new, multiscreen cineplex being built in town.

"I asked him to rate his exertion level on a scale of six to twenty," Quinn said, referring to the Borg Scale used for sports and exercise testing. "He said sixteen, so I think he gave it a real effort."

Still observing Carter, Mark slowly shook his head. "I still can't believe this."

Quinn gave a knowing sigh. "He…told me you were the one to go to his house afterward."

"I'm surprised he mentioned it. He's been pretty close-mouthed." Hesitating, Mark appeared somber. "It seemed like every photographer in LA who wasn't camped at the hospital was outside that big house of his, like buzzards waiting for death. The doctors had prepared us."

Quinn touched the sleeve of his dress shirt. Mark had seen too much tragedy.

"I regret how long Carter and I were estranged," he said. "Something like this brings home how much time we wasted."

She thought of the rift that had been caused by Carter and Shelley's high school fling, something that had begun behind Mark's back while he was away at college.

"You two weren't always so close," she agreed softly. "With good reason."

"And you and Carter were *closer* than I ever realized." His subtle but pointed comment caused her face to heat.

"He finally told you." Focusing on her iPad, she gave a small, dismissive shrug. "It was a meaningless, one-time thing."

"You should've come to me, Quinn. You were too young, and you should've been way off-limits." He sighed regretfully and pushed his hands into his pockets. "You should know Carter feels bad about what he did."

She tried to make light of it. "Oh, I don't know. I'm sure there're worse things than having your first time be with a future *People* magazine Sexiest Man Alive."

"I'm *serious*. Knowing what I do now, you're an even better person than I thought for taking this on."

"Don't give me so much credit. I'm more mercenary than that. I needed a job." Uncomfortable with the discussion,

Quinn fidgeted with the lap counter as she searched for a change of subject. "Maybe I'm overstepping, but has Carter mentioned anything to you about the dreams he's been having?"

"No." Mark looked at her. "About the attack?"

She relayed what Carter had told her about his dream, about the bathroom door in his home being locked and him trying to get to Bianca Rossi, unresponsive on the other side.

The fine lines at the corners of Mark's eyes deepened. "That doesn't make sense. There's no way she could've locked the door with a mortal injury like that. She would've collapsed immediately."

Like pretty much everyone, Quinn had heard the excerpts from the 911 recording, which had been released to the media. The tape had ended with Carter, distraught, following the operator's instructions to help the dying actress until he, too, was stabbed. Thinking of the audio, she felt a chill. "I shouldn't have mentioned it. It's probably just some crazy, medicated dream."

Mark blew out a breath. "I hope so. What happened that night…he's better off never remembering."

He peered again at Carter, who had reclaimed his cane from Ethan. Carter ruffled the child's hair, then slowly stood. He bent his tall frame toward Olivia, who kissed his cheek. His weary gaze met Quinn's.

"I'm surprised, but I'm glad he's talking to you," Mark said. "He needs to open up to someone."

***

It was late afternoon by the time Carter and Quinn entered through the rear of the beach home, then took the elevator up to the main floor. His strength depleted, Carter leaned heavily on his cane. Quinn stood beside him, holding a package that had been left in the parcel box at the home's gated front. It was addressed to Craig Staten—the alias he used during times when he needed anonymity, such as when he had rented the house. He could tell from the Burbank address it was the script Elliott had sent by express mail over the weekend. Elliott had mentioned it that morning during their phone call, claiming it was the best he had read in years.

As the elevator doors opened, they were met with the clicking of nails over the hardwood flooring. Doug danced in happy greeting.

"It doesn't look like he destroyed anything." Quinn looked around, sounding relieved as they entered. She laid the package on the coffee table and removed her coat.

"Told you he'd be fine."

Carter shrugged free of the leather bomber jacket draped over his shoulders to accommodate the sling. Then he sat on the sofa in front of the fireplace while Quinn went around the room, turning on lamps and filling the space with light.

"You're exhausted," she said, returning to him.

"You should be pleased." He discarded the baseball cap he'd worn to try to conceal his identity, then ran a hand through his shaggy hair. "Torturing of the prisoner accomplished."

"And another torture session begins tomorrow. I'm giddy."

Carter looked up at her, her soft smile breaking through the weariness that dulled his senses. He had always liked Quinn's hair—thick and glossy in the lamplight, loose russet tendrils framing her face. She was petite, probably only about five-four, and while definitely fit, there was also a lushness about her body, her breasts full and hips shapely. Carter lightly cleared his throat and looked away.

"I noticed the refrigerator's stocked," she said. "I'm going to make you an early dinner before I go. Maybe an egg omelet?"

"I thought you were vegetarian."

"That doesn't keep me from cooking it. Besides, I'm lacto-ovo."

He rubbed a hand tiredly over his face. "That's not necessary, Quinn."

"Food *is* necessary, for building your strength. Even when you don't feel like eating. In fact, I'd like to start supplementing with some high-calorie protein shakes." When he didn't respond, she sat on the sofa beside him. Her eyes softened.

"This *will* get easier," she promised. "These first few days will be hardest, but you'll start getting accustomed to the routine. If you give it your all like you did today, we'll make progress." She added carefully, "If you're open to it, I'd like to teach you some meditative breathing techniques. To help with pain and anxiety."

He'd tried, but he had been unable to hide his worry about the walk test that afternoon, fearful of pushing his heart too hard. His apprehension embarrassed him, and he was glad Quinn had kept his mother and Ethan out of the ballroom. Quinn had been a soothing presence, calmly assuring him nothing bad would happen, that his heart and lungs could handle the exertion. Still, she had pointed out the automatic defibrillator the St. Clair had installed in the ballroom as a routine safety feature. Quinn was certified in CPR and knowledgeable about the system.

"Vegetarian, meditation," he noted wryly. "And I thought

I'd escaped California." Then, becoming serious, he murmured, "Thank you."

The corners of Quinn's mouth tilted up slightly. "For torturing you?"

His eyes held hers. "For doing this."

She shrugged. "As I reminded Mark earlier, you're paying me a lot of money. But thank you for trusting me today." She tilted her head at him. "And for not being a special snowflake. I was expecting some serious celebrity A-list attitude."

Despite his fatigue, Carter chuckled. "Least I can do."

"Carter…there's also something else I want to talk to you about. You need to be wearing that medic alert necklace."

He felt his dignity slip another notch. She had seen it on the kitchen counter, no doubt, next to the revolving spice rack. Exactly where he'd left it after Mercer had presented it to him yesterday morning.

"My sister's idea of a going-away gift," he said dourly. "She's apparently confused me with an eighty-six-year-old."

"It's a good idea, especially with you here alone so much. At least until we get some of your strength and agility back."

"I don't need it."

"If you fell, could you get yourself up?"

Carter pressed his lips together, unsure of the answer. "Let's say I did need it. What then? It calls emergency services, and suddenly I'm on the news again."

"I looked at it—this one's advanced. There's a secondary button you can use to contact someone for lesser emergencies, like Mark or me. You just have to program in the number." When he didn't answer, Quinn said, "Just think about it, all right? I don't want to show up in the morning and find you facedown on the floor."

She stood, picking up the remote and handing it to him. "I'm going to make that omelet, you're going to eat it, and then Doug and I have to get going."

"Why don't you start leaving him here?" He knew the story about how the dog had come into Quinn's possession. Doug had taken a spot on the area rug, but raised his head, apparently aware he had become a point of discussion. Rising, tail wagging, he padded over to Carter. "Your mother doesn't want him underfoot, right? And you'll be here most every day, anyway."

Quinn bit her lip. "You're sure?"

He rubbed the dog's head. "Yeah."

"I have enough food for him in my duffel for tonight," she said, although she still sounded unsure. "I can bring more, and the rest of his things, tomorrow. But if you change your mind, you can just—"

"I won't." He watched as Quinn headed into the kitchen. Carter turned on the television and laid his head back against the cushions, Doug now seated beside him on the sofa. A short time later, he sat up again. The overnight package on the coffee table seemed to stare back at him. He leaned forward and picked it up, put it on his lap and awkwardly opened it, sliding out the three-ring binder. The movie script was titled *The Rainy Season.* On its front, Elliott had scrawled, *Forget the Others and Read This Now*, in bold, red ink.

Carter tossed it onto the coffee table and closed his eyes.

***

By the time Quinn departed, the sun had dropped almost completely below the horizon. Waiting for the gate to open, she pulled from the home's inlaid-brick drive onto the road. As the Mercedes's headlights swept across the wooded, undeveloped property adjacent to the beach house, she noticed a nondescript black sedan, lights off, tucked into the jungle of palmettos, palm trees and loblolly pines. Decelerating, she squinted at the car as she passed, fairly certain she saw a shadowed figure inside. Locating her cell phone, she called Carter and warned him about the car as she drove, suspecting it might be a photographer. If so, she wondered if they had been tailed from the resort. She hoped not, since so far, none of the paparazzi had located the home Carter was renting.

Once the call ended, Quinn laid the phone on the passenger seat, the dark plane of ocean on her left as she drove the several miles back into town.

You were too young, and you should've been way off-limits.

Mark's words echoed. Her first time hadn't been particularly pleasant. The sex had hurt. But at that point in time, she hadn't cared. Her fifteen-year-old self had been too taken with the idea of *being* with him—her sister's ex and the cutest, most popular boy in school. A filmy recollection of their time alone on the beach, Carter's mouth on hers, tasting of beer, sprang without invitation into her mind. His insistent erection against her swimsuit bottom as they'd made out had both scared and thrilled her. Thinking of how he had pressed her down onto the cool, white sand, the weight of him on top of her—even now, it caused a pulling sensation low inside her. Annoyed with herself, Quinn brushed the recollection away like gritty sand stuck to her skin.

When she reached the B&B a short time later, light shone from its interior. But based on the lack of cars, it appeared the houseguests were out somewhere. Nora was at Bible study, Quinn already knew.

As she cut off the car's engine in the driveway, she noticed the large flower arrangement sitting at the front door under the porch light's aura. Intuition tightened her stomach. Quinn gathered her things inside the car. On her way into the house, she paused on the porch to pick up the heavy arrangement. Placing it on the kitchen counter, Quinn's pulse quickened as she read her name typed on the small envelope tucked into the mass of red roses. With a tense breath, she opened the envelope and took out the card.

I'm not giving up on us. I want you back.

Jake

Quinn checked her watch, noting that even though the winter sky had darkened, the time was just after six. There was a chance the local florist that had delivered the roses was still open. Dialing the number under the logo on the envelope, she waited through several rings before someone answered.

"This is Quinn Reese, calling from the Reese House Bed & Breakfast. You delivered flowers here today—"

"I remember," the woman said, pride in her voice. "Two dozen red roses. Is there a problem?"

"No, they're lovely. But could you tell me if they were purchased in person?"

"I believe it was a wire order. Hold on a second, hon." She paused, as if checking her records. "The order came through a San Francisco florist. Pacific Heights Floral Designs."

Quinn recognized the high-end florist boutique. It was one Jake had used before. Relief washed through her. Confirmation he had returned home.

"Thank you," she said, then disconnected. Quinn disliked roses. They reminded her of funerals. She had told Jake that before and wondered if he had forgotten. She knew only that she didn't want Nora to see them. To her, they would be another indicator that her daughter was making a mistake. Picking up the vase, she went out to the backyard through the kitchen door. A garbage receptacle sat discreetly behind a latticework fence at the patio's edge. Balancing the arrangement on her hip, Quinn lifted the receptacle's hinged lid and removed the bag of trash inside. She then dropped in the flowers and replaced the bag on top, hiding them from view.

Jake wanted her back. He'd made that abundantly clear. He had cajoled, begged and, finally, threatened. The latter was the reason Quinn had fled San Francisco.

Standing in the shadowy backyard, her gaze fell on her mother's collection of garden gnomes. They loitered among the lifeless stems of last summer's vegetable garden. Looking at them, a faint chill ran across Quinn's nape. Their dead eyes and leering grins gave her the creeps.

Nora's a fragile thing. I wonder how she'd like knowing what her little girl is really into.

Crossing her arms over her chest against the chilly night air, she hurried back inside.

CHAPTER TEN

"You're up early." Nora stood at the kitchen counter, putting out food for a continental-style breakfast for the two houseguests, who were still in their room upstairs. Quinn had just come down, dressed in yoga pants and a sleek, zip-up athletic jacket. As she packed her things into her duffel, her mother admonished, "This is your fourth day at this job, and every morning you run off without breakfast. Sit down and eat."

Quinn tucked a loose strand of wavy hair behind her ear. "It's supposed to be warmer today, almost like spring. I want to get in some yoga at the beach before leaving."

She went around behind her mother and filled a black-handled teakettle with water, placing it on the stovetop. "I'll take some tea with me. I've been getting breakfast on the square."

"Why, when I have all this food here?" Nora picked up her coffee mug that sat next to a wooden knife block, taking a sip as she regarded her daughter over its rim. Relenting, Quinn selected what looked to be the healthiest item—a bran muffin—from the platter of pastries and breads, then picked off a section and popped it into her mouth. As she chewed, she stared at a trio of potted herbs that sat next to the window before speaking.

"My dinner with Emily is tomorrow night," she reminded. Quinn had mentioned it several days ago, encouraging her mother to come along. "You still haven't said if you're going with us."

"I can't." Nora busied herself with removing several jams and jellies from the refrigerator. "I volunteer at the library on Fridays."

"It still closes at seven, right? We can wait to go until then."

"It isn't a good time, honey." Having placed the jars on the counter, Nora reached into a cabinet and began pulling out juice glasses. "You know we have guests—"

"Who are on their *own* for lunch and dinner. I know the house rules, Mom. Complimentary breakfast and a snack at night." When Nora continued working, Quinn put down the muffin she'd been picking at and moved closer, frustrated. "Look at me?"

With a sigh, Nora faced her. Quinn gentled her voice. "Emily is *Shelley's* daughter. *Your* granddaughter. I don't understand. You should want to see her as much as possible. She's only eight. Surely you're not holding it against her that Mark—"

"She calls that woman *Mommy*, right in front of me." Nora's expression tightened with hurt and indignation. "The last time I had Emily here, all she talked about was *her*. I just can't take how they've all forgotten about our Shelley."

"I know it's hard," Quinn said sympathetically. "But try to think of Emily. She was just a toddler when her mother died.

She's a little girl who needs a mother, and Samantha's filled a big void in her life. Mark still wants *you* to be part of Emily's life, too. He told me you haven't asked to see her in months. You can't act like they're trying to keep you out. You're the only one doing that."

Nora bit down on her bottom lip, looking away.

Quinn released a breath. The teakettle had begun a low whistle. Moving to the stove, she dropped a sachet of green tea—a favorite blend she had brought with her from San Francisco—into her stainless-steel travel mug, then poured steaming water over it.

"You're working for them, aren't you?"

She turned to her mother again.

"I guessed as much," Nora said unhappily. "Mark wanting to talk to you. That fancy car outside. There've been rumors Carter St. Clair's in town. He's this mystery patient, isn't he?"

Quinn felt guilt for her secrecy. "I didn't tell you because they're trying to keep his presence low-key. I was worried you might mention it to someone."

"Are you seeing him alone?"

"I'm *treating* him alone, yes. That's how private therapy works."

"It's unseemly, Quinn." Nora squinted at her harshly. "You're still a *married* woman. And you know how those actor types are—"

"I'm legally separated," she reminded, tense. "And my relationship with Carter is professional."

"I never liked him when he was going around with Shelley. And I saw one of his movies—one was enough. I don't care if it did win some big award. It was pure filth, like everything that comes out of Hollywood. You ask me, the whole family should be ashamed."

Quinn stiffened, thinking of her own shadowed backstory. Nora also seemed oblivious to the parallels between the professional sports and entertainment industries. Nor had she inquired about Carter's health. Instead, she shook her head, self-pity in her voice. "It wasn't enough the St. Clairs stole Shelley. Now they're working on you, too."

"No one's working on me." Quinn's jaw clenched as she screwed the top onto the mug. "And no one *stole* Shelley, Mom. I'm pretty sure she married Mark of her own free will."

Nora gave her a pained look. "Do you think I don't know she preferred them to me? And who could blame her? I was here all alone. With them, she had a big, new family, not to mention all that money and prestige. I always played second fiddle."

"That isn't true," Quinn said, although she couldn't bring herself to look her mother in the eye.

"Shelley inherited that baby grand piano from your Nana," Nora recounted, referring to Quinn's paternal grandmother, Fiona. "She didn't even ask me about keeping it here. She moved it into that ostentatious mansion of Olivia's. I swear that woman thinks she lives at Tara."

"The Big House *is* on the St. Clair property, where Shelley lived," Quinn tried to reason. "The piano's too big for the bungalow, and it was probably just more convenient to have it nearby since she played so often." Hesitantly, she added, "Shelley also knew how much you disliked Nana Fee, even more so once you and Dad divorced. She probably thought you wouldn't want the piano here."

Nora appeared doubtful. Putting down the mug, Quinn walked to where she stood and laid her hand on her mother's drooped shoulder. When Nora didn't respond, she suppressed a sigh. Retrieving her mug, she picked up her things, including her yoga mat bag that sat nearby on the floor. Their disagreement had shown her once again how intractable, how judgmental, her mother could be. Quinn's throat tightened.

She still loved her, however.

Before departing, she made a final plea. "Think about having dinner with us tomorrow night? I...know Emily would like to see you."

***

It was midafternoon by the time Carter returned with Quinn from the orthopedics appointment in Charleston. He stretched out in the Mercedes's passenger seat, no longer wearing the sling, since the specialist had agreed with Quinn's assessment that the immobilization could be making things worse. As she drove them on the two-lane highway that ran beside the ocean, he stole a look at her from beneath the brim of his baseball cap. She had worn her russet hair loose today, and it tumbled around her shoulders, her slender fingers grasping the steering wheel.

They had already fallen into something of a routine. Mornings began with a supervised walk on the treadmill, then Quinn performing the rather unpleasant scar massage. Another treadmill session followed in the afternoon. Today, however, she had also instructed him on what she called mindful breathing. Carter had felt silly, sitting with his eyes closed and trying to focus his thoughts on his breath. But Quinn was insistent it would help once he got the hang of it. For now, he was indulging her.

"How's your shoulder?" she asked.

The physician had given a cortisone injection deep into his

shoulder to help with the inflammation. Carter squinted through his sunglasses at the brief flashes of ocean appearing between the beach houses lining the shore, most of them sun-bleached and ramshackle. "Numb."

"The injection probably included an anesthetic for immediate relief," Quinn said. "The corticosteroid should start kicking in over the next several hours. If we can get some of the pain to ease, we should be able to start some shoulder work." She glanced over at him. "I'll admit you took the injection like a champ. I've seen three-hundred-pound defensive linemen get woozy when that massive needle comes at them."

Carter thought of his lengthy hospitalization. "Not my first rodeo," he murmured.

Quinn gave him a sympathetic look. A short time later, she spoke again. "I noticed you brought the script with you—the one your agent sent. Is it any good?"

After avoiding it for days, Carter had begun reading it last night. Elliott had been right—it was enthralling, a tense domestic thriller about a man in an unhappy marriage who gets involved with his child's nanny, then later becomes a suspect in her disappearance.

"It's pretty great," he admitted, aware it was Elliott's bait for getting him interested in working again.

He had begun to doze in the warmth of the car's sunbathed interior when he heard the blinker come on. Carter opened his eyes as they neared one of the Rarity Cove public beach access points. "What're you doing?"

Quinn decelerated and turned into the parking lot.

"Your afternoon cardio." She pulled into one of the marked spots and turned off the engine. "I've already been on the beach today, and it's really nice. The windbreaker you're wearing should be enough. Who knows how long this weather will hold out? I thought we'd go for a walk."

Carter stared at the waves rolling onto the shoreline. Shifting in his seat, his mind fluttered uneasily. "I can't use my cane out there."

"I'll be your support when you need it." Quinn took a tortoise-shell clasp from a tray in the armrest, then used it to secure her hair into a messy bun. Unsnapping her shoulder belt, she turned to him, reassurance in her voice. "We'll go slow and take breaks. I've learned what you're capable of at this point, and I won't let us go so far you can't get back."

He ran a hand over his facial scruff, tense and uncertain.

"Remember what you said when we first talked about what you really wanted?" she reminded. "You said you wanted to walk on the beach. The steps at your place are a bit much right now, but I remembered this place. There're only a few steps down to the sand."

His throat ached at her thoughtfulness.

"With the off-season, there aren't too many people out," she continued. "I've also been watching in the rearview mirror. I'm fairly sure no photographers tailed us from the medical center, despite whoever it was camped across from your house the other night."

Carter had gone to the windows after Quinn called to warn him about the car, but he had been unable to see anyone parked on the undeveloped property.

"So what do you think?" Encouragement shimmered in her gray-green eyes. The same color as the ocean that spread out in front of him, he realized. Carter had seen too much of hospital rooms and physician offices. Despite his anxiety, the sand and sea called to him.

"You're kind of small to be my only support out there." He was only half joking.

"I'm well trained and stronger than I look. *Trust me*, Carter." She issued an ultimatum, however. "It's this or the treadmill. Your choice. You still owe me a second walk today."

Carter shook his head in amused disbelief. He *had* begun to trust Quinn, as much as he had trusted anyone in a long time, outside of close family. Celebrity and the brutal politics of Hollywood had leached much of that ability from him. Maybe Mark was right. Maybe it was because she had been a part of the St. Clair family, at least peripherally, for so long.

"Screw the treadmill," he muttered under his breath.

Her sunny laugh caused his heart to lift. She exited the car, closed her door and went around to open his. Holding his right shoulder carefully, he climbed out to stand in front of her. The salty breeze met his face as seagulls cawed in the air overhead. Squinting up at him, loose tendrils of her hair tossed by the wind, Quinn smiled.

"Let's do this," he said with quiet determination. Leaving the cane in the car, he took the arm she offered.

CHAPTER ELEVEN

Quinn sat at the rustic dining table in the beach home's living area, using her iPad to begin the process of transferring her National Physical Therapy Exam scores to the South Carolina licensing board. The shadows outside the wall of French doors had deepened, but she was in no hurry to return to her mother's—partly due to their argument that morning, but also because the B&B's wireless Internet was down, something Nora considered a low priority for repair. Instead, Quinn had worked here in solitude while Carter napped upstairs.

He had come down for dinner a short time earlier and now lounged on the sofa in front of the hearth, long legs propped on the coffee table, movie script in his lap and Doug's head on his thigh as the dog snored softly. Nearby, the television was on, although its sound was muted.

Carter had done well at the beach, Quinn thought, a sense of accomplishment filling her. He had walked for a good amount of time without assistance, although he had leaned on her a bit more on the way back.

A short time later, she powered down her device and stood. Arms crossed loosely over her chest, she went to where Carter sat, intent on his reading.

"Doug's been fed, and the kitchen's cleaned up. I'm leaving soon. Thanks for the wireless access."

He looked up at her from the sofa, a pair of preppy reading glasses on his nose. Unsurprisingly, he looked good in them. Quinn thought of the nerdish spectacles she had worn nearly until college.

He nodded at her comment. "Thanks for dinner."

Since she had stayed later tonight, she had cooked for them both, bypassing the takeout cartons from Café Bella inside the fridge. She had made a lentil and brown rice dish and also sautéed a chicken breast with rosemary for Carter. He had eaten rather well, she'd noticed. Perhaps the outdoor exercise had piqued his appetite, or the cortisone injection was beginning to provide some relief.

"Isn't that what personal assistants do?" she asked lightly. "Make dinner?"

"In LA, they make dinner *reservations*. And you're thinking of a personal chef—two different people."

"Which reminds me, there's only one of me and I'm going to run those errands tomorrow morning." She planned to go to the BI-LO for groceries, then to McSwain's drugstore on the town square to have two of his prescriptions refilled. Carter had also asked her to drop off some papers to Mark at the St. Clair. "We might not get started until after lunch."

"Torture session delayed—duly noted." He returned to the script. She went to gather her things, but he spoke again, causing her to turn back to him.

"Quinn…today was okay," he said, a vulnerability about him. "It felt good to be on the beach, and for you to have my back. I'm sure I looked like some geriatric case—"

"You looked like someone recovering from a traumatic injury," she corrected, earnest. "Like someone who's finally starting to fight his way back."

His gaze held hers. Unsettled by her lapsing objectivity, Quinn searched for something to say. "Let's hope this weather holds out. Maybe we can trade the treadmill for another walk on the beach tomorrow."

His full mouth quirked faintly, the grooves of his dimples deepening. "Are you going soft on me, or am I falling into some kind of Stockholm-syndrome situation here?"

Quinn smiled back. "Don't worry. You'll start hating my guts again soon enough. I'm hoping to start your shoulder work…"

She stopped at the image that appeared on the television. The national news had moved to an entertainment segment, and her stomach dipped as Bianca Rossi posed on the red carpet in front of them. His features sobering, Carter removed his glasses and leaned forward for the remote, upping the volume as he appeared in the footage, as well.

"Filming on the sitcom has been halted since Rossi's murder in November at the home of actor Carter St. Clair, who was also seriously injured in the stalker attack," the voiceover stated as the screen switched to a clip from the show in which the young actress had starred. "The network announced today Rossi is being replaced by twenty-four-year-old actress Serena Ruben-Reyes…"

Once the segment ended, Carter cut off the television, their lightness of earlier vanished. Leaving the cane against the sofa's arm, he rose, causing Doug to leap from the couch and trot off to the kitchen.

"You can go, Quinn," he said quietly, seeming distracted.

As he walked slowly to the row of French doors that led to the deck overlooking the beach, Quinn's heart beat dully. A voice inside her pointed out she had just been dismissed like a servant, that she should do what he asked and leave him alone. But some stubborner, more compassionate part of her remained. Moving closer, she could see Carter's profile as he stared onto the dark plane of ocean. Sensing his anxiety, she gave a gentle reminder. "Deep, slow breaths."

His eyes squeezed closed, and he said with a slightly breathless forced patience, "I'm fine, Quinn. I'll see you tomorrow, all right?"

At his rebuff, she took a step back, prepared to leave. But as she reached for the duffel she had left on the table, he spoke again, his voice troubled.

"The footage was from the charity gala we went to that night. I remember that much, at least."

Quinn turned. Carter remained at the doors, his back to her. Unsure of what to do, she hesitantly returned to where he stood.

"We'd been seeing each other for about a month." The perfect symmetry of his pensive features reflected back to her in the door's glass. "Our studios set us up. That's not unusual. I'm not sure, but I think maybe she was also sleeping with her show's producer. I'd seen some texts between them."

Quinn thought of the photos she had seen of the actress with Carter in the weeks leading up to the stabbing, the same images used repeatedly in its aftermath. Like the rest of the world, she had assumed they were in love.

"I never confronted her about it," he admitted somberly. "I guess it really didn't matter that much to me. I was leaving for Perth to start filming a movie in two weeks. I figured whatever was going on between us would end once I left." He continued to stare out over the water. "I suppose I haven't changed all that much to you, have I, Quinn?"

She heard the self-recrimination in his voice.

"I'm not here to judge you," she said quietly, peering up at him. "But, Carter, you can't…surely you don't think her death is your fault."

He looked at her then, his eyes like twin pools of indigo. "If she hadn't been with me that night…if I'd broken things off with her sooner, she'd still be alive."

Jaw clenched, he bowed his head and swallowed.

The mood was subdued as she departed the house a short time later. As she waited for the electronic gate at the top of the drive to open, Carter's admission weighed on her. She wondered now if the dream he'd had about trying to get to the actress through a locked door wasn't a recalled memory at all, but was instead his subconscious still trying to find some way to save her. Quinn believed she now understood why he had been so apathetic toward his recuperation.

He felt guilt for his survival.

But what he had revealed was also a cautionary tale. Bianca Rossi wasn't the first actress, the first supermodel, to whom Carter had been linked. She thought of the serial dating in Hollywood, the constant cycle of celebrity pairings and breakups. Although he hadn't said it directly, it sounded as though his relationship with Rossi had been more of an *arrangement*, created at least initially for the PR buzz.

Regardless, the lifestyle seemed superficial and lonely. Not unlike the world she had left behind.

It had grown dark, the road that ran alongside the beach illuminated only by the Mercedes's headlights and spill of moonlight in the cloudless evening. Where the subtropical foliage was low, Quinn could see the silvered sheet of the ocean's surface as she drove. To her right, roads that traveled inland were marked by street signs. Hers was the only car on the thoroughfare. The oceanfront property on the north side of town was undeveloped in stretches, and what had been occupied was owned by the wealthy, who had constructed vast homes—many just for summer—on large lots of land. Nor were there public beach access points, which were mostly in town or to its south.

Quinn glanced briefly down to change channels on the radio. But as she looked up again, she startled as headlights entered her peripheral vision, shooting toward her from a side street.

There was no time to react.

She screamed at the bone-jarring impact and crunch of metal as the cars collided.

CHAPTER TWELVE

Stunned, her chest heaving, Quinn tried to process what had just happened. Whether she was injured. Upon impact, the Mercedes had spun off the asphalt before coming to a stop in the undergrowth of an undeveloped property, broadsided by a car that had driven through the stop sign on the interconnecting street. The car that hit her sat in the road, hood crumpled and smoke rising from its mangled grille.

Releasing her seat belt with trembling fingers, she heard a car door opening and approaching feet.

A dark-haired man wearing sneakers and jeans strode toward her, his eyes locked on hers through the windshield. Sudden realization prickled her nape. The car. It was the one she had seen across from the beach house earlier that week. A warning bell sounded in her brain.

Quinn locked the Mercedes's doors and grabbed for her purse that had slid off the passenger seat. She searched frantically through it, finding her cell phone just as the man yanked at the door handle where she sat. He cursed when he found it locked.

"Open the door, bitch!"

This was no paparazzo. Heart slamming inside her chest, Quinn began to dial for help on her phone as the man pulled something from his pocket. A second later, she flinched and cried out as the window glass shattered.

The door flew open. Hard hands dragged her from the car despite her struggling and screaming. The man smelled like nicotine, his grip on her bruising. Quinn kicked as hard as she could, landing a solid blow to his right kneecap. He bellowed in pain, and she wrenched free. But his large frame blocked her path to the road. She fled in the opposite direction toward the shoreline. Thorns and bramble tore at her clothing as she ran deeper into the shadowy undergrowth, through a stand of tall bamboo, her breath rasping out of her, her hand still gripping her cell phone.

Daring to look back, she felt her heart lurch. The man was coming after her—gaining on her. Gasping, Quinn broke free of the scrub a minute later. She half stumbled, half fell down an outcropping of rocks before her feet sank into soft sand. Ahead, waves crashed onto the beach. If she could make it to the water's edge where the sand was hard-packed, she could increase her speed.

But as she gained purchase on the firm sand, something jerked her backward with violent force. Her feet flew out from under her as pain seared her throat, the cell phone flying from her grasp. It took a second to realize what had happened. The man had caught up to her, used her jacket's hood to lasso her. Sprawled on her back, Quinn clasped her throat, coughing and wheezing. As he stood over her, cold terror poured through her. She attempted to scream, but her lungs had lost power and only a hoarse croak emerged.

"Fucking bitch," he snarled, winded, his chest heaving.

Quinn skittered away, crawling backward from him like a sand crab. But instead of coming after her, he picked up her cell phone that lay among streamers of seaweed washed onto the shore. He lit up the screen.

"Give me the code!"

Quinn stared at him in confusion. She cried out, recoiling and shielding her face with her arm as he advanced on her, his hand curled into a fist and drawn back as if to strike her. "Give me the fucking passcode!"

"Eleven…" she stammered, panting. "Eleven seventeen!"

Her stomach soured in realization as he worked the screen, no doubt deleting her saved voice messages. Then he turned to the water and threw the device as far as he could. The ocean swallowed it.

He had something else. The key fob for the Mercedes. As he hurled it into the water next, Quinn glimpsed the small tattoo on the inside of his wrist, visible in the strong moonlight beneath his jacket sleeve. She had seen the tattoo before.

He spat on the sand. A look of victory in his stony, dark eyes, he turned and stalked off, back into the thicket at the edge of the beach.

She couldn't stop shaking. Quinn remained on her knees on the wet, cold sand. She touched her face, and her fingers came away with blood.

The messages she had threatened Jake with were gone. Tears crowding her vision, Quinn nearly choked on her frustration and hate. The flowers he had wired from San Francisco had been a subterfuge so she would let down her guard. Jake *had* returned to California, but he'd sent someone else to do his dirty work here.

She managed to stand. Quinn thought with dismay of the

Mercedes. She pressed her hands to her face, knowing she could have been injured or killed tonight. Thinking of the car accident that had taken Shelley's life, she trembled harder.

She didn't dare go back to the road, in case the man was still there. And even if the Mercedes was drivable, she no longer had the key. She was still several miles out of the Rarity Cove township, but Carter's beach house was only a mile or so back.

She was fearful of being alone on the isolated beach.

Arms hugged around herself, not knowing what else to do, Quinn began walking northward along the shore.

CHAPTER THIRTEEN

"It sounds like things with Quinn are working out," Mercer said over the phone once Carter had given her the requested rundown on his day. Her nightly calls to check on him were becoming a ritual. "I won't say I told you so."

"Thanks," he replied dryly.

"You okay? You seem a little down."

"I'm just tired," he lied, wishing his sister couldn't read him so easily. The last thing he wanted was for her to worry about him. Thinking of his brother-in-law, he changed the topic. "Tell Jonathan to hang in there. I'm glad his recent scan showed improvement. I know he's happy to have you back home."

"I'm happy to be here, too," she admitted. After they talked for another few minutes, she said, "Okay, gotta go. Love you."

"Love you, too." Carter disconnected. Leaning forward to place his cell phone on the coffee table, the medic alert pendant that hung on a cord around his neck bumped against his chest. He had conceded to himself days ago that it made sense to have the device on him when he was here alone, and he had put it on soon after Quinn's departure.

Quinn. Suppressing a sigh, he massaged his closed eyelids. He wondered why he had bared his soul to her like he had tonight. It surprised him it mattered so much what she thought of him.

Carter sat back in tense silence. Seeing Bianca on television had his mind grasping again for some memory of that night. He recalled the gala, then driving them to his home afterward, even though they were scheduled to attend an afterparty. He hadn't been in the mood to go. He remembered them entering his foyer, but the memory ended there, as if it were film on a projector that had stopped working, leaving the theater dark.

Barking erupted from somewhere else inside the large house, pulling him from his thoughts. When it didn't stop and the dog didn't come when called, Carter reached for his cane and went to investigate. He found Doug pacing in front of the tall windows in the solarium, his attention on the beach below.

"What is it, boy?" Carter approached the windows, too. Moonlight illuminated the stretch of pale sand, but he saw nothing except the whitecaps of breaking waves. He scanned the area again, certain there had to be a reason for the dog's alert. A moment later, his skin tingled. He had been looking too far out. A shadowed figure was much closer to the property, at the gate closing off the high wood stairs that led up from the beach.

He squinted in bafflement. Quinn?

He couldn't see her face or body, only the russet mass of her hair being whipped by the wind. Doug's whine indicated he recognized her, too.

What the hell was she doing down there? She had left nearly an hour ago by car.

She had the passcode to the beachside entrance, which was the same code used to gain access at the front drive. Still, Carter went to the wall console and buzzed the gate where she stood so it unlocked. Then he took the elevator down to the bottom floor and went out to the rear terrace, Doug at his side.

"Quinn?" he called, cursing his slow pace with the cane. He was coatless, and the day's mild temperature had dropped with nightfall. Doug raced ahead of him on the terrace, meeting Quinn at the top of the steps.

As Carter neared, his concern grew. Her face appeared pale, and what looked like droplets of dried blood flecked one cheek.

"Quinn," he murmured, breathless from his trek. "What happened? Are you all right?"

"The car…I'm sorry," she stammered, her reddened eyes meeting his for only a moment before she averted her gaze. Did she have an accident? Why did she return on foot instead of using her cell to call for help? But the questions died in his throat. Quinn covered her face with her hands.

Dropping his cane on a nearby chaise, Carter closed the distance between them.

"Hey," he said softly, pulling her against him. He used his left hand to cup the back of her head and stroke her tangled hair. She shook like a freezing child, not fighting his embrace, instead pressing her face into his chest.

"It's okay," he said, his heart tugging as she tried unsuccessfully to contain a sob. Quinn had been a source of strength for him these last several days. Seeing her distraught caused a swell of protectiveness inside him. "Are you hurt? Do you need me to call for paramedics?" He indicated the medic alert pendant he wore, trying to show her, to do something that would stop her tears. "Look. I'm fully wired. You need them, I'm your man."

He felt her head shake against his chest. "No," she whispered.

Despite his need to know what had happened, he remained silent, holding her as firmly as his injured shoulder would allow, until finally she released him and took a small step back, wiping her eyes, appearing embarrassed. "The car's about a mile down the road. I don't know how much damage—"

"I don't care about the car, Quinn. Are you okay?"

She nodded, her arms clasped around herself. "I-I think so."

Gently, he cupped her jaw and tilted her face upward so he could get a better look at the small cuts on her cheek under the terrace lights. "What happened?"

She wavered before speaking. "There was another car. The driver crashed into me from a side street. He…wasn't hurt."

"You're sure?" Carter frowned. "Where's this guy now?"

She rubbed her forehead. "I-I don't know."

He listened in bewilderment. "He hit you and just took off?"

Quinn bit her lip, and he noticed her shivering had increased. Intuition made his heart beat harder. He didn't like this.

"Let's go inside where it's warm. And then you're going to tell me exactly what happened."

***

Seeing the house from the beach, its interior drenched in warm light, had been like a beacon to Quinn. But as she had neared, dread over what to tell Carter had taken hold. She had been at the gate trying to gain her composure when he had buzzed it open. Humiliated by her breakdown, she now sat upstairs on the sofa. Carter had taken a seat in the adjacent chair, pulled so close their knees nearly touched. Leaning forward, he slid the crystal tumbler on the coffee table closer.

"Here, drink this. It'll help."

Hesitating, Quinn picked up the glass. As she swallowed, the aged scotch nearly stole her breath. Wiping her hand over her lips, she set the glass down again, feeling the alcohol's slow heat slide down her throat and into her stomach.

"What's going on, Quinn?" Carter asked, his brow creased. "Full disclosure."

He had a right to know. The car had been leased through his production company. Police and insurance reports would have to be filed. She had to tell him. Quinn stared at her hands, twisted together in her lap. "The car that hit me…it was the one I saw outside here a few nights ago."

"A pap hit you?"

She knew the anger in his voice was concern. "It wasn't a photographer. And he was here watching me, not you. I know that now. Probably establishing a pattern, my comings and goings. I'm…sure Jake sent him."

Carter sat rigidly as he waited for her to continue.

"The driver hit me on purpose." Fresh anxiety coursed through her. "When he got out of his car and started coming toward me, I knew something was wrong. I locked the doors, but he had something—it looked like a small baton. He used it to shatter the window."

When she had gone into the powder room to try to clean up, she had seen the small cuts on her cheek from the flying glass.

"Did he hurt you?" Carter's jaw clenched. "He didn't try to—"

"No. He pulled me out of the car, though. I thought at first that..." Her voice thickened, and she stopped. When the man had thrown her down on the beach, she had been certain she was going to be beaten, raped or worse. She forced herself to continue. "I took a self-defense course in San Francisco. They taught you the most vulnerable places—the eyes, groin, knees. I got away from him, but the only path was to the beach."

She stole a look at Carter, her stomach tense. As he listened, his eyes were stormy, his mouth a hard line.

"I-I tried, but I couldn't outrun him. But instead of attacking me, he took my cell phone. He deleted my messages and threw it in the water, along with the car keys." She shook her head, still in disbelief. "Then he just turned and walked away."

"What were in the messages, Quinn?" Carter pressed.

She hung her head, unable to bring herself to tell him what the messages had said. How, in the last message, Jake had described in lurid detail the things he had done to her and gloated that she had liked it. He had also threatened to bring her back home by force and imprison her in his house.

"It would be enough to get a restraining order this time." She clenched her hands together harder. "Jake came to my mother's last weekend to try to get me to go back to San Francisco with him and stop the divorce. I told him if he didn't leave town, I'd give the messages to the Rarity Cove Police."

But she knew what had happened tonight was about more than just getting rid of the messages. Jake had intended to scare her, to let her know he was still in control. Carter was speaking to her, she realized dully.

"You said *this time*," he repeated, a tightening around his eyes. "I've heard things about Medero. Was he abusive to you? God. You didn't lose the baby because—"

"No." Her brain was in tumult. She couldn't tell him about her sex life with Jake. It hadn't been *abuse* at first—the dominance and submission games, the roleplaying had all been consensual. The abusive part had come when Jake had repeatedly violated the boundaries she'd set, pushing her limits. When he had given his best friend permission to have her.

"It's not what you think," she managed.

"*Then tell me*."

Quinn was angry with herself that she had let it slip that she had tried to get a restraining order once before. She had desperately wanted to dissolve her marriage to Jake with minimal drama. It was the reason she had kept quiet about Mike Buczek. But following the break-in at her apartment, she felt she had been left with no choice. Fortunately, the press hadn't gotten wind of her filing with the court.

"I tried to get a restraining order after we were separated," she recounted. "I'd already moved out of his house and into an apartment in the Mission District, where I lived before. But Jake was watching me. I'd see his car outside almost nightly, when he wasn't on the road with the team." At the memory, her stomach clenched. Jake's Maserati had been impossible to miss. "One night, I went out onto the street and confronted him. I couldn't take it anymore."

"What happened?"

"Nothing. He left." An ache entered her throat. "But the next night, I came home to find my belongings destroyed, most of the clothes in my closet shredded." She passed a nervous hand over her eyes. "My...bedding had been urinated on. I knew in my heart Jake was behind it, just like tonight."

Carter shook his head, a mounting anger in his eyes.

"The judge denied my request," she said on a small sigh. "Jake had an alibi—the night of the break-in, he was out of town for a game. There was no evidence connecting him. There were no prints, and the DNA profile from the urine wasn't a match. The judge treated Jake like a hometown hero who was being inconvenienced." Quinn took a breath, her hands fidgeting in her lap. "Jake approached me outside the courtroom afterward. He again claimed his innocence and voiced his concern for me. But he also warned me my neighborhood was dangerous and that I should come back home before something worse happened. I took it as a threat."

"How long ago was this?"

"Two weeks ago." Weariness settled over her. "I put my things—what was left of them—in storage and booked a flight home. I didn't know what else to do. I only knew I had to get away from him."

"And then Medero showed up here." Carter ran a hand over his mouth, his features hard.

"He's back in San Francisco now." Quinn picked at her nails. "The Breakers are in the playoffs."

"But what about this guy tonight? If you can describe him to the police, they may be able to pick him up. If they find him, he might fess up that Medero hired him."

"I doubt he's from around here. More than likely, he's already gone."

Aware she needed to explain, Quinn nervously raked a hand through her hair, tangled from the ocean breeze. "If you follow sports, you probably know Jake had a bad childhood. The press loves his story." Thinking of how she had at first been so deeply moved by his background, bitterness pooled inside her. "He grew up in poverty in Sacramento, and ran with a gang before sports gave him a way out. The man who hit me had the same tattoo on the inside of his wrist that Jake has. It's a gang sign. I found out after Jake and I were married that he still keeps connections to them."

Carter appeared resolute. "We have to call the police."

Her insides quivered. She thought of the crashed Mercedes. Her wallet and other belongings were still inside it, unless they had been taken. For all she knew, the car that had hit her wasn't drivable and could still be there, as well. If it had been left behind, there could be fingerprints or other evidence. The man had touched the door handle of her car, too. He had been a gang member, so there was a good chance he would be in the system.

"I know we need to report this." Still, Quinn briefly covered her eyes with her hand.

"It's going to be okay." Leaning closer, Carter slipped a hand under her hair and gently cupped the back of her neck.

The secrets she had brought with her from San Francisco were beginning to seep out. Feeling almost nauseated, Quinn waited in silence as Carter used his cell phone to call the Rarity Cove Police.

CHAPTER FOURTEEN

Quinn watched as the two police officers who had been dispatched to the house used their cell phones to snap selfies with Carter. Despite his smile and easy demeanor, she could see the faint lines of fatigue visible around his eyes. She knew he didn't want to be photographed while appearing frailer than his public persona, and she felt horrible for having drawn him into her problems.

Prior to their arrival at the house, the police had located the crashed Mercedes, although the other car had disappeared. The officers had returned her personal items, which, miraculously, had been left untouched inside the car. Quinn had described her assailant and his vehicle to them in as much detail as she could. And while she had haltingly stated her belief that the man had been hired by her soon-to-be ex-husband, she had no proof. She had noticed the officers exchanging glances when she'd given them Jake's name.

As Carter escorted the policemen to the door, Quinn went to check on Doug, who had been placed in another room until they were alone again.

"You okay?" he asked when she returned with the dog.

"I'm so sorry about this."

"Don't be. You didn't do anything wrong." He turned back to the entry hall as the door opened again. Mark and Samantha entered, their expressions indicating they had seen the officers outside. Tail wagging, Doug went to greet them.

"The police said you were in an accident." Samantha looked worriedly at Quinn. It appeared they had been out somewhere, since Samantha wore a cocktail dress underneath her coat, and Mark was in a business suit.

"I'm fine." Quinn lowered her gaze.

Mark came over and embraced her. "What happened?"

"What're you doing here?" Carter's question kept her from having to explain.

"We had a Chamber event," Mark said. "We thought we'd come by on the way home to check on you. The police were leaving as we pulled in."

"Quinn got T-boned," Carter supplied.

"We saw a tow truck down the road." Laying her purse on the table, Samantha slid out of her coat. "There was a silver Mercedes in the brush. It looked pretty banged up."

"That would be me." Quinn attempted a weak smile, but it faltered. "If you'll excuse me, I'm going upstairs to put some cool water on my face."

She went up the staircase, bypassing the elevator. On the landing, she turned into the first bedroom, knowing Carter had the master suite on the other side of the hall. The room was elegant, with an ironwork bed and antique furniture. She closed the door behind her. Sinking onto the mattress edge, she released a weary breath. Her body felt sore from the impact, and she pressed her fingers to her closed eyelids. What Jake had done—risking her life to make a point—proved again that whatever it was he felt for her, it wasn't love.

She hadn't meant to break down in front of Carter like she had. His kindness to her made her throat ache.

A knock sounded on the door. Quinn looked up to see Samantha standing on its threshold.

"Carter suggested I check on you," she said, her eyes soft. She looked sophisticated in her evening attire, her raven hair pulled back into a bun to reveal diamond drop earrings.

"What happened tonight wasn't just a random car accident," Quinn confessed quietly.

Samantha sat beside her. "I gathered that from what I heard between Carter and Mark. I think Carter sent me up here so they could talk."

"I'm sure Jake—my husband—was behind it. We're legally separated, but..." Quinn faltered. "It's gotten messy." An understatement. She shook her head. "I don't know what you must think of me, bringing all this insanity here."

"I know more about insanity than you think." Samantha touched her arm. "Quinn...we don't really know each other that well yet. But if you need a friend, I'm here."

***

"Do you think he did something to cause the miscarriage?" His features taut, Mark kept his voice low. "That would explain the separation so soon after losing the baby."

Carter was seated on the sofa. He had taken the opportunity of Quinn's absence to fill Mark in on what had really gone down tonight. He had told him pretty much everything he knew, including the break-in at Quinn's apartment that had spurred her exodus from San Francisco. "She says no. I asked her flat out if he'd ever abused her."

But her evasiveness, the way her eyes had averted from

his, bothered him.

"If he was behind what happened tonight, that's pretty abusive." Mark paced a few steps. "Her car took a hard hit. She should be checked out by a doctor."

"I agree."

"What do you know about Medero? Beyond the whole pro ball thing?"

The professional sports world and Hollywood overlapped. Although their paths had never crossed directly, Carter had heard of Medero's presence at LA parties and high-profile nightclubs. "There was some talk about him beating up a sound editor at a wrap party a few years ago. Medero supposedly got rough with a woman, and the guy stepped in. Nothing came of it, though. No charges were filed."

"How's that possible?"

Carter shrugged as much as his weakened shoulder would allow. "Money and handlers have a way of making things go away. It might seem like everything a celebrity does goes public, but you'd be surprised what still manages to get swept under the rug." At the possibility of Medero getting rough with Quinn, anger laced through him.

"The question is," Mark said, "how do we stop something like this from happening again? How can we protect her?"

Carter had kept his apartment in Manhattan after relocating to LA. "We can send her to my place in New York. She can stay there as long as she wants."

"I'm not leaving."

Carter looked up to see Quinn on the upstairs landing, having obviously overheard. She came down the stairs with Samantha following. When Quinn reached the main floor, her still-bleary eyes met Carter's.

"Not unless you want me to. I'm talking about the job, I mean. I would certainly understand if you don't want this kind of situation."

"That's not it, Quinn." He slowly stood. "I just thought you'd be safer if you're somewhere Medero can't find you."

She still appeared vulnerable, but her distress seemed to be giving way to anger. "I've already left California because of him. I won't give him any more power. Besides, Jake made his point tonight. I don't think he'll be back anytime soon. He's in the playoffs, and he'll be tied up even longer if the Breakers go to the Super Bowl."

"The playoffs didn't stop him from coming here last weekend," Carter reminded. "Or sending someone after you tonight."

Quinn released a breath, appearing at a loss for words. Then, "I'll be better prepared. I'll carry pepper spray or a stun gun. And if Jake shows up in town again, I *will* ask for a restraining order, even without the voice-mail messages."

"If you're staying because of me—"

"You can fire me. But I'm not leaving Rarity Cove."

Despite Quinn's need to stand her ground, her gaze was questioning, even pleading, as she looked at Carter. Mark touched Samantha's shoulder and guided her to the kitchen, apparently sensing the conversation had taken a private turn.

"I want to keep working with you, Quinn," Carter told her once they were alone. "If it comes to it, we'll both go somewhere else."

She shook her head. "You should be here with your family. You need their support—it's why you came back home. Rarity Cove is *my* home, too. My hometown. If I can't feel safe here, I'll never feel safe anywhere again."

A short time later, Carter entered the kitchen with Quinn. Mark leaned against the counter as Samantha fed Doug small bites of leftover chicken she had taken from the refrigerator. He sat obediently, his tail sweeping the tile floor as he awaited the next morsel.

"Quinn's staying for now," Carter said. "I'm having another car delivered for her use tomorrow."

"It's the low season, so we're slower right now. Why not have the St. Clair limo take her anywhere she needs to go?" Mark suggested. "I'm sure we can arrange a schedule between guest pickups and drop-offs at the airport in Charleston."

"Carter suggested that, but I don't want to interrupt business," Quinn interjected. "Or lose my independence."

The men shared a look, and Carter knew his brother was fighting the urge to insist she be locked away in an ivory tower somewhere. But Carter was reluctantly with her on this. He understood her need for defiance in the face of Medero's stunt. But understanding it didn't erase his unease.

"We'll try it like this for a while," Carter said. "If we sense any kind of threat, we'll ask for your help."

***

"You could stay *here*," Carter offered quietly to Quinn once they'd all returned to the main living area. Mark was helping Samantha into her coat on the other side of the room. "This place is a compound. It'd be the simplest solution."

Biting her lip, Quinn looked up at him. Tired, Carter now used his cane. "Like you said before, we're both adults. You can have your pick of bedrooms."

"I don't think it's a good idea." Her voice was halting.

It had been an impulsive thought. "The offer stands if you change your mind."

She nodded, and he saw gratitude, as well as pain, in her eyes. She briefly touched the medic alert pendant that lay against his chest. He'd nearly forgotten its presence.

"Get some rest," she said softly. "Tomorrow's business as usual."

"Ready?" Mark asked. He and Samantha were going to take Quinn to the twenty-four-hour urgent care facility in town to be checked out, then drop her off at her mother's. The St. Clair limo *would* pick Quinn up tomorrow, since she was temporarily without transportation.

Carrying her purse and duffel, Quinn trailed them to the foyer, then stopped, a strain entering her voice. "I forgot. I have a dinner date with Emily tomorrow night. I don't want to disappoint her, but after what's happened, I'd never risk putting her in harm's way."

Carter spoke up. "We'll work something out. Right, Mark?"

He gave a nod. "Absolutely."

As Mark opened the door for the women, Quinn looked back at Carter. She appeared fragile to him, her russet hair disheveled and the small cuts visible on her cheek. He swallowed. For the second time that night, protectiveness rose up inside him, her desire for independence be damned. But he also felt a helplessness in his current state.

Leaning on the cane, he watched as the door closed behind them.

CHAPTER FIFTEEN

Yesterday's cortisone injection had provided some relief, at least enough that Quinn could begin Carter on some light stretches for his shoulder. They had done across-the-body stretches and side reaches—avoiding resistance exercises and weights until more of the inflammation had subsided.

"Don't force it," she reminded as he completed the last set of overhead reaches, a move that required him to face the wall and repeatedly slide his hands up it as far as he could. "Hold the last rep for ten seconds."

Eyes on her wristwatch, she touched his T-shirt-clad back to let him know when the time had elapsed. Carter lowered his arms and stepped back from the wall, his brow drawn tight by the morning's exertion. Prior to stretches, he had also used the upper-body ergometer—or arm bike—for several minutes, making slow rotations. Other than a muttered curse or two, he hadn't complained or asked for a break, but Quinn could see he was nearing his limit.

"We're done for now. How're you doing?"

"You warned me about the shoulder work," he said, sounding a bit breathless. He rubbed his right shoulder.

"Things just got real."

She indicated the massage table, where he sat so she could once again take his vitals. Quinn remained physically aware of him, but over the past week, she had gotten fairly used to touching him, to their being in intimate proximity to each other. She laid two fingers against the carotid artery in his neck and silently counted the beats as she looked again at her watch. While elevated from the exercise, his pulse was steady and strong.

"You don't look like you got much sleep," he noted a short time later as Quinn removed the pulse oximeter from his left index finger. Since her arrival a couple of hours ago via the St. Clair limousine, they hadn't talked much about what had happened last night. She had meant what she said about keeping things business as usual—she didn't want her problems to interfere with his therapy.

"I suppose I didn't." Stepping to the credenza, she entered his vitals into her iPad.

"Did you tell Nora what happened?"

There hadn't been much choice. Her mother had seen her being dropped off by Mark and Samantha last night, carless. She had also noticed the small cuts on Quinn's cheek. "I played it down. I didn't want to upset her."

Carter frowned. "So, you didn't tell her Medero set the whole thing up?"

"No," she said, still typing. The wreck had caused Nora to fixate on the accident that had killed Shelley, and she'd gotten emotional. Quinn had told her as little as possible—assuring her she hadn't been seriously hurt and relaying only that the other driver had been at fault and left the scene. "Mom hasn't changed. You know how high-strung she is. The less she knows, the better."

Carter said nothing, but as she went about her tasks, she was aware of his scrutiny. Thankfully, the wall intercom buzzed, signaling that someone had arrived at the front gate. Quinn went to the console and asked who it was, finding out it was a representative from the car dealership in Charleston, delivering the replacement vehicle. She buzzed him in, as well as the driver of a second car who would take the representative back once the delivery was completed.

Another silver Mercedes, identical to the first, appeared in the rear drive, where she had told the man to bring the vehicle. When she looked at Carter, he merely gave a tight-lipped smile.

"My own act of defiance—everything stays the same. Medero can kiss my ass."

Quinn looked away, not wanting him to know how deeply his support affected her.

"Why don't you go out and sign for the car?" He stood from the table and reached for his cane. Doug, who had been lying on the floor nearby, got up, as well. "I'll meet you upstairs."

***

Ending the latest call on his cell phone, Carter returned to the kitchen where Quinn was cleaning up after lunch. She had rearranged her schedule around the car's delivery, moving her errands to midday.

"Your phone's really been blowing up," she noted over her shoulder as she rinsed dishes and placed them in the dishwasher.

"Yeah." Elliott had called again about the spec script, letting him know two major studios were interested, but only under the condition that Carter was attached to the project. He had also heard from Ariel Carrington, his publicist, who had been fielding calls from the media, asking for an update on his recuperation. Ariel had been calling every few days, in fact. His last call had been from the Rarity Cove Police. Carter watched as Quinn moved around the kitchen, gracefully sidestepping Doug, who was underfoot.

Except for when her work necessitated conversation, she had been quiet since she had arrived at the house, even distracted. He couldn't blame her. Carter reflected on what he knew. He didn't get it. Medero had come here last weekend to try to win Quinn back, and when he had failed, he had countered with violence? He thought about the stories of exes who developed an *if I can't have her, no one can* mentality.

"You don't have to run errands today," he offered as she placed leftovers in the fridge. "Samantha can pick up my prescriptions."

"No, I'm going as soon as I clean up here."

"I'll go with you. I'll wait in the car while you go inside."

Quinn wiped the granite counter with a damp dishtowel, not looking at him. "I gave you quite a workout this morning. You should stay here and recharge. When I get back, we'll go to the beach for our walk. The same place we went yesterday. We'll take Doug—"

"Quinn."

The firm tone of his voice caught her attention. She turned to face him, and for a moment, the façade of normalcy she had been holding on to slipped. Carter could see it in the tightening around her eyes.

"I need to do this. Alone," she said, insistent. "It's just a simple drive in full light of day. I need to rip off the bandage.

And like I said last night, I believe the danger's gone."

Carter stared briefly at the counter stool, where he'd left his cane after they had come upstairs. Then he looked at Quinn again. "One of the phone calls was from the police. They took prints off the car's door handle. The guy who hit you is in the national crime database—drug trafficking, assault, among other things. And you were right. He's a member of a gang called The Mayans. They started in Sacramento, but now have bases around the country, including in Atlanta, which is probably where he came from. Regardless, the local police have an all-points bulletin out for him."

The information seemed to upset her. She swallowed, then rubbed the back of her neck.

"You're sore from the crash. You should've told me."

"The doctor said I'm fine, just a little banged up. I still managed to get in my yoga practice this morning." At her words, her face clouded, and she slowly shook her head. "You must think I'm full of it. All my talk about yoga, meditation, breathwork—none of it's working."

"I just think you're overwhelmed," he said with honesty.

Her discomfort nearly palpable, he felt compelled to move to another topic. "Mark called, too. About tonight. I know it won't be the same as taking Emily into Charleston, but he said he could put something special together at the St. Clair."

Quinn nodded her agreement. He knew she understood that if there was even the slightest risk to Emily's safety, it had to be avoided. She looked up at him, uncertainty in her eyes. "Would you like to have dinner with us?" she asked tentatively. "I invited my mother, but she isn't coming. Emily's wild about you, and I'm not myself right now. I could use some help in keeping her entertained."

"Well, I am her favorite uncle."

"You're her *only* uncle." She smiled for the first time that day. It faded quickly, however. "I know you're trying to keep your presence low-profile, so if you'd rather not—"

"I'll talk to Mark. I'm sure we can keep things on the down-low."

Their eyes held, and Carter felt it again—that delicate thread that seemed to have formed between them over these last few days. He admired Quinn for her keen intelligence, her compassion and how centered she seemed. Medero's stunt last night had rattled her badly, though.

"Take this when you go. Just in case." He picked up his cell phone from the counter where he'd left it. When she tried to refuse, he said, "The house has a landline, and I have the medic alert pendant. And you'll be doing me a favor. I'm tired of hearing the damn thing ring."

She hesitated, then accepted the phone.

"While you're out, use the credit card I gave you to get a new phone. There's a Verizon store in the same plaza as Café Bella."

"I'll pay for it myself, but thank you."

She went back to her cleanup, but Carter touched her shoulder, needing her to understand how serious he was. "I also want you to find somewhere that sells pepper spray or a stun gun. You said last night you'd start carrying self-protection. I'm holding you to it. If I had it my way, you'd start packing a gun."

Unspoken pain appeared in her eyes. "You're being incredibly kind and understanding."

"I'm being *human*. Believe it or not, I am capable."

The tension on her face eased as she touched his shirtfront, then went back to what she was doing.

Once she left the house, Carter laid his head against the sofa cushions. The pain medication dulled the soreness in his shoulder, aggravated by the workout that morning. Except for the noise Doug made as he trotted back from the door Quinn had departed through, the house was quiet.

He didn't like her being out there alone, but she was strong-willed, and it wasn't like he could stop her.

He wondered again what the full story was behind Quinn and Medero. Their short-lived marriage now seemed more insidious with the knowledge of his threats and violent behavior.

Regardless, Carter's gut told him this was far from over. Whether she saw it as such, Quinn had a stalker of her own, a dangerous one, in the form of her soon-to-be ex-husband.

CHAPTER SIXTEEN

"This is lovely," Quinn said, looking around as Mark led them onto the covered loggia with its stone columns and outdoor fireplace. Holding Emily's hand, she matched her pace to Carter's, who had needed his cane for the rather long walk through the hotel.

"We had to do some reconstruction after Hurricane Gina, so we added this at the same time." Mark walked ahead of them, the crisp ocean air that entered through the arched breezeways ruffling his hair.

Tables with cushioned seating were situated around the dramatic space, although only one had been set for dining. It was located in front of the crackling fire in the stone hearth while, below them, the Atlantic spread out in a dark plane. A bar was located against one exposed-brick wall, but it was unlit and unused that evening. A sign, in fact, had been placed outside the loggia's double doors, stating it was closed for a private event.

"They're called fairy lights. It's like there's a thousand fairies around us," Emily exclaimed as she looked up at the high ceiling. Tiny white lights on strands—a sea of them—hung down from it. A large antique mirror over the bar magnified the effect. Releasing Quinn's hand, Emily twirled under the lights, her blond hair swirling around her coat collar. "This is my favorite place in the whole hotel!"

"I can see that," Quinn commented with a smile.

"Which is why you're having dinner out here. At night, in January," Mark deadpanned to Quinn and Carter. "Are you warm enough? I had them start the fire and outdoor heaters an hour ago."

"I'm good." Carter wore a navy pea coat over a sweater and gray slacks.

"Me, too." Quinn's fingers smoothed the beautiful pashmina shawl wrapped around her shoulders. After much of her clothing had been destroyed in San Francisco, she had purchased only a few basic items outside of active wear. She wore a simple midcalf skirt and turtleneck, garments she had picked up at the B&B when she had gone out to run errands. But Samantha had suggested she borrow the wrap, just in case, when Quinn and Carter arrived to pick up Emily. Mark had still been at work and was awaiting them here.

"Emily, stop turning circles," he admonished. "You're going to get dizzy and fall."

"And then I'll barf?" she asked with a grin.

Carter chuckled. "And then you'll kick off a chain reaction. I'm a sympathy hurler."

Emily giggled, but stopped twirling. As she and Carter went to the railing to look down onto the beach, Quinn spoke to Mark.

"Ethan really could've come, too. You and Samantha could've had a grown-up dinner alone."

"Carter offered the same thing, but Em vetoed it. She's

thrilled about having the two of you to herself. She almost burst with happiness when she found out Carter was coming, too. She made it clear she wasn't sharing either of you with her brother."

Quinn thought of Ethan. He was a beautiful child, with his mother's dark hair and soft-brown eyes. "Emily's entitled. I'm sure she's had to give up some of the spotlight."

Mark's tone grew serious. "I'm sorry about this. I know you'd planned to take her into Charleston, but—"

"I understand," she assured him. She looked around the space, taking in the scent of the cool, briny sea air and the sounds of the waves breaking below. "And this is a pretty perfect substitute."

The doors opened, and a white-coated server entered, rolling in a cart with several trays covered with sterling-silver lids.

"I'll let you get to it," Mark said. "I took the liberty of starting you off with appetizers—including a few vegetarian choices, now that I'm clued in. The lowcountry purist in me revolted a bit, though."

Quinn smiled. "You're sure you don't want to join us?"

"I don't think Emily wants *me* here, either. Besides, it's been a long day. I'm looking forward to getting out of this suit and being at home." He peered somberly at Carter, who was still engaged in conversation with Emily. "He doesn't look too worse for wear right now. If he's up to it, why don't you two stay for a bit when you bring Emily home? You and Samantha can have coffee. I need to talk to Carter about that envelope you dropped off today."

She gave a nod. As Mark exited, she turned back to Carter and Emily. After Shelley's death, Emily had stopped speaking. Hearing her niece's happy voice now, a sound that for so long had been silenced, her heart filled.

She had surprised herself today when she had asked Carter to come with them in Nora's absence. Now, he was seated near the fireplace, laughing at a joke Emily told, completely at ease with her. In that moment, he seemed remarkably normal. Quinn had to look away to reorient herself.

If it wasn't for his famous profile silhouetted by the firelight, it would be almost possible to forget the entire world adored him and awaited his return.

***

"I figured you hadn't looked at the papers yet," Carter said as he stood on the bungalow's covered porch with Mark, who had ushered him outside so they could talk alone.

"Well, I did. Right before you got to the hotel. I didn't want to bring it up in front of everyone."

His face serious, Mark indicated the pair of rocking chairs across from the rattan porch swing. Repressing a sigh, Carter leaned his cane against the wall and sat in one of the rockers, Mark taking the one beside him.

"Want to tell me what this is about?" Mark asked.

"The document my attorney drew up is pretty explanatory. I want to give you and Mercer my share in the hotel."

He waited as Mark looked out over the neat lawn with its circular drive and Bermuda grass. Farther out, sand dunes were visible against the darkened night, their sea oats waving in the evening breeze.

"I'm worried you're depressed, Carter." Mark's concern was visible as he looked at him in the filmy glow emanating from the porch light. "Giving away your belongings is a classic sign of—"

"I'm not suicidal," Carter interjected. "I'm of sound mind,

if not body, at least."

Mark frowned at the comment. "Then why would you do this?"

"Because I have more money than I'll ever need." He tipped the rocker slowly back and forth. "Because the St. Clair means more to you than any of us. You've put your whole life into this place, Mark. I also want to be sure Mercer's well taken care of. Jonathan's a lot older than her."

"I don't know what to say. I'm thrown by this," Mark said.

Carter rose and went to stand at the porch railing. Hands shoved into the pockets of his coat, shoulders hunched against the chill as he stared into darkness, he spoke quietly. "All this wealth and fame—a few years ago, I would've sold my soul for it. But now..." Lips pursed, he shook his head. "I guess my perspective's changed. Now I just keep wondering what's the point of all this excess."

He felt Mark's presence as he came to stand beside him. Carter's mind turned to the barely controlled chaos that had been his life before the attack. He had done four movies in just over two years—two of them bona fide blockbusters—and had been preparing for a fifth. Add in the promotional obligations and there were times when he'd awakened not knowing what city, what country, he was in.

"Don't get me wrong. I'm grateful for the opportunities I've been given. I know how lucky I am. And I'm sorry if I worried you. I'm just trying to figure things out."

Stillness settled between them, until Mark spoke. "When you were in the ICU and they'd just taken you off the ventilator, do you remember what you said to me?"

Carter looked at him.

"I didn't think so. You were pretty drugged. But you grabbed my hand, and there were tears in your eyes." Mark's voice roughened. "You said you talked to Dad. That he said you had to come back to us. That it wasn't your time."

Carter swallowed. He wondered what synapses had been misfiring in his brain to make him say that. Had it been the drugs talking, or something more?

"You've been through a lot these past few months," Mark conceded. "I can see how it might call for some serious self-reflection. But you have a *gift*, Carter. All of us have always known that. I'm just saying it'd be a shame not to use it. If you feel guilty about the excesses, then do something about it."

He clasped Carter's uninjured shoulder. "You've changed, little brother. I remember you wanting to sell this place for profit not long ago."

"I was wrong," Carter admitted, regretful.

"And just like I said no to selling back then, I'm saying no to you on this." Despite Mark's authoritative tone, his eyes were soft. "I appreciate the gesture. It's a big one. But you're keeping your share of the hotel. I'm speaking for Mercer here, too—I know she'd be with me on this. The three of us are connected by blood and by this place. It's going to stay that way."

Clearing his throat, Mark pounded his fist on the porch railing like a gavel. "The eldest St. Clair has spoken." Then, with feigned disapproval, he tugged at Carter's facial hair. "What's up with the hipster look? You're about a week away from going full lumberjack."

Carter ran a hand over his lightly bearded jaw. It *had* been a while since he'd shaved. "It's not that bad."

Mark rolled his eyes good-naturedly. Then, "You're cold. Let's go back inside."

"I'll be there in a minute."

Conversation and children's laughter floated outward as Mark opened the door and stepped inside. Carter turned up his coat collar. It had been a long day, and fatigue made him feel sluggish. Still, he had enjoyed the dinner he had shared with Quinn and Emily, the three of them tucked under the stars, the sea air invigorating. He and Quinn had exchanged amused glances at Emily's nonstop conversation. But they had shared another look, as well, and it was one that remained on his mind. Their gazes had held in the firelight, more serious this time, until Quinn had shyly lowered her eyes and focused again on Emily.

The phone in his coat pocket chimed, indicating he had received a text. Taking the device out, he looked at the screen.

Coming, little brother?

Smiling softly, Carter stared out over the resort property once more before heading inside. It felt strange to be home again, and yet, also perfectly natural. Here, he wasn't famous.

He could just be himself.

CHAPTER SEVENTEEN

"Their son was the one caught up in that embezzlement scandal," Nora recounted to Quinn as they entered the B&B, having returned from Sunday-night church service. "You remember him—Charlie? I believe he graduated a couple of years before you."

"He was a couple of years ahead of Shelley, actually," Quinn corrected, sliding out of her coat. The house was quiet, the weeklong guests having departed that morning, and she could hear the ticking of the grandfather clock in the foyer as she placed the garment in the closet, which smelled faintly of mothballs. She took her mother's coat and hung it there, too.

"He's serving six years in federal prison for stealing nearly half a million dollars from his clients." Nora shook her head as Quinn trailed her into the kitchen. "I don't know what happens to some of these kids when they leave here. It's like they lose all their morals."

She began removing items from the refrigerator for dinner. "Let me tell you, it took Peggy down a notch or two. She was so proud of her stockbroker son with his big job on Wall

Street. Always bragging about him—Charlie this and Charlie that. They had to get a second mortgage on their house to help pay his legal costs. It's true what the Bible says—*pride goeth before a fall*."

Uncomfortable with the piety in her mother's voice, Quinn changed the subject. "What can I do to help with dinner, Mom?"

"Just put out plates and silverware. Everything's ready, mostly. I made the lasagna this afternoon while you were out." Nora took the bakeware covered in tinfoil from the fridge. "It's spinach—no sausage or ground beef—so you can't turn up your nose at it. I just need to reheat it in the oven while I put the salad together."

Quinn had the weekend off from therapy. She had gone for a run on the beach that morning, then traveled into the quaint downtown that afternoon, where she had done some shopping for clothes in a small women's boutique and then web-surfed on her iPad at the Coffee Cabana. She checked her wristwatch, her stomach knotting as she thought of the football game taking place in San Francisco. It was probably close to being over by now.

"Quinn, are you listening to me?"

Her mother was speaking again. "I'm sorry. What?"

Nora appeared contrite. "Thank you for going to church with me tonight, honey. I know things have been tense between us because of that dinner with Emily. I've thought about it, and I *will* try to do better. You're right, Emily is Shelley's daughter. She's as much Reese as she is St. Clair, and I need to make sure she remembers that. I'll call Mark this week and see about taking her out for a hot chocolate."

"That'd be great."

As Quinn finished setting the dinner table, Nora said, "Tell you what else you could do. The garden club is having a garage sale, and I cleaned out the upstairs closets looking for things to donate. There're a few boxes in my bedroom. Could you bring them down? My bursitis is acting up, and those stairs are a bit much sometimes."

"Sure," Quinn said.

"No need to do it right now. It can wait until morning."

"No, I'll take care of it now."

As Nora turned on the radio beside the coffeemaker and began chopping lettuce for the salad, Quinn went upstairs. She located three cardboard boxes on Nora's bed. Curious, she shuffled through the items her mother was planning to contribute to the sale. The first box held old bedding linens and a Christmas tree skirt Quinn fondly recalled as a child, although the snowman depicted on it had yellowed with age and lost the gold braiding from its felt hat. While the second box contained mostly bric-a-brac—a crochet tissue box cover, old perfume bottles, a decorative cloisonné plate—the third held men's clothing. Items her father had apparently left behind and Nora was finally letting go of. Quinn hoped it was a healthy sign.

One of her father's cardigans lay on top. She picked it up, sniffing it to see if she could catch the bergamot scent of his cologne that lingered in her memory, but nothing remained. Returning the sweater to the box, she looked through the other garments before uncovering several silk dress ties and a leather belt. Quinn flashed on an image of herself, nude, helpless, lying on the large bed she had shared with Jake, her wrists and ankles bound to its carved-wood posters using his designer ties. Jake stood over her, his face shadowed, the buckle end of the belt wrapped around his fist as he trailed the strap over her breasts.

She shoved the mental picture away, her face hot.

Burying the ties and belt under other clothing, Quinn picked up the box. But as she passed the upstairs den, her steps slowed. Hesitantly, she entered, then put the box down and picked up the television remote from the coffee table. Taking a tight breath, she clicked it on.

The playoff game had started at one p.m. Pacific Time. It was already after seven here. Her mouth dry, Quinn located the game on channel four. It was still daylight in San Francisco, the sky a cerulean blue. A female journalist held up a microphone as a perspiring Dion Washington, the Breakers's quarterback, talked about the merits of the defensive team. Confetti swirled in the air as the stadium crowd roared. A celebration had overtaken the field, with members of the Breakers back-slapping and chest-bumping one another in the background. Quinn tensed as she saw Jake from behind, the number forty-four visible on his jersey. He appeared even more imposing with his shoulder pads, his helmet off and dark hair wet.

She recognized jersey number thirty-six, as well. Built like a bull, Mike Buczek strutted beside Jake, pounding him on the back. A cold sickness spread through her.

Despite the buzzing in her ears, she heard Nora call up to her from the downstairs.

"Quinn? Did you hear? It was just on the radio—the Breakers are going to the Super Bowl!"

CHAPTER EIGHTEEN

Three Weeks Later

"Easy." Quinn heard his faint hiss of pain, and she reached for the dumbbell in Carter's right hand, helping support its weight as he lowered it again to shoulder height. He sat on a bench in the workout room, performing overhead presses with five-pound weights. They had been working together for a month now, and Quinn had gradually increased the exercise intensity. At the same time, Carter's care team had begun to taper down the pain medication.

"Let's make that your last one. You're tired, and you're starting to compromise your form."

He shook his head. "I'm finishing this set."

Quinn pressed her lips together, having become acquainted with Carter's competitive side, even against himself. "Arms at shoulder height and a forty-five-degree angle," she reminded. She supervised him through the remaining reps, then took the weights. He scrubbed a hand over his face.

"We can ask to re-up your meds a little. We may have been too aggressive—"

"No." He tested his shoulder. "I'm tired of the fuzziness."

They had already done their morning cardio—indoors on

the treadmill since the February day had brought with it a chilly rain.

Once he rested, Carter stood and pulled his T-shirt over his head, his movements a bit less restricted now, but still slow and careful. Walking to where Quinn waited, already warming the oil in her palms, he sat on the massage table. Moving behind him, she began the slow, deep glide of her fingers, applying pressure and stretching the scar on his shoulder. With his shirt off, Quinn believed she could see some evidence of the several pounds he had gained back.

Carter looked out through the window as she worked. "Typical lowcountry winter," he said on a sigh.

"The rain's supposed to be with us for a while." Quinn was disappointed, too. She looked forward to their walks along the shore with Doug.

"Can you hit me in those spots?"

As she often did for patients, Quinn performed body massage, since it released endorphins and helped to naturally manage pain. Once she finished with the scar on his shoulder, she rubbed the tight muscles in the back of his neck, a smile touching her lips as she heard his grunt of pleasure. A short time later, she moved her focus to beneath his left shoulder blade, where a stubborn knot had taken up residence for the past several days. As she massaged, Quinn studied his hair, which remained untrimmed. It was thick and carelessly tousled, the color of dark honey, and curled at his nape.

"Elliott needs a decision on the script," he said. "He can't put the studios off much longer."

That would explain the tension he carried. "What're you going to do?"

"I don't know. Filming will start in September."

Quinn had read the compelling script at Carter's invitation. It wasn't an action movie, but would still be physically demanding. He had told her shooting on a film could sometimes go fifteen to sixteen hours a day. Once she finished the work on his neck and back, she returned to stand in front of him, and Carter held out his right hand to her.

"Fall *is* still a long time away." She applied the oil and put pressure over the scar on his palm, rubbing in a circular motion. "You've been working hard. Your endurance is improving, and you're using the cane less all the time. If you keep working like you have, I think you'll be up to the challenge by then."

"What if I'm not sure I'm ready to go back?"

Quinn looked up from what she was doing, her eyes meeting his. Inside them, she saw uncertainty that went beyond his physical condition. She had seen firsthand the pressure being put on him—countless phone calls from his agent, his publicist, the studios—all inquiring as to his health but also letting him know, both subtly and not so subtly, that money and his brand were at stake. She had begun to see the stress that coiled beneath the movie-star façade.

"Don't let them push you," she urged. "Do what feels right to *you*. If you pass on this film, there'll be others."

He seemed to consider what she said, his gaze somber and assessing. Then, "Have you heard from him, Quinn?"

She lowered her eyes to focus on his palm. It wasn't the first time he had asked. The Breakers had won the Super Bowl on Sunday, four days ago. Jake had been named MVP. She shook her head, a tightness in her chest. "No. Maybe he's finally accepted it's over."

But she didn't really believe that, and she suspected Carter didn't, either. Jake's MVP status meant he was in demand—interviews and sports talk shows, not to mention the parties that were no doubt taking place. But sooner or later, she expected he would get back around to her.

She became aware that, somehow, her fingers had tangled with Carter's. His thumb stroked lightly over her knuckles, creating a swooping pull low inside her. She dared to look up at him again, but his gaze was down, his head bent. He frowned slightly as he seemed to study their joined hands, almost as if he were as surprised as she was. But the sound of the elevator opening and recognizable voices in the hall jolted them back to reality. As Quinn stepped away, smoothing the long-sleeved yoga tee she wore over her leggings, he cleared his throat, reaching for his shirt in an attempt to cover the scars on his chest before Jolene and Olivia entered. Doug had taken to following Jolene around as she worked, and Quinn could hear his padding trot accompanying the conversation.

"I figured we'd find them down here," Jolene said as they turned the corner.

The women halted in the doorway. Carter pulled the T-shirt down over his chest. But it was obvious by the shock in Olivia's eyes he had been too late. Jolene recovered more quickly.

"Carter, your mother brought the most beautiful cupcakes from Café Bella."

Carter had risen from his seat on the massage table. Olivia moved to where he stood. Staring up at him, she cupped his face. Quinn saw him swallow at her touch.

"Hi, Mom," he murmured.

***

"You know the cupcakes were just my excuse to see you."

Olivia stood in the main living area as Carter sat on the sofa. Her discarded raincoat lay across its back.

"You're welcome here anytime. You know that."

She paced before sitting beside him, her face tense. "I'm sorry about my reaction downstairs. I saw you in the hospital, but—"

"It's okay, Mom."

"It's not," she fretted. "The violence—what that woman did—it still takes my breath away." She placed a hand on his sweatpants-clad knee. "How're you feeling, darling?"

"I'm doing a little better every day. I'm getting stronger." Through the French doors, Carter could see Quinn outside on the covered porch. She had added a cozy sweater over her clothing, and she sipped from a mug—green tea, no doubt, since he'd never seen her touch coffee—as she watched the rainfall.

"I'm so happy to hear that." Olivia looked out at Quinn, too. "It's because of her, isn't it? Mark was right. That young lady knows her stuff."

"She does. But I've still got a long way to go."

"I haven't a doubt you'll get there." Olivia twisted the sapphire ring on her finger. "I did come by for a reason, Carter. I…need to tell you something. I talked to Mark last night and to Mercer by phone this morning."

Her nervous tone concerned him. "Are you all right?"

"Oh, health-wise, I'm fit as a fiddle. I wanted to talk to you about Anders and me." She took a breath. "He's asked me to marry him."

"Mom," Carter said, surprised.

She pushed several strands of her silver bob behind her ear, emotion in her clear blue eyes. "I know you and your father were especially close. Harrison was my first love, and I miss him every day. But Anders has been so good for me. I didn't realize how lonely I was until he came into my life. I…do love him."

Carter's gladness for his mother mingled with a sadness. Still, he smiled. Putting his left arm around Olivia, he pulled her close and kissed the side of her head. "I think that's great, Mom. Congratulations. You deserve to be happy."

"Thank you, sweetheart." Relief brightened her voice. "I know this might seem sudden, but we've been talking about it for a while. I just didn't want to say anything until I was sure you were on the mend. Now that all of you know, Anders wants to have us to his home for a celebratory dinner. You don't have to worry—it will just be us, Anders's daughter and her family, and a few friends."

"When?"

"Next Saturday night. Mercer and Jonathan are going to try to make it in for the weekend."

"My calendar's pretty full these days, but I might be available." He gave her a wink. Just then, Jolene called to Olivia from the kitchen.

"I'll be right there," she responded, then stood. She laid a hand on Carter's shoulder and looked out through the French doors again. "You should consider bringing a date," she said before heading into the kitchen.

Quinn had placed her mug on the porch railing and assumed a yoga pose that he imagined required a great deal of strength and flexibility. He had witnessed her slipping in her practice before—in the solarium, on the terrace by the pool—during the empty spaces of time between their work. She was mesmerizing to watch and had clearly been at it for years. A short time later, she moved into another graceful pose that resembled a standing backbend, her long hair falling behind her like a russet waterfall. Carter felt something sexual stir inside him. He looked away, swallowing down guilt. Perhaps it was just another sign his health was improving.

But that didn't explain how he had ended up holding Quinn's hand downstairs. He had seen the worry in her eyes when he had asked her about Medero. He had only been attempting to comfort her, hadn't he?

The police had failed to locate the man who had assaulted her on the beach. Like Quinn, he now believed the gang member had left town after carrying out Medero's order. Still, Carter insisted Quinn call him each night when she arrived back at her mother's home from his, and that she also call him each morning before leaving the B&B to come here. At least that way, if she didn't arrive, he would know something was amiss. It wasn't foolproof, but it was the best he could get her to agree to.

He looked out at Quinn again.

While the reduction in pain meds might be the reason for his reawakening libido—dormant since the attack—it didn't seem to be having an impact on his lucid dreaming. He'd had the same dream last night he'd had before. It had recurred several times now over the past few weeks, the one where he was trying to get into the bathroom through the locked door. But in last night's dream, Carter had had a key, and he had opened the door. He'd come awake at seeing Bianca, nude, sprawled on the bloody floor.

The violence—what that woman did—it still takes my breath away.

He couldn't shake the feeling it was more than a dream.

CHAPTER NINETEEN

As it had for the last four days, dreariness dominated the Monday afternoon. Quinn sat in the cardiology office's waiting room on the fifth floor of the medical center in Charleston. She glanced through a magazine as she tried not to listen in on the conversation of the older, African-American couple seated nearby. The husband was being treated for heart failure and had a mobile oxygen tank. Quinn's throat tightened at the way he and his wife held hands as they awaited his appointment.

It also made her think of what had happened between Carter and her last week.

Her fingers had felt so natural inside his. Neither of them had mentioned it since, though, and she told herself it would be foolish to construe it as anything more than a show of support. Even in his recuperative state, Carter's physical magnetism was strong. She had simply been temporarily caught in its pull.

The older couple looked up along with Quinn as the door leading to the exam rooms opened and Carter appeared, escorted by a nurse wearing scrubs. From the couple's surprised stares, it was clear they recognized him. Quinn picked up his leather jacket from the seat next to her and helped him into it, then handed him his baseball cap as well as the cane she had kept while he was inside. Sliding on her own coat, she went with him into the hall.

"How'd things go?" she asked as they awaited the elevator. The bay had a large plate-glass window, and a boating marina on the Ashley River was visible below, swathed in gray mist.

"You mean other than having my chest hair ripped out?"

She knew he was talking about the electrodes that had been attached with sticky pads for the echocardiogram.

"No different from having my chest waxed—God knows I've been through that a few times." He grew more serious once the elevator doors opened, and they entered. Carter held the cane, but so far hadn't used it. "The doctor says my heart function has improved since my last echo. My EF numbers are up."

Her spirits lifted. "That's great."

As they traveled down to street level, he dug into the pocket of his jeans and handed her two prescriptions that required filling. "My heart meds are being reduced, too," he said just before the doors opened into the lobby.

"Hey, you're Carter St. Clair, right?" Two men approached as Quinn and Carter walked across the marble floor toward the automated doors. One of them, an African-American, walked with a limp, and Quinn suspected he had a prosthetic leg. The other wore a baseball cap with U.S. Army Special Forces emblazoned on it. The cap partially hid a burn scar that ran down his temple and across his left cheek.

"I wasn't sure at first, but it really *is* you," the one in the baseball cap said, sounding in awe.

Carter greeted the men, shaking their hands and finding out through conversation they were both former military, at the hospital for a weekly support group for disabled veterans. He thanked them for their service.

"Would it be too much trouble to stay a few minutes and say hello to our group?" the one with the prosthetic leg asked. They had learned he had lost his limb in an IED explosion while serving in Afghanistan. The other had been injured in a fire when his plane had been shot down. He'd spent months in an Iranian prison. He indicated a meeting room, its doors closed, at the other end of the lobby. "It'd be a real thrill. Most everyone's inside already."

Carter bobbed his head. "I'd be happy to."

Quinn waited in back of the room, holding Carter's jacket and cane, as he was introduced to the group. More than a dozen men with physical disabilities—many missing limbs—were in attendance. Modest and self-effacing, Carter talked with them, signing anything thrust at him and having numerous photos taken. A few asked questions about the stalker attack, and he answered honestly. He asked Quinn for his cane only after he'd been on his feet for nearly a half hour.

***

"I think you made their day," Quinn said as she pulled the Mercedes from the pay lot where they had parked.

"They made *mine.* Those men are real heroes." Carter stared pensively out through the windshield. "Their injuries put mine into perspective."

It was clear the experience had affected him. Before they'd departed, Quinn had seen him giving his contact information to one of the vets.

"Would you mind taking a detour before we go back?"

She looked at him. "Where to?"

"The Battery."

The palm-tree-lined promenade in Charleston Harbor appeared in front of them a short time later. Its waters were rough, rippled by the wind and as gray as the late afternoon sky. A little farther down, antebellum mansions painted in cheerful pastel hues lined the waterfront.

"I can't believe how long it's been since I've been here." Quinn felt a pang. In her youth, prior to her parents' divorce, trips into Charleston had been a regular family occurrence. As they reached East Battery Street, she saw sightseers in front of an ancient church, climbing aboard a horse-drawn carriage for a guided tour. "Any reason we're here?"

"You heard Mom's getting remarried."

"Olivia told me last week. Anders seems like a nice man."

"His house is here. I looked up the address." Carter pointed out the location up ahead. Quinn slowed the car as they drove past the elegant Greek Revival mansion with outsized colonnades and double porticos. Twin, high staircases that led up to the main floor were located on its front, and the wrought-iron fence surrounding the property featured a pineapple design—a longtime symbol of Charleston hospitality.

"They're having the engagement dinner here Saturday night. Those stairs are going to be a bitch," Carter mused as he peered up at them.

Quinn heard the anxiety in his voice.

"We were going to start tackling stairs soon, anyway. They'll definitely up your cardio. I'd hoped to increase your elevation on the treadmill a bit more first, but plans change. We can make it our focus the rest of the week." When he didn't respond, she glanced over at him. "You *could* mention it to Olivia. They probably haven't even thought about it. Maybe they could move the dinner to the Big House? Or the St. Clair?"

"I know she wants to have it here. She talks about Anders's home all the time—it was featured in *Garden & Gun*. I don't want to be the reason they have to change plans."

While the house Carter had grown up in was large and quite grand itself, Quinn wondered if his mother wanted to have the party here since it was neutral ground. Both the hotel and home Olivia lived in had been in the St. Clair family for generations. It was where she had raised her children with her husband, Harrison. Perhaps there were too many memories, and celebrating her engagement there didn't seem right.

They drove past White Point Gardens. Quinn recalled its oyster-shell pathways and displays of Civil War mortars and cannons among the centuries-old live oaks. Then she turned the car around and headed back to Anders's home for another look. As they passed it again, she estimated there were at least twenty steps. "You really *are* ready, Carter. You're barely using your cane these days. You'll do fine if you just take your time and—"

"Go with me."

His intense blue gaze held hers before she again looked at the road. Quinn shook her head. "The party's for family."

"As Mark has reminded me, you are family. And Mom sort of already suggested I bring you."

The comment surprised her.

"Besides, it's not just family. There'll be others. Mom assured me the gathering would be small, but she has her own view of what *small* means." He paused for several heartbeats.

"I could use your support there, Quinn," he said seriously. "This will be my first time in front of a lot of people. I probably can do the stairs, but I'd feel more confident knowing you were with me."

Quinn felt herself relenting. "Mom *does* have guests arriving later this week. I suppose you'd be saving me from an evening of white zinfandel and canasta."

Carter smiled. The matter apparently settled, he laid his head back against the headrest. But as she accelerated the car onto the causeway a short time later, his cell phone that he had placed in the cubby between them sprang to life. Quinn glanced down at the caller's identity displayed on the screen.

Los Angeles Police Department.

He picked up the phone. Before answering, he said, "They're returning my call."

Quinn drove as she listened to his side of the conversation. When he disconnected, she asked, "Is everything all right?"

"That was Detective Warren. He was one of the leads on my case. I called him a few days ago with a question. He had to go back and look at the files before he could give me an answer."

Quinn glanced over at him.

"Remember the dream I told you about? About the bathroom door being locked? I had it again, but it went further. I had a key to the door, and I unlocked it." He rubbed a hand over his jaw. "Something kept telling me it wasn't just a dream. I asked the detective if there was a key recovered at the scene. It turns out there was a key in the bathroom door's lock. It's visible in the forensics photos."

Her stomach fluttered.

"I kept that key in a drawer of the nightstand. It's a master key that fits all the interior doors. Which means I must've used it to get in."

She recalled Mark's observation that it wouldn't have been possible for Bianca Rossi to close and lock the door in her condition. Carter's thinking must have been on the same wavelength, because he said, "I think Kelsey Dobbins was in the bathroom all along. She locked the door. The bathroom's pretty big, and she could've been hiding in there."

Quinn was confused. "Which would mean what, exactly?"

"That she locked the door to keep me out." He hesitated, seeming to measure his thoughts. "She didn't want me to see what she'd done. But when I got inside, she had no choice but to attack me, too. She couldn't escape without me seeing her, and I would've been able to identify her."

"So, you're saying she stabbed Bianca out of jealousy? That she never planned to hurt you?"

"I don't know." He sighed softly. "I'm not sure any of this matters. Dobbins still did what she did. But maybe it means some of my memory really *is* returning."

The skies had grown darker. Although the forecast had indicated the rain was on its way out, fat drops splattered the windshield. "Are you sure that's something you want?" Quinn asked.

"I didn't say I want it. I just said it might be happening."

CHAPTER TWENTY

The engagement party had begun winding down inside as Carter located Quinn in the courtyard of the Charleston mansion. She had been with him for most of the evening, but had slipped away at some point when he had been in discussion with other guests. He had wandered the residence's well-appointed rooms until spotting her through the window of Anders's wood-paneled study.

Arriving at the edge of the formal garden, he stilled. Quinn wore the lavender cocktail dress she had bought several days ago when they had gone into Charleston together to find suitable attire for the dinner. The dress set off her auburn waves and porcelain skin and melded against her curves.

"You have to be cold out here," he said, making his presence known. She turned at his voice, and he emerged from between the hedges of yews and boxwoods.

"I'm sorry I stepped out. I've never been much for crowds."

"I warned you about Mom. She likes a gathering. Nothing like an intimate dinner for twenty-plus."

Quinn smiled at the comment. "You made it down here

alone. And you haven't used your cane all night."

"Don't be too impressed about the stairs. Getting back up is the hard part," he joked, although Quinn had been right. He had done well on the stairs that led up to the front entrance. He'd feared getting out of breath and embarrassing himself, but he'd been just fine.

"I was talking to Jonathan earlier. I like him," Quinn said. "You have a wonderful family, Carter."

"I do." He clasped the back of his neck, feeling the newly trimmed hair at his nape, courtesy of one of the stylists at the St. Clair salon who had come to his home that morning. At his mother's strong suggestion, he had also gotten a shave. He chuckled. "Although Ethan's doing his best to tarnish the family name. You missed his epic meltdown. He got himself and his sister banished to one of the guestrooms."

Quinn's face brightened at the image. "He's probably exhausted. It's getting late for a little one."

Recalling her miscarriage, his heart pinched. She crossed her arms against her chest, probably to ward off the chill, and he began to shrug out of his suit jacket, even if a bit awkwardly due to his shoulder. "Here. Take this."

Ignoring her protest, he stepped closer and wrapped the jacket around her. Even with the darkness pressing in on them, her eyes were luminous as she stared up at him.

"Now you're cold," she pointed out.

"It's not too bad tonight. And I haven't had much opportunity to be a gentleman to you. You've been opening doors for me, driving me around and carrying my things. I'm trying to repair my male ego."

She seemed to assess him before directing her gaze to the evening sky. "I've never seen so many stars. After a straight week of rain, everything is so—"

"You look beautiful tonight, Quinn."

Appearing uncomfortable, she looked down at the flagstone path. "You really don't have to—"

"I said it because you *do*," he emphasized. "Whatever Medero did to hurt you, to make you leave him, he's a fool."

Carter was stone-cold sober. He was on no pain medication tonight, nor had he accepted the wine served with dinner. Whatever it was he felt for Quinn, he couldn't keep denying it much longer. It was different from anything he had felt for a woman in a long time. He enjoyed her companionship, and he looked forward to being with her. The beach house seemed empty when she wasn't in it. A reckless part of him thought of sifting his fingers through the glossy waves of her hair. Of lowering his mouth to hers. He swallowed. They stood so close.

"We should probably go back inside," she murmured, her eyes uncertain as they searched his.

With a small release of breath, he nodded. "They're doing the toast soon. That's why I came to find you."

He took his time on the steps leading back up to the main floor, Quinn beside him. As they reached the piazza—its ceiling painted a traditional lowcountry *haint blue* to ward off evil spirits—light spilled from the home's interior, as did the sound of laughter and voices. He and Quinn made their way through double French doors that led into the wide hallway, then entered the elegantly decorated parlor where the guests were gathered. His cane lay across the seat of one of the upholstered chairs that had been pushed back to make room. Quinn removed his suit jacket and laid it over the cane.

"We've been waiting on you two," Mark said upon their

entry. A stemmed glass in hand, he stood in front of the crowd along with Samantha, Anders and Olivia. Mercer and Jonathan came to stand with Carter and Quinn. A butler offered them crystal glasses of champagne from a silver tray.

"To my mother and Anders," Mark toasted as the others lifted their glasses. "Here's to your joy and ours from this day forward. Welcome to the family, Anders."

Carter sipped the champagne, his thoughts on what he had nearly done outside. Nearby, Jonathan slipped his arm around Mercer, adding his well wishes to the others echoing in the room. But Mercer was looking at Carter, he realized, a question in her eyes. Beside him, Quinn focused pensively on her champagne glass, its stem clasped in her fingers.

***

Quinn had been telling herself any attraction she felt to Carter was foolish and one-sided. But tonight, in the courtyard when she had lifted her gaze to his, she had again sensed his carnal interest in her. Their conversation on the drive back from Charleston had been stilted, not their usual easy discourse. Small talk about the dinner had punctuated the stretches of silence.

"We need to talk," Carter said now, as Quinn fed Doug in the kitchen.

Her back to him, she halted and briefly closed her eyes. "About what?" she replied as casually as she could, wishing she hadn't come inside to see to the dog and to collect her iPad, which she had left here by accident.

"Tonight in the courtyard. I wanted to kiss you. But I think you already know that."

It became hard for her to breathe. She wanted him to take the words back. They ensured nothing between them would ever be the same again. Quinn faced him, aware of the hard beat of her pulse. He stood in front of her, tall and handsome, wearing the crisp, white shirt and tailored slacks, his tie undone. He looked like he had stepped out of some high-end men's fashion journal. Quinn had gotten used to his bearded, scruffy appearance—dressed in jeans or sweats, maybe even house shoes, sometimes sporting a case of bedhead after a nap. But when she had arrived at the house to pick him up tonight, he'd no longer appeared to be the semi-invalid she had been working with for these past weeks. He had gained back more weight and was looking more each day like the idol women worshipped on a movie screen.

He had wanted to kiss her. The fact that Quinn had wanted him to frightened her.

"Then why didn't you?" The question escaped her before she could leash it in.

"Because it's *you*, Quinn. When you stopped me by saying we should go back inside..." He made a small, helpless gesture with his hands. "I choked. I want to make sure I do things right with you—"

"Your instincts were on target. It would've been a mistake," she interjected, her voice thick. "You don't want me, Carter. You're just confused because of our situation."

"I disagree," he said adamantly.

That night on the beach all those years ago resurfaced in Quinn's mind, as did his callous dismissal of her afterward. Hurt, long dormant, sparked. "I'd just be another of your conquests. I've already been that once. I...I can't do it again."

Despite the pain in his eyes, he closed the small distance between them, his hands slipping up her arms. Her skin tingled where he touched her. "When I saw you again after all this time, I felt something. Something *real*, Quinn. It's just taken me some time to admit it to myself."

His nearness was overwhelming. A hopefulness laced his words. "I'm asking whether you feel something, too."

"I can't do this," she whispered, dropping her lashes so he couldn't see the truth.

"Why? Because of what I did to you in high school? Because of Jake Medero? You're legally separated—"

"Because of who *you* are." Her voice shook with the admission. "Don't you understand? I'd be crazy to let myself be vulnerable to someone like you. You go through women like water, you always have. You can have *anyone* you want. Women who are so much more—"

But her protest was silenced as he kissed her hard, sending a hot wave of shock and ecstasy through her. Then, raising his mouth from hers, he gazed into her eyes. "Tell me you don't feel something," he repeated hoarsely.

She felt drugged, caught in his undertow. Quinn tried to throttle the dizzying current running through her. But her body overruled her brain. Looking at him, defeat welled inside her. Then, lifting on tiptoe, she wrapped her arms around his neck and pressed her lips to his again. This time, she opened her mouth to his, groaning as he slipped his tongue inside.

She was his physical therapist. There were protocols and ethics. But none of this situation between them had been normal. He walked her backward, his disability seemingly forgotten. He pinned her against the refrigerator door with his weight, still kissing her. When his mouth dropped to her neck, sucking at the column of her throat, Quinn shivered, melting under his touch. Her hands encircled his back, and she could feel his heat through the cotton of his dress shirt.

She struggled for rational thought even as the hot ache inside her spread. She was vaguely aware of Doug walking around the room as well as her own ragged breathing.

"Carter," she murmured shakily, trying to gain some purchase in reality. But he hushed her by taking possession of her mouth again, his hands moving slowly up her body, stopping at the sides of her breasts. Instinctively, she arched into him.

The wall intercom buzzed. Someone was at the gate. Carter swore softly and dragged air into his lungs. "It must be Mercer and Jonathan. I thought they were staying at the hotel, but they must've changed their minds."

Quinn felt dazed. Unsure if his sister's arrival was a curse or blessing, she slid out from between him and the refrigerator and walked to the console, pressing the button that opened the electronic gate. As she turned to Carter again, he cupped the back of his neck, still breathing hard. Their eyes met and held in the room's silence.

"Mercer has the gate code," he said, sudden realization on his features.

She went quickly into the foyer and looked out through the beveled-glass door onto the front drive. The headlights of a large SUV nearly blinded her. As she squinted against their glare, her stomach turned rancid at the powerful figure who emerged from the driver's side of the vehicle. *Oh, God.* She felt Carter's presence behind her.

"Who is it?"

Quinn's voice was breathy with fear. "It's Jake. I didn't know. I let him in."

CHAPTER TWENTY-ONE

"Stay inside and call the police."

Carter attempted to go around Quinn, but she blocked him, her hands on his chest, her face pale. "You can't go out there. You don't know him—"

"I'm just going to talk to him." But his surprise over Medero's arrival had given way to a quiet fury. Gently but firmly, Carter moved her out of the way. He could stay inside and wait for the police, but he refused to do so. He needed Medero to know Quinn had a protective circle of people around her. "Do as I asked. Lock the door behind me."

He stepped onto the wide, wraparound porch, closing the door behind him and cutting off Quinn's pleas. Medero stalked up the paved-stone walkway, his face and body silhouetted in the headlights' glare. He was about Carter's same height, but had the hulking, overly muscled physique of a pro football player.

"This is private property. The gate was opened by mistake. Go back to your vehicle and leave."

Medero halted at the bottom of the porch steps. From this distance, his face was visible, topped by raven eyebrows drawn down over stony, dark eyes. "I want to talk to my wife. I know she's in there."

He had lost the right to call her that. "Quinn isn't coming out. We've called the police. They're on their way."

Medero tilted his head on his well-developed neck as he squinted up in recognition. "*Carter St. Clair.*" He smirked, his tone derisive. "I knew she had a family connection, but I never thought you're who she's been—"

"Leave now," Carter repeated, his pulse beating in his temples. "She doesn't want to see you. You need to accept things are over."

"Quinn and I are none of your business." Medero's chin jutted upward, his stance wide. "But *my* business is finding out whether you're fucking her."

He placed one foot on the bottom step, preparing to come onto the porch, but Carter came carefully down instead, not wanting him to get any closer to Quinn.

Medero eyed him coldly. "Are you stupid enough to be tapping that? Knowing who it belongs to?"

Carter felt a nerve jump along his jaw. "Quinn doesn't *belong* to anyone. She's a person, not a thing. And I'm receiving physical therapy from her—"

"Bullshit." He scowled as he took in Carter's attire. "Looks to me like I broke up a date."

"You don't care about her. That car crash you orchestrated could've gotten her killed. You know that?"

He gave an innocent shrug. "I don't know what you're talking about. But I do know this. You've got about ten seconds to get her out here before I go in and drag her out myself."

Tight-lipped, Carter stood his ground. "You're not going

in there. Think about it, Medero. Neither of us wants to end up on the news. I'm telling you again to leave, before the police get here. It's over between you and Quinn."

With a snarl, Medero grabbed Carter by the shirt collar, but he shoved away from him hard, breaking his hold. He grunted as pain lanced through his right shoulder. Medero lunged for him again, but stopped at the sound of Quinn's voice.

"Don't do it, Jake!" Both men looked up to where she stood on the porch. She indicated the home's roofline. "There're security cameras. You hurt him, and we'll have it on video."

Medero glared up at her. Sirens wailed in the distance. He took a step back, pointing a finger at her.

"I warned you to be careful how you treat me." His next threat was directed at Carter, who clasped his shoulder with his left hand. "When I do get around to you, you'll wish that crazy stalker bitch had finished you off."

Carter watched, breathing hard as Medero retreated. Halfway down the walk, though, he turned back to him.

"Didn't figure you for being into the lifestyle, St. Clair," he called out. "Here's a tip—use hand gestures instead of a safe word. That way you can use a gag on her. The sounds she makes through it will go straight to your balls."

Reaching the SUV, he got in and started it, gunning the engine. Wheeling the vehicle around, he roared out. He drove through the closed gate, sending sparks flying as it burst outward with a metal bang. Face hot, outrage warred with the pain in Carter's shoulder.

Quinn rushed down the steps. Worry pinched her features as she touched Carter's chest, his shoulders, trying to assess the damage. The sirens were louder now, coming closer.

"Are you crazy?" Concern ratcheted up her voice. "You're in no condition to stand up to him. He could've just set back weeks of therapy."

"What was he talking about, Quinn? That stuff about gags and me being into the lifestyle?"

She dropped her gaze, but Carter held on to her with his left hand. "Look at me."

Her eyes were pained.

A black-and-white pulled into the driveway.

CHAPTER TWENTY-TWO

"You can pick up a copy of the report at the station on Monday, Mr. St. Clair," the younger of the two policemen said as he stood in the driveway with Carter and Quinn. The other was already at the patrol car, using the radio to report to dispatch. They were the same ones who had come to the house over a month ago. A second unit had also responded, but had since left.

The officer's gaze moved to Quinn. "I'm sorry about the restraining order, ma'am."

Carter watched as Quinn merely nodded before looking off to the rustling palms on the eastern side of the property. He shared her frustration. They had been told that obtaining a domestic-violence restraining order across state lines would be a more complicated process, since it would first have to be filed and granted in a court where the accused resided before a similar order could be issued here.

"His laying hands on you is enough for third-degree simple assault in South Carolina, though, if you want to press charges," the officer said to Carter. "It's a misdemeanor—maximum thirty-day jail term and a five-hundred-dollar fine."

He peered at the broken gate. "We can haul him in for property damage, too."

Quinn's voice held a plea as she looked at Carter. "I don't want to drag you further into this—"

"I want to press charges," Carter said to the officer.

The man gave a nod.

"That's it? You're leaving, then?"

"Not just yet. I need to write up a few things. But we'll be going shortly. My partner is putting a bulletin out on the SUV's make and model now."

"It's probably a rental from the airport in Charleston," Carter told him.

"We'll check into it." Politely, he tipped his cap to Quinn before walking to the squad car and entering on the passenger side.

"This will only make Jake angrier," Quinn reasoned once they were alone. "I know you're doing this for me, but you don't want this kind of publicity. And even if they find him, an arrest like this will only tie him up for a few hours until he's processed and makes bail."

"He needs to know we mean business." Carter tested his sore shoulder. Inside the squad car, the interior light had been turned on and he could see the officer they had just been talking to scribbling on a clipboard. Half in dread, he took their moment of privacy to readdress what he'd asked earlier.

"I'm no prude, Quinn—far from it. I know what Medero was implying." At the look of misery on her face, his voice gentled. "Is that the kind of relationship you were in?"

She colored fiercely, her eyes downcast. "I don't want to talk about this."

His jaw tightened. The idea of Quinn being treated like

that, even consensually, disturbed him. It was clear Medero had a sadistic side. But it didn't fit with the strong, independent woman who stood in front of him, although she now appeared cowed. Her eyes still hidden from his by her thick lashes, Carter's gaze fell on the swell of her cleavage revealed by the neckline of her dress. The thought of Medero hurting her sickened him. He bent his head closer to hers.

"You can talk to me. I can handle whatever you tell me. If you've gotten in over your head—"

"I'm going home." She appeared dazed when he gently gripped her arm.

"I'm not letting you leave alone. Medero could be out there waiting for you."

"I can't stay here." As she looked up at him, he saw the deep shadows in her eyes. Reluctantly, he let go of her, letting his left hand fall to his side. Wrapping her arms around her midriff, Quinn walked to the patrol car. The officer on the driver's side rolled down the window as she approached.

"Officers? Can you give me a ride to the Reese House B&B?"

"Yes, ma'am."

"*Quinn*," Carter entreated as she walked back to him.

"Take ibuprofen." Her voice trembled slightly. "Put an ice pack on your shoulder. If it doesn't feel better by Monday, call Dr. Patel."

"Forget about my shoulder, all right?"

Disbelief appeared on her face. "You're in no condition. He could've killed you tonight."

She went past him and into the house, presumably to get her purse and the iPad she had come inside for earlier. Doug greeted her at the door. Carter released a slow breath. Their relationship had changed tonight. It had been his doing. But when he had crushed his lips to hers, once her shock had passed, Carter had felt the shiver of need that had run through her. The kiss had raced through him like a wildfire, too.

But this new part of Quinn, this darker side he had learned about, confused him.

She returned to the porch, wearing her coat, clutching both her iPad and evening purse against her chest. She came down the steps and attempted to walk past, but he touched her again, stopping her. His voice lowered. "After everything that's happened tonight, *after what happened between us*, you can't just shut me out."

"I need to go home," she whispered shakily.

Defeated, he let her pass. He stood beside the Mercedes, a throb in his shoulder. As she neared, one of the officers got out and opened the rear door of the patrol car for her. Carter's breath fogged in the chilly air. A moment later, the vehicle exited through the gate that now hung awkwardly open like a broken maw.

***

"Quinn, what on earth?"

Nora met her at the door. It was late, nearly midnight, but her mother must have seen the patrol car from her bedroom window. Nora peered worriedly at its receding taillights.

"Why did the police bring you home?" Clutching the edges of her housecoat against her chest, she trailed Quinn into the darkened house. At least it appeared the new houseguests—four of them, two older couples vacationing together—were upstairs in bed.

"I'm fine. They just gave me a ride."

"Why? What happened to your car? Don't tell me you had another accident!"

"I left it at Carter's. He didn't want me driving here alone." Nerves worn thin, Quinn removed her coat and laid her things on the sofa. "Jake's back in town, but I think you know that. He came to Carter's."

Nora's expression was telling. Still, she shook her head, emphatic. "I didn't tell him where you were or who you were with, I swear! I only told him you'd gone out for the night. How did he find you?"

If her mother hadn't told him, then the gang member Jake had hired a month ago had. The man had probably given Jake the address of where Quinn had been spending time. Tiredly, she rubbed a hand over her burning eyes. "It doesn't matter."

"What happened? And what does it have to do with the police?"

"Carter went out to talk to Jake, and Jake got violent. I had to call 911."

Nora gasped. "Oh, no! They didn't arrest him, did they?"

She stiffened. "He left before they arrived, but they're looking for him. You couldn't have told me Jake was here?" she asked angrily. "You should've called to warn me."

"I didn't think it was necessary. Jake was fine when he was here. He stayed for a glass of wine and signed autographs for the guests. He said he would come back in the morning to see you. I was going to tell you when you got home."

So Nora had let him into the house again, despite Quinn's warning. But she also knew her mother's fondness for Jake. She couldn't expect her to be rude to him. Not without knowing the real reason for their breakup, or that Quinn feared for her safety. Thinking of what Jake had gleefully disclosed to Carter, it felt as though a stone had lodged in her chest. As much as she dreaded it, maybe it *was* time she told her mother the truth. Quinn hesitated, her throat dry. "Mom, we need to talk—"

"All I can say is you reap what you sow. I don't know how you can blame Jake for his behavior tonight." Accusation shone in Nora's eyes. "He's heartbroken over you. He comes here to try to plead his case a final time and finds out you're running around with some movie star."

"I told you. I went to Olivia's engagement dinner with Carter *only* to assist him." Quinn's face had grown hot. "With who he is, he knew people would be watching him, and—"

"What kind of physical therapist goes out with her patient?" Nora glanced to the low cut of Quinn's dress. "Look at you, all dolled up. I can only imagine what Jake thought, finding you there with him. It's no wonder he lost control!"

Her mother's voice had risen, and they both turned at a creak upon the stairs. One of the houseguests, a matronly looking woman who Quinn knew as Mrs. Kent, peeked down at them. Realizing she had been noticed, she tightened her bathrobe's belt. "I heard voices. Is everything all right?"

Embarrassed, Quinn looked away. She wondered how much the woman had heard and what Nora had told the guests to explain Jake's appearance.

"I'm sorry, Betsy," Nora apologized. "It's a family quarrel. I didn't realize we had gotten so loud. Can I make you a cup of herbal tea or some warm milk to help you get back to sleep?"

Mrs. Kent came down the steps. "That'd be nice."

Giving Quinn a weighted stare, Nora led her into the kitchen. Quinn stood in stunned silence before going upstairs to her room and closing the door.

Jake was out there somewhere. He could be watching the beach home right now, could be on this very street. Whatever he'd said to Nora tonight, it was clear he had once again invoked her sympathy.

But despite that knowledge, despite her mother calling her out for what she believed to be inappropriate behavior, Quinn thought of Carter. Shrugging out of the cocktail dress, she tried to erase the memory of his mouth on hers, his hands roaming over her body. The garment pooled at her feet, the room's cool air touching her too-hot skin. She had repeatedly assured her mother their relationship was professional. But that was no longer true. And despite Carter's declaration of feelings, what did he expect from her? Some kind of dalliance while he finished healing?

Use hand gestures instead of a safe word. That way you can use a gag on her.

Humiliation tightened Quinn's throat. Admittedly, though, she hadn't seen judgment in Carter's eyes, only concern.

Quinn tensed at the sound of footsteps in the hall, knowing them to be her mother's. She waited as they stopped briefly in front of the closed door before continuing on. Apparently, Nora didn't want to continue their discussion. Quinn didn't either. She didn't have the strength for it. She finished undressing. Too tired to even put on pajamas, she pulled back the bed linens and slid under the sheets, wearing her panties and bra.

She feared the coming morning.

CHAPTER TWENTY-THREE

Carter pushed himself up against the headboard with a grimace, the ice pack on his shoulder now tepid. Quinn was probably right about him having set his therapy back last night, but he wasn't angry with himself, only Medero. His gaze fell on the vial of pain pills on the dresser, next to the medic alert pendant he no longer needed. He had a temptation to take a pill to ease the pain, but the meds made him feel numb and sluggish. He had come too far to get lost in that haze again.

Pushing back the duvet under which he had fitfully slept, he rose and went to stand at the glass wall. The sun was burning away the morning mist, exposing the sand and sea below.

As his fingers absently traced the raised, vertical scar on the center of his bare chest, he couldn't stop thinking about something Quinn had said. She had told him to call Dr. Patel on Monday if his shoulder hadn't improved. Typically, that was a task she would handle.

He looked at Doug, who lay curled into a circle at the foot of the bed. The canine had taken to sleeping with Carter, shunning his own bed on the floor. Doug's nose was tucked under his hind leg, but his sad, brown eyes studied him.

"What do you think? Have we been abandoned?"

Doug thumped his tail on the rumpled bedding in response.

Carter's poor sleep couldn't be completely attributed to his shoulder. He had thought a lot about Quinn last night. She was in the midst of a contentious divorce from a man whose behavior was increasingly dangerous. And Carter had complicated her situation—even if he believed she felt the same desire. Sighing, he dragged a hand through his hair.

It was no wonder she had flown the coop on him.

***

"Quinn, there's someone here to see you!"

The excitement in Mrs. Kent's voice as she appeared in the B&B's open rear door caused Quinn's stomach to flip-flop. Wrapped in a thick sweater, she put down her teacup and rose abruptly from her seat on the back patio, where she had gone to think and take solace in the late winter sunlight.

"I answered the door since your mother isn't back from church yet." Mrs. Kent motioned for her to come quickly, then returned inside.

Quinn steeled herself. Her mother had told her of Jake's intent to return today, but she'd prayed he would decide against it considering last night. She had no choice but to go inside and deal with him.

Entering the kitchen, she considered calling the police, but she hoped Jake would just leave if she threatened it in private. She didn't need a showdown in front of everyone.

Conversation came from the dining room, where the houseguests had been lingering over the breakfast Nora had laid out before departing. As Quinn neared, however, surprise and relief washed through her. It was Carter who was talking with the guests, explaining to them his relationship to the Reese family. He appeared low-key in jeans and a zip-up sweat jacket as his eyes met Quinn's.

"I don't know if Nora's told you, but Quinn's a physical therapist—one of the best. She's been helping me get back on my feet."

He talked with the guests for another few minutes, autographing paper napkins before excusing himself and following Quinn into the kitchen. She had already glimpsed the silver Mercedes through the dining room window. She had left the key fob at Carter's, but certainly hadn't expected him to use it.

"You shouldn't be driving," she admonished once they were out of earshot of the guests.

"You're right. My shoulder's pretty jacked."

Quinn frowned. "Then why are you? And why are you here?"

Leaning against the counter, he peered at her. "I called your cell twice. No answer."

She had left her phone in her bedroom. "Why were you trying to reach me?"

He lowered his voice. "For one, the police called. Medero turned his rental in early this morning—but at the airport in Myrtle Beach, not Charleston. He took a flight out from there."

Quinn bit her lip, the implication clear. Jake had traveled nearly two hours north to avoid the local police. She wondered if Nora had alerted Jake to the fact they were planning to arrest him. Her mother hadn't asked her to attend church with her that morning. In fact, they hadn't spoken. Quinn had stayed in her room until she had heard the Buick start up and leave. Regardless, it meant Jake was no longer here.

"Quinn." Carter dropped his voice further. "I know a lot happened last night. I got the feeling you might not show up for work tomorrow." He sighed softly. "I'm sorry for what I did. For…kissing you. I shouldn't have, not with all you're going through."

Quinn's throat tightened. She glanced toward the dining room. She was sure the houseguests couldn't hear, but they were still sneaking looks at them. It occurred to her they had been treated to surprise visits by two famous people in less than twenty-four hours.

"You said 'for one.' What's the other reason you needed to reach me?"

"I need a driver. I'm going to the St. Clair to have lunch with Mercer and Jonathan before they go back to Atlanta."

"You could've sent for the hotel's limo service. Or just kept going since you're already halfway there."

"I want *you* to drive me," he persisted, although the seriousness of his gaze told her this was about more than transportation. "You can have lunch with us. And then you and I can talk somewhere private. We'll go for a walk on the beach. I've got Doug with me. He's in the car with the window rolled down. How about it?"

Recalling Carter's mouth on hers, how perfectly her body had molded to his, she shook her head. "I don't think—"

"We'll talk here, then." His midnight-blue eyes pinned hers. "But we're going to talk, Quinn."

She looked again to the houseguests. Her mother would be back any time now. Quinn released a breath of defeat as Carter dug into his jeans pocket and handed her the car key.

***

"I want you to file for the restraining order tomorrow," Carter said as he walked along the shoreline with Quinn, Doug romping ahead of them, chasing seagulls. They'd had lunch at Mark and Samantha's home, the children still dressed in their church outfits and Jonathan and Mercer's car already packed for the return trip to Atlanta. Carter had brought the cane with him just in case, but had left it back at his brother's house. They had used the path from the cozy bungalow to reach the beach, then headed away from the St. Clair property. He wore his baseball cap and sunglasses to detract attention, although there were only a few others out walking.

"I've done some research online." He pushed his hands into his jacket pockets, shoulders hunched against the breeze. "We can download the forms from the San Francisco County Courthouse's website and file electronically. That'll at least get the process started. We'll also enlist the help of an attorney there."

"But eventually, I'll have to face him." Quinn stopped and looked at him, shoving her wind-whipped hair from her face. "If I do this, I'll have to go back for the hearing."

Dread settled over her features. They had been walking for a while, and she went to sit on the bottom step of an unoccupied lifeguard stand. Knowing she wanted to give him a break, Carter sat beside her. He fervently hoped a courtroom would be the next time she came face-to-face with Medero. It would mean he would be out of her life until then.

"How the hell did you end up with him, Quinn?" he asked as they watched the sigh and drag of the ocean.

"He was a client at Brookhaven." Regret dulled her voice. "He was charming and intense, and I fell hard." Pensively, she shook her head. "He asked me to marry him within a few weeks of meeting. We eloped. Now I know marriage was just another form of control."

Carter hesitated, but he had to understand. "So he sees himself as some kind of *dominant*?"

Her face clouded, and she stared down at her hands. "It started out pretty tame, just some light bondage, some spanking, nothing too extreme."

Carter studied her, his voice careful. "And you liked that?"

She shrugged, floundering. "It was taboo and exciting, at first."

He could sense her becoming more uncomfortable. Her windblown, russet hair partially hid her face. "Once we were married, though, things started changing. Jake wanted more. He kept pushing my limits, getting rougher with me…"

His jaw tightened. "How badly did he hurt you?"

"Bruises, mostly." She looked at him then, her gray-green eyes liquid and filled with shame. "But I allowed it. I wanted to please him, so I went along with it."

Carter wondered if the ocean's roar was louder than the demons he believed she heard inside her head.

"I don't think our marriage would have lasted as long as it did if he hadn't been on the road so much," she confessed. "There were other problems—parties at the house, him wanting to know where I was all the time. He wanted to pick out my clothes, tell me how to wear my hair and who I could see…I left my job at his insistence."

Carter ran a hand over his mouth, forcing himself not to say the things he wanted to. He wanted to believe Medero had trapped Quinn in some way, had kept her tethered to him with fear or some kind of brainwashing. He didn't want to believe someone like her could let herself be used in that way. But he had seen a lot, and he had experienced a lot himself when it came to sex. Hollywood was a screwed-up town, and he understood better than most that people had perversions and kinks. He had played around with handcuffs himself at one point, but he could never intentionally hurt a woman.

"Why'd you finally leave him?"

Her face closed for a time as if guarding a secret. "Jake wanted to have a three-way. He wanted to bring in another man. I refused. It was one of my hard limits."

A warning sounded in Carter's brain.

"Jake had been on the road for over two weeks." Quinn tugged the sleeves of her sweater down over her fingers, her words halting. "He had a group at the house the first night he was back. His friends and teammates were there, as usual. Women, too. I'd stayed away from where they were partying." She stopped then, her eyes distant with the memory. Carter placed a hand on her knee, reminding her that he was with her.

"But as I was going upstairs to the bedroom, one of Jake's friends...Mike Buczek...cornered me."

Anticipating what was to come, he felt his face grow hot with anger.

"He pinned me to the wall...he ripped my blouse open and started groping me." Shaken, she rubbed a hand over her forehead. "He was so strong, but I managed to get him off me. And then I saw Jake. He was watching us."

"God, Quinn," Carter murmured, feeling sick.

She stared blindly at Doug as he darted into the ocean foam. A group of terns fishing there took noisy flight. When she spoke again, her words had thickened. "I think he and Mike…I think they planned it."

Carter sat on the left side of her, and he put his arm around her. Quinn laid her head against his shoulder.

"I fled the house that night. I miscarried a few hours later."

He swallowed heavily.

"Jake didn't know I was pregnant. Our marriage was over, but I still wanted the baby." She shook her head, her voice breaking. "It was my fault I lost it. If I hadn't been involved in—"

He hushed her. "It's not your fault, Quinn. I'm so sorry."

They sat like that for a long time, Carter trying to process what she'd told him. Holding Quinn and trying to keep her from shattering into a million pieces. His instincts told him no one else knew. That she had told no one else the truth, including Nora Reese.

He vowed to keep Medero away from her.

CHAPTER TWENTY-FOUR

"I was about to send out a search party," Mark said to Carter once Quinn had gone indoors to look for Samantha. Carter sat on the bungalow's covered porch while, bundled in jackets, Emily and Ethan played ball with Doug against a backdrop of sand dunes and the placid ocean.

"I guess we were out for a while. My stamina's building."

"Everything okay? Both you and Quinn seemed a little distracted at lunch."

Carter removed his sunglasses and clipped them onto his sweat jacket. "After we got back from Charleston last night, Medero showed up at my place demanding to see Quinn."

Mark frowned. "What happened?"

"Let's just say the police are looking to arrest him for assault and property damage."

"He assaulted Quinn?" Anger tightened his brother's voice.

"No, me. And it was nothing. Barely a misdemeanor, but I'm not missing the opportunity to press charges. Unfortunately, Medero left town before the police could find him."

Mark called out a reprimand to Ethan, who had made a

wild throw, narrowly missing his sister. "What can I do to help?"

"I wish I knew." Carter watched pensively as Doug danced and barked in front of Emily, who now had the ball. He thought of all his brother didn't know. But what Quinn had told him was deeply personal. He turned his attention to the door as it opened. Samantha and Quinn came outside.

"You know you're just adding pressure for us to get them a dog." Samantha's tone was light, however.

"Sounds like a good idea. Hey, kiddo," Carter said as Ethan scampered onto the porch. Small hands grasping his uncle's knee, he launched into an exuberant account of how high Doug could jump. Carter nodded, eyebrows raised, listening intently.

"Thank you again for lunch," Quinn said to Samantha before turning to Carter. "Ready to go?"

"Yeah."

Touching Mark's arm, Quinn stepped off the porch. She walked to Emily to give her a good-bye hug, then opened the rear door of the Mercedes so Doug could jump in before she got in on the driver's side. Announcing that it was nap time, Samantha took Ethan by the hand and ushered him indoors despite his protest.

"You're looking stronger every day," Mark said as Carter stood, retrieving the unused cane he had leaned against the chair's arm.

"I'm feeling stronger."

"*But you're still healing.*" Mark's eyes held concern. "You don't need a war with Medero."

Carter gave him a pained smile. "Too late, bro. I think I already have one."

He laid his hand affectionately on Emily's blond curls as she came onto the porch. "Later, Em."

Carter got into the Mercedes. As he closed the door and reached for the seat belt, the strain must have been visible on his face, because Quinn said, "I'll call Dr. Patel tomorrow."

He was capable of setting his own appointments, but keeping Quinn busy meant keeping her nearby. They left the resort and rode in silence as, overhead, the afternoon sun had dropped in the sky that was streaked with fingers of white clouds. As they traveled through downtown a short time later, Carter took note of Café Bella's striped awning and sidewalk tables, although the business was closed on Sunday. He thought of Samantha, how just a few years ago she had shown up in town, alone, an enigma. But she had changed Mark's life for the better. Carter had kept her secrets, too.

"If we hadn't talked today, were you planning not to show up tomorrow? Or the day after that?" he asked.

Quinn's lips pressed together as she formed a response. "I would have had to come back eventually. You have my dog."

He chuckled.

The mood between them seemed to lighten a bit, until they arrived at Carter's. The broken gate hung open, a sobering reminder, and pieces of metal and plastic were scattered over the drive.

"Something else I can call about tomorrow." Quinn navigated the car around the debris. She parked in front, since there was no longer a need to go around back so Carter could take the elevator.

"Do you want to come in?" He released his seat belt.

She shook her head. "I'll see you in the morning."

He turned to her, serious. "Quinn...I've lain my cards on

the table. I'm attracted to you. There's no taking that back."

Her lips parted as her gray-green eyes searched his.

"But I meant what I said. I don't want to add to your burden. And I don't want to ruin what we had before I pushed you against the fridge and had the hottest kiss of my life. What I *do* want is to help you, however you'll let me."

Reaching for the cane, he exited the car and opened the back door for Doug, who bounded out. Quinn's eyes briefly met Carter's through the door's glass before she drove away.

Aware of her uncertainty, he watched her go.

***

"Good evening, young lady." Mrs. Kent's husband spoke as Quinn entered the B&B's foyer. The two pairs of houseguests stood with Nora in the living room. Mr. Kent peered theatrically at the door Quinn had just come through. "I thought you might just turn up with another star—they seem to be in big supply."

Quinn forced a smile as they all laughed, with the exception of her mother. She noticed they wore coats and the women held their purses.

"We were just leaving. We're going to have dinner at that little Italian place on the square." Mr. Kent zipped up his jacket. "Nora's coming, too. Would you care to join us?"

Quinn was glad her mother had something to do, although she was surprised she was missing Sunday-night church. Nora made a point of not looking at her, instead fussing with something inside her purse. Quinn thanked them for the invitation, but declined. "I'll stay here. But have a nice dinner."

The group filed outside. Quinn watched from the living room as they piled into a station wagon with Tennessee license plates and pulled away from the house. She felt relief that, at least for an hour or two, she would have some time to herself. Picking up the glasses that had been left on coasters on the coffee table, she carried them into the kitchen. As she washed them, she caught a faint reflection of herself in the window over the basin in the fading light of day.

Quinn had never considered herself beautiful, not like Shelley. She never imagined being caught between two famous, powerful men. Nor would she have ever thought Carter would be a source of comfort, someone she could confide in. She had poured her heart out to him on the beach. But she had no illusions. He would soon return to his life in Hollywood. Even if he didn't plan to, she knew getting involved with him would only end up breaking her heart.

The dishes done, she looked through the refrigerator for something to eat, then removed a container of her mother's homemade vegetable soup. As she looked through the cabinets for a pot to heat it up in, she heard the chime of her cell phone inside her purse, which she had left in the living room. It indicated she had received a text. She went to retrieve the phone. When she saw the screen, her stomach clenched.

WORTHLESS SLUT.

The message was from Jake. She had gotten yet another new number when she had replaced the phone thrown into the ocean. Had Nora provided him this number, too? The phone chimed again. Quinn's breath shuddered out of her.

I WARNED YOU.

HE CAN HAVE YOU.

THEY ALL CAN.

CHAPTER TWENTY-FIVE

"There's nothing you can do?" Irritation made Carter pace in front of the coffee table where his cell phone lay. Jolene had opened the shutters wide upon her arrival, and morning sunlight washed the spacious, high-ceilinged room.

"Not this time." Through the phone's speaker, Elliott's voice had the roughened croak of a bullfrog, reminding him how early it was in California. "*Celeb Snitch* bought the photos as an exclusive—otherwise, they'd already be online."

Briefly closing his eyes, Carter squeezed the bridge of his nose. "When's the issue dropping?"

"A week from today. And you can say she's just your physical therapist all you want. My source has *seen* the photos. I'll say this—it didn't take you long. Rossi's barely dead for four months, and you're cuddled up on the beach with some curvy little redhead. The wife of a pro baller, no less."

"They're legally separated," Carter pointed out. "And my personal life is no one's business."

Elliott let out a laugh. "You're Carter St. Clair—you're everyone's business. Expect some backlash. The tabloids will paint you as insensitive for not adhering to some reasonable mourning period. Hell, they'll probably spin this as you being the reason for Medero's marriage breaking up. Thank God I'm your agent and not your publicist. Speaking of, Ariel will be calling you later, and she's not a happy camper."

Carter silently cursed the telephoto lenses and high-tech drones that paparazzi used. He could take the blowback, but he didn't want this to come down on Quinn.

"So what do you want from me?" His patience was wearing thin. "There must be a reason for this heads-up."

"I want your cooperation. My thinking is we let the gossip sites run with this for a few days, then we announce your impending return. *The Rainy Season* was on the bestseller lists for months. The film adaptation is big news. Your signing on as the lead will dilute the fervor over this."

Carter looked at Doug. The dog was lying on the hardwood floor, but his ears had perked up. A second later, he rose and trotted off to the foyer.

"I'll call you back later." His eyes met Quinn's as she entered the space.

"I'm holding you to that." Elliott sounded tired and frustrated. "You're saying *yes* to the film. The world's a fickle place. The tide can turn on anyone, Carter. Even you."

"That sounded dire," Quinn said once he disconnected.

Barefoot, wearing sweatpants and a T-shirt, he drew in a slow breath. He had to tell her. It was better than being blindsided.

"Quinn…we were papped at the beach yesterday."

***

She had taken the news with grace, but Carter could read the disquiet in Quinn's eyes. He'd had to tell her how the gossip sites would most likely spin the photos. "This is just a part of my life that I have to deal with. I didn't want to pull you into it. I'm sorry."

"You don't understand. I…think Jake might've alerted the paparazzi to get revenge."

Carter frowned. "What makes you think that?"

She had dropped her duffel onto the sofa, but she moved to it and retrieved her cell phone. Lighting up the screen, her features taut, she handed it to him. Reading the texts, an angry heat coursed through him.

"He just gave us more cause for the restraining order," he said tightly. "I'm assuming the *he* is me, but what does he mean by *they all can*?"

She shook her head. "I don't know."

It *was* possible Medero had given his location to the photo agency and clued them in on Quinn and him. Carter had let his guard down here. It was likely the paps had followed him yesterday to the Reese B&B and then to the St. Clair without his being aware.

"Maybe the photos are just of us walking on the beach," Quinn suggested hopefully. "That doesn't mean anything. It's part of your therapy."

"Elliott knows someone who's seen them. I think they were taken while we were sitting at the lifeguard stand."

She released a soft breath of realization.

It was ironic that now that Carter had taken a step back from her romantically, they would most likely be presented as lovers by images taken out of context. Quinn looked over her shoulder at the sound of Jolene's vacuum cleaner starting up in another room.

"So what do we do?" she asked, returning her troubled gaze to his.

"I'm going to borrow your phrase. We keep it business as usual. We file for the restraining order, just like we discussed. At least we have time to prepare family before the magazine hits."

At the dread in her eyes, he asked, "What is it?"

"Mom's been insistent my relationship with you isn't professional." Nervously, Quinn scraped a hand through her hair. "She hasn't been happy about our spending time together. She keeps hoping I'll change my mind about the divorce. You could say she's Team Jake. He's gone out of his way to charm her."

Carter's lips pinched together, his suspicion confirmed. "Nora doesn't know why you left him, does she?"

At his scrutiny, she bowed her head. "She doesn't know anything. I can't tell her what I told you. And when the photos come out, she's going to think I've been lying to her about you and me." With a weary breath, she added, "I guess I have been."

He knew she was thinking of what had happened between them.

"Quinn," Carter entreated softly, moving closer. "She's your *mother*. She needs to know the truth about your marriage, even if it upsets her."

She looked away.

"I'm just sorry you've been dealing with this on your own." He wanted to touch her, but instead he left his hands at his sides. "If you want to skip work today, you can."

"No, I agree with what you said. I'd rather be busy." She switched into physical-therapy mode, despite the worry that remained in her eyes. "I called Dr. Patel's office while I was in the car. He can see you at three today. Until he checks you out, we should avoid any shoulder work. How's the pain?"

"A little better."

"Good. The ibuprofen and ice packs are helping. We'll get in your cardio this morning. I was thinking maybe we'd walk the beach here. We've been avoiding the steps down from the terrace, since they're pretty steep, but that doesn't seem to be a problem anymore."

They should enjoy the beach while they could. Once the photos were out, he expected their privacy to end. Carter needed a shower. He had been lured downstairs by the aroma of coffee Jolene had made in the kitchen, but had gotten sidetracked by Elliott's call. "Take Doug with you, and I'll meet you by the pool in fifteen minutes?"

She nodded, and he turned to go upstairs. Carter had been making a point of no longer using the elevator, and as he made his slow but steady climb up the staircase, he looked down at Quinn, who had turned away from him. Arms hugged around herself, she looked absently out through the French doors. She appeared rattled and alone. Thinking of what Medero had said to her in his text, anger rekindled inside him.

***

Carter hadn't significantly reinjured his shoulder, but Dr. Patel still advised Quinn to take it easy on that aspect of his therapy for the next several days. She now sat in her car in front of her mother's home, the night sky a dark blanket over the sleepy beach town. She had turned off the car's engine, but remained looking up at the glow emanating from the house's windows.

She's your mother. She needs to know the truth about your marriage.

Quinn knew Carter was right. Her mother's ignorance

about her relationship with Jake was the cause of the widening chasm between them. The only way Nora would ever see past Jake's façade was for her to learn the truth about him, even if Quinn had to expose her own culpability.

The dashboard clock indicated it was well after eight. Gathering her courage, she exited the car and locked it. Quinn entered the house to conversation and laughter once again coming from the dining room. Although the B&B's practice was to serve only breakfast and a light snack at night, it appeared Nora had made a farewell dinner for her guests before they traveled on to the Florida Keys the next morning. She had gotten out the fine china, and each place setting held what appeared to be the remnants of a pork loin with cornbread dressing. She recalled the meal from her youth, one of her mother's specialties. The quintet was so involved in their lighthearted discussion that Quinn stood there for a time unobserved. Her throat tightened at the rare sound of her mother's laughter and how much younger she looked with the tension gone from her face.

"Quinn," Nora said upon seeing her. "We've been having such a good time I didn't hear you come in."

The warmth in her voice had replaced the chill that had been there whenever she had spoken to Quinn over the last several days. Perhaps the two empty wine bottles sitting in the table's center were responsible. Quinn placed her duffel on the brocade-upholstered settee just outside the dining room. "I didn't mean to interrupt."

"Would you like to eat? I'll get you a plate. I know you won't touch the pork, but there're side dishes." To the others at the table, Nora said with an air of disbelief, "My daughter took off to San Francisco and returned a vegetarian."

"It looks good on her." Mr. Kent toasted her with his glass. Quinn smiled politely, then returned her eyes to her mother, who was about to stand up from the table. Quinn indicated for her to remain seated.

"Thanks, but I've already eaten. And if you don't mind, I'm going upstairs to my room. It's been a long day."

"All right, honey. I want you to stay long enough tomorrow to see off the Kents and the Pickwells, though. They're leaving."

She said she would be there. Bidding them good night, she left her duffel where it was and went upstairs. What she had to tell Nora could wait until tomorrow, after her guests were gone. Her mother appeared too happy for Quinn to pull her away. The morning sun would reach her windowsill soon enough.

With some guilt, she skipped her evening yoga practice, the day too much of an emotional drain. Despite the still-early hour, she changed into pajamas and readied for bed, planning to give in to her exhaustion. After leaving the doctor's office in Charleston, she and Carter had gone to the Rarity Cove Police Station to pick up the police report from Saturday night. Then they'd returned to the beach house and, over dinner, taken the first step of filling out the online forms for requesting a domestic violence restraining order. Carter had also scheduled a phone call for tomorrow between Quinn and an attorney in San Francisco, whom his own counsel in LA had recommended. The attorney would assist her through the court's various steps and would also try to get a temporary emergency restraining order that would go into effect until a formal hearing could take place. The attorney was from one of the top firms in San Francisco and was far more than she could afford, but Carter had insisted on covering the cost. The first time she had attempted to get a restraining order, she had done so without counsel. Perhaps this time she would be successful.

The truth behind her marriage wasn't the only thing she would have to talk to Nora about in the morning. Quinn had to forewarn her of the photos that would be published next week.

She *had* been lying to Nora about her relationship with Carter. Even before their heated kiss, he had become much more than her employer. Working together required close physical contact, but over these last weeks, they had also developed an emotional bond.

Carter was getting better. He wouldn't be needing her for much longer.

Still, as she drifted off to sleep, she couldn't help it. She thought of his lips, hard and searching, over hers.

CHAPTER TWENTY-SIX

Going to bed so early had been a mistake. Quinn was awake and restless by midnight. Not wanting to wake the household, she left her bedroom and trod quietly down the hall in bare feet. She had been reading a book on her iPad and could use it to pass the time, but she'd left the device in her duffel.

Avoiding the creaks in the staircase, she went to the settee where she had left the bag. As she rummaged through it in the darkness, she heard a noise and looked up, her eyes drawn past the dining room to the kitchen and door leading out to the back patio. Her throat went dry. Someone was outside. At nearly the same second, the doorknob clicked as it turned. Quinn's heart clenched.

The door eased open, and a large man entered. He wasn't one of the male houseguests, and he carried some kind of sack. Breath trapped in her lungs, Quinn shrank back against the wall, out of sight. She could scream to alert the others, but what if he had a gun?

I warned you.

Whoever the intruder was, Jake had sent him, she was sure

of it. She just didn't know why.

She willed herself into action. Reaching over the settee's arm, Quinn searched blindly again through her duffel, her fingers finally curling around the canister of pepper spray she had purchased weeks ago. Back pressed against the wall, fingers trembling, she managed to release the canister's safety as footsteps approached. She prayed the intruder wouldn't hear her shallow breathing or the hammering of her heart.

He passed over the threshold into the living room. At the moment he saw her, Quinn sprang. Finger on the canister's button, she sprayed him in the face. She screamed as the man howled, dropping the sack and stumbling backward as he clawed at his eyes. Quinn picked up a vase from a table and threw it at him. It bounced off his forehead, knocking him down as the vase shattered. A small trickle of blood ran down his temple.

"Stay on the floor!" She held the pepper spray pointed at him. Her voice sounded high and unnatural, adrenaline pumping through her body. "Don't move, or I'll spray you again!"

"Are you *crazy*?" He writhed on the oriental carpet runner amid the broken china, his face screwed up in pain. He appeared to be in his mid-forties, with a receding hairline. Above her, Quinn was aware of panicked voices and footsteps coming down the stairs.

"Is this some kind of setup?" the man demanded from the floor, trying to open his eyes. "Are you fucking *robbing* me?"

"What the hell's going on?" Mr. Kent was the first to reach them. Clad in pajamas, he stared down at the intruder as he flipped on the overhead light. Mr. Pickwell, Nora and the other women rushed down behind him.

Seeing the man, Nora cried out in alarm. Then, "Arnie, there's a baseball bat in the foyer closet—go get it!"

Mr. Kent was a large man himself, but he moved fast. He returned with the bat and stood over the intruder, waving it menacingly as Nora dialed 911.

"Someone just broke into my home!" She gave the street address to the operator. "We've got him down, but you need to hurry! Please!"

None of this seemed real—the houseguests and her mother in distress, all of them in nightclothes, while the man on the floor squinted up at them with reddened eyes. Tears streamed down his cheeks. Now that the lights were on, he didn't look at all like someone Jake would send to do his dirty work. He appeared confused, even scared. What had he been talking about earlier? Why would she try to rob someone who had broken into her home? Quinn attempted to swallow but couldn't, her throat like sandpaper. Mrs. Pickwell touched her shoulder. As the woman guided her to the couch across from the settee, Quinn realized she was shaking.

"Sit down, honey," she said, gently prying the canister of pepper spray from Quinn's grip. "It's going to be okay. The police will be here soon."

Mr. Pickwell had picked up the cloth sack—a pillowcase, actually—that the man had carried inside with him. He looked through the items it held, his features hardening.

Although she was still on the line with the emergency dispatcher, Nora asked, "Is that his? What's in there?"

"You don't want to know, Nora." Frowning, he looked at Mr. Kent. "Keep that bat on him, Arnie. If the sick son of a gun moves an inch, use it on him."

***

"Who is he?" Nora demanded. She and Quinn stood in the driveway with one of the responding police officers. After being briefly treated by paramedics who had also arrived at the scene, the intruder had been handcuffed and placed in the backseat of a patrol car. Wearing a coat over her pajamas, feeling drained and edgy, Quinn was aware of the neighbors who watched curiously from their yards, having been drawn outside by the sirens and flashing lights.

"According to his driver's license, his name's Samuel Dunbar," the officer said. "He's from Charleston. Says he's an accountant."

The B&B's houseguests had returned inside, although Quinn could see them watching from the window. Nora pulled her bathrobe more tightly around herself. "This makes no sense! Why would an *accountant* break into my home?"

The officer hesitated, looking at Quinn. "He's claiming you and he were emailing each other—said you invited him here. Even told him where the key was hidden on the patio."

Outrage tightened her lungs. "That's not true. I haven't emailed him. I don't even know him!"

"Officer, I don't know what's going on, but if my daughter says she's had no contact with this man, she hasn't!" Nora's voice rose. "Now I need you to do your job and find out why he would come here and make these wild claims!"

"Why don't you go back inside with your guests, Mrs. Reese? I need to talk to your daughter alone."

"No. I'm staying right here."

"Go inside, Mom," Quinn said, dread filling her. "It's okay."

Nora stood there for another moment, then turned and went into the house. The officer indicated for Quinn to follow him to the rear of one of the police cars. The trunk was open, and the pillowcase the man had been carrying was inside. Its edges had been rolled back to reveal its contents—rope, a ball gag, condoms and several sadistic-looking sex toys. Quinn blanched, feeling sick.

"What else did he tell you?" she asked, a strain in her voice.

The officer was older than the others, with graying hair and a slight paunch. Awkwardly, he cleared his throat. "He said you put an ad on the Charleston pages of e-Rendezvous.com, under Women Seeking Men."

Quinn's heart began to pound. She was familiar with the website, which connected people for dating and sexual activity. It included a personal ads section. Although the site was national, it segmented users into geographic areas.

The officer's face reddened a bit. "He said you exchanged emails earlier today, and you were, um, pretty specific about what you wanted. Said you gave him your address. He claims you wanted to role-play. He was supposed to break into your home and..." He glanced uncomfortably at the contents of the patrol car's trunk.

Quinn worked to hold on to her control. "I've never had any communication with him, and I didn't post any ad. This is my mother's home. It's a B&B, and we have guests. Why would I plan something like that here?"

His voice gentled, a possible indication he believed her. "Look, we're going to check into the ad when we get back to the station. Try to get this whole thing figured out. We'll also contact the website and get the ad taken down."

She bowed her head, humiliated.

"Miss Reese, we're a small department, and word gets

around. You've become something of a frequent flier with us. I know you've had two other incidents within the past couple of months. Seems like you've got yourself some trouble."

Quinn sighed, her breath fogging in the cold air. She figured the officers who had come to Carter's home had been talking to others on the force.

"You're in the employ of Carter St. Clair?"

"I'm his physical therapist. I'm also going through an ugly divorce," she admitted. "I know my husband's behind this. I'm trying to get a restraining order against him."

"Jake Medero," the officer said knowingly. He lifted his cap and scratched his head before replacing it. "Well, if there's evidence he really did post the ad, there may be more than a DVRO in his future. Since he did this from another state, it could be grounds for what's called felony interstate stalking. Depending on the outcome of our investigation, that could get the feds involved. A conviction comes with a prison term of up to five years."

"How hard is it to prove?" There had been no way to tie Jake to the car accident or her attacker on the beach.

"Our force here is too small for resources like that, but the experts can most likely track where the emails were sent from."

"My email was spoofed?"

"No. Otherwise, you'd be seeing replies in your inbox. My guess is someone set up an email account and claimed to be you."

Another officer who had been across the street, talking to neighbors, joined them.

"We'll leave a car here for now," he said to Quinn, indicating the arrestee in the patrol car's backseat. "In case he's not the only one who shows up."

He can have you. They all can.

Quinn's lungs squeezed. She now understood Jake's texts. This was his perverse way of exposing her to her mother. He had finally accepted they were over and had gone into full revenge mode.

The older of the officers handed her his card and said he would be in touch. As they closed the trunk and got into their car, Quinn stepped back. The man who had answered the ad stared at her from the backseat as the vehicle pulled out. Face hot, she looked away. One other squad car departed, while another one turned its lights off but stayed behind. The show over, the neighbors began filing back into their homes. As much as she didn't want to, Quinn turned and went inside, her stomach tense. Nora sat on the couch, a laptop in front of her on the coffee table, while the houseguests stood nearby, their eyes on anything but its screen. Nora looked at Quinn, her face and neck flushed a vivid red. Awkward silence filled the room. In that moment, she wished her mother hadn't gotten the B&B's wireless router repaired.

Nora got up and, hand pressed over her mouth, rushed past Quinn.

"Mom?" Quinn called as her mother went up the steps. The guests glanced away, except for Mr. Kent. Clearing his throat, he came to her and placed a hand on her shoulder.

"I…heard the police talking about e-Rendezvous. I mentioned it to your mother, and she got out her laptop."

"I didn't place that ad." Embarrassment choked her. "And I-I swear I've had no communication with that man."

"I believe you, dear. I'm sure your mother believes you, too. She's just confused and in shock."

"I'll go check on her," Mrs. Kent offered. She stood and went up the staircase, Mrs. Pickwell following. Meanwhile, Mr. Pickwell had closed the laptop, as if that would erase what was on the Internet. Quinn didn't ask to see it. Instead, her limbs like dead weight, she retrieved her duffel from the settee and took it up to her room.

Once inside and the door closed, she got out her iPad and booted it up, her pulse pounding in her ears.

Based on what the officer had told her, she found the personal ad quickly, under the heading Petite, Pretty Sub Seeking Hardcore Dom. She wanted to vomit. Still, Quinn clicked on the link. Her heart sank at the photo of herself. It was one Jake had taken of her on his cell phone, early in their marriage and in the privacy of their home. Quinn wore a sheer negligee, her hair tumbling around her shoulders. When she had voiced concern about the image, Jake had deleted it…or so he had said.

Thinking of her mother, the houseguests, seeing it, she drew in a shaky breath. Quinn pulled her gaze from the image of herself and read the ad.

My dom and I have broken up. Looking for a new master. Total power exchange. No safe words. No limits.

The email address for inquiries wasn't hers.

CHAPTER TWENTY-SEVEN

Quinn had waited until the women left her mother's bedroom. Now, standing outside its closed door, she drew in a breath and knocked before entering. Nora sat on the bed, sniffling as she grasped a crumpled tissue. Quinn hated to see her mother cry, something that had occurred often during her divorce and after Shelley's death. It felt worse than it did in her memories, since this time she was the cause of it.

"Mom, are you all right?"

When she didn't respond, Quinn sank onto the bed beside her and touched her knee. "You know I didn't post that ad, don't you?"

Her mother merely shook her head. "*Who* would do something so vile?"

Her shame felt like a steel weight. A quaver entered Quinn's voice. "It was Jake."

Nora looked at her, disbelief on her face.

"I should've talked to you about our marriage sooner so you would understand why I left him, but I...couldn't. I didn't want to upset you."

"What're you talking about? Jake still *loves* you. Why would he post something like that, saying you're looking for men to abuse you?"

"I'm trying to tell you." Quinn's mind fluttered with anxiety. "When I met Jake, he swept me off my feet in every way. But he isn't who he seems."

Nora stared at her, a flush rising on her skin. Her mother had never been comfortable talking about sex, and Quinn hesitated. "You know we got married too quickly. I didn't know him at all. There were things he wanted, sexual things, that I went along with. I…wanted to please him, but some of the things were too much—"

"What kinds of things?" Nora nervously clasped at her throat, as if she were suffocating. "That ad said you had broken up with your *dom*. I know you think we're backwoods around here, but I know what that means. You're telling me Jake was…that you let him…"

"Mom." Quinn tried to calm her. "This is why I couldn't tell you. But I *left* him. It wasn't the kind of situation I wanted. Jake…he's dangerous."

Nora closed her eyes. Quinn remained silent, letting her think through what she had been told.

"He knew where the key to the back door was," her mother admitted finally. "It just came up in conversation. I was telling him how safe our town is. I told him I keep a key under the flowerpot on the patio, in case a neighbor needs to come in and check on things when I'm traveling."

According to the intruder, the email had told him about the house key.

"How could he do this? I believed him. I believed he cared about you. I feel like a fool."

At her mother's upset, Quinn's heart ached. "Jake took

the photo of me on his phone. I asked him to delete it. I thought he had. I'm sorry. The last thing I wanted was to embarrass you."

"The houseguests, the police—they all know about this." Although her voice was soft, Nora's eyes held a glazed look. "You know how this town is. People *gossip*. You might just be passing through on your way to better things, but I still have to live here."

Guilt flowed through Quinn as her mother wiped at her eyes.

"The police are working on getting the ad taken down. They're keeping a patrol car parked across the street…" She hesitated. "In case anyone else shows up."

Nora began to cry harder.

Quinn's throat tightened. "If you're afraid to be here, I'm sure Mark can put you up at the St. Clair until this blows over. If I tell him not to ask questions, he won't. As soon as the guests leave in the morning, I can—"

"Maybe *you* should stay at the St. Clair for a while," her mother said, not looking at her. "I…think maybe it's best."

Standing, Quinn swallowed down her anguish. Nora climbed under the bed's coverlet and turned onto her side, facing away from her daughter. Turning off the lamp on the nightstand, Quinn left the room on weak legs. She didn't know if Nora meant for her to leave immediately, but she only knew she had to. Humiliation caused her insides to churn. Jake had exposed her to her mother in the worst possible way.

The guests had gone to their rooms, although all the lights remained on, as if to keep away whatever might be lurking outside. Quinn couldn't face them in the morning. Going into her room, she changed into jeans and a sweater, then pulled her suitcase from under the bed and began shoving her things inside. The task was all that was keeping her from curling into a fetal position on the floor. Fighting back tears, she lugged the suitcase and her duffel down the stairs and outside.

A cold rain had begun to fall. Her hair and clothing getting wet, Quinn placed the items in the Mercedes's trunk, then got into the vehicle with her purse and started the engine. As she neared the police car, its driver's side window rolled down. Quinn did her best to hide her upset and stopped beside it. She rolled down a window, too.

"Everything all right, miss?" the officer asked. There was an officer on the passenger side, as well.

"I'm taking a room at the St. Clair. Please stay here and keep a watch on my mother's house?"

To her relief, he nodded and let her go. Quinn pulled from the neighborhood and headed south toward the resort. But a few minutes later, tears clouded her vision. She had to pull over. While rain pounded the car's roof, she sat there for a time, sobbing. Then, pulling herself together as best she could, she made a U-turn and went north instead.

It was after two a.m. Still, she took her cell phone from her purse.

"Quinn?" Carter answered on the third ring, his voice rough with sleep. "What's wrong?"

She told him everything.

CHAPTER TWENTY-EIGHT

Carter met her at the door. Rain fell in a solid sheet as Quinn stood on his porch, wet and shivering. Then she stepped inside and into his arms. A hot ache in his throat, he held her against him. He cursed Medero for his torment of her. He cursed Nora Reese, too, in disbelief that she would turn her daughter away in the middle of the night.

When she finally took a step back from him, he asked, "What can I do?"

"Pull out that scotch from wherever you hide it?" Her reddened eyes revealed her anguish. "I want to get drunk."

Maybe a strong buzz was what she needed. "You're soaked. Leave your things in the car. You can go up to my room for some dry clothes. They'll be big on you, but they'll do. Quinn…you're safe here."

She looked at him, damp waves of russet hair framing her pale face. "Thank you," she murmured.

He swallowed, watching as she went upstairs with Doug trailing her. She could have gone to the St. Clair tonight, to any of the smaller hotels dotting the shoreline, but she had come to him. Carter had looked at the website while he had been on the phone with her, trying to keep her calm enough to drive. It infuriated and worried him, as did the intruder who had come for her. He set the security system and went to retrieve the scotch.

When she didn't return, he went up to find her still in his bedroom, staring absently out through the rain-streaked glass wall. Doug wagged his tail upon seeing him.

"You found something," he said, making her aware of his presence. She had on the soft plaid shirt he'd worn earlier that day. Its sleeves had been rolled up to accommodate her smaller frame, and a pair of his sweatpants bagged down to her ankles. The oversized clothing made her look even more fragile to him.

Barefoot, wearing jeans and a V-neck T-shirt—what he'd pulled on after Quinn's call—Carter held the bottle of scotch by its neck and a single glass in his left hand. He indicated the adjoining sitting room, and she followed. They sat beside each other on the sofa.

"Did you see it?" Her gray-green eyes appeared stricken.

Carter poured a measure of scotch into the cut-lead crystal. He wouldn't lie. "Yeah," he rasped. Fresh hate for Medero festered inside him. "He has to pay for this."

The revealing photo, along with what the ad said, was likely to attract a range of men, from simple sexual deviants to the truly dangerous. And the email correspondence Quinn had told him about had been even worse. He handed her the glass, and she took two large gulps.

"Easy." Sliding the tumbler from her fingers, he had a sip himself and handed it back. Quinn drank again and wiped her fingers over her lips before speaking.

"The police said if the ad or the emails can be traced to

Jake, he could be charged with felony interstate stalking."

Carter thought of other, even more serious charges, like conspiracy to commit rape, although Medero had no doubt known how the situation would play out with Nora and her guests also inside the house. Still, his heart thrummed with silent anger. He watched as she took another gulp, then breathed out against the alcohol's burn.

"This *is* going to get better. He's gone too far this time, and he's going to get caught."

She reached for the bottle and splashed in another generous portion. Drinking deeply, she coughed.

"That's no way to treat a twenty-five-year-old scotch," he chided gently.

They were turned toward each other, her shin propped against his jeans-clad thigh. She wore a pair of his socks, as well. Her eyes were watery, whether from the scotch or from her tears, he didn't know. Quinn studied him somberly.

"What?" he asked.

She shook her head. "You know so much about me. All my dark, humiliating secrets, things I never wanted anyone to know…and I know practically nothing about *you*."

He chuckled lowly. "I'm an open book, honey. A web search can give you every detail of my life. Every woman I've dated, my favorite color, what I eat for breakfast. The fact I broke my arm when I was seven, although I'm laying that on Mark and a game of dare."

"I mean something *real*," she persisted.

It was the scotch talking, loosening her up, but this turn in conversation seemed to distract her. "Okay." He blew out a thoughtful breath. "I have a motorcycle in LA—three of them. High-end performance machines. I ride around the canyon at night sometimes, really open those babies up."

Taking a sip from the glass, she lifted her eyebrows faintly.

"No one knows it's me under that helmet, especially not the paps. My property has a hidden rear gate off the main road, so I can come and go without anyone who might be camped out front seeing me." He thought of those lone rides, a way to escape the pressures of his career. "Don't tell Mom, though. She'll have my hide. She abhors bikes—she calls them donor cycles."

When she continued to look at him with serious eyes, he tilted his head at her. "Not good enough?"

Her fingers traced the cut-lead pattern of the glass she held. She took another drink. "Considering things, no."

She was at once familiar and also alluring to him. All his life, he had glutted on women because he could—his looks, the St. Clair money and, later, his fame—had afforded him that. But Quinn was different. He would rather take a beating than see her hurt, he realized.

"How about this?" His voice was low and husky. "I'm the biggest fool in the universe. All those years ago, I didn't see how special you are."

Her gaze traveled over his face, as if sifting for truth. Then, slowly, Quinn leaned into him, pressing her mouth to his. Carter returned her kiss, the feel of her breasts against his chest causing a slow heat to rise inside him. In one forward movement, she straddled his lap, and he settled against the cushions with her, his hands at the small of her back, slipping under the oversized shirt to reach the warm silk of her skin. He instantly hardened as she released a kittenish moan into his mouth. She tasted of scotch, their tongues mingling, her hands threading through his hair. Carter's hands grazed her narrow waist and moved upward to the sides of her breasts. She wore no bra, having apparently dispensed with it along with her other damp clothing. Quinn ground against him, her breath warm against his face, her beautiful long hair hanging around him like a curtain.

He wanted her. *God, he did.* But not like this, he realized with resignation. He didn't want her decision to be confused by alcohol or careening emotions. For the first time, he wanted to take care of a woman more than he wanted to fulfill his own needs. Reluctantly, he broke their kiss, breathing hard. When he did, she buried her face against the hollow of his throat, sucking at his skin there. He stifled a groan of pleasure. "Quinn. *Quinn*, honey. No."

She straightened, her eyes confused and dazed by lust or alcohol, or both. She panted along with him. Her already full lips appeared swollen from their kissing.

"I want you," he said hoarsely. "But not tonight. You've been drinking, and you're upset. I'd be taking advantage."

Pain entered her eyes, and he reached for her hands.

"*Quinn*," he appealed to the hurt on her face, but she pulled her fingers from his. She managed to get off him, although she stumbled a bit as she stood, an indicator he had accurately assessed her intoxication.

"I have to go," she mumbled, appearing lost.

Carter followed her across the room. Reaching for her, he ignored the strain in his shoulder and turned her around to him. "You're not going anywhere. You can't drive like this."

"Just a few days ago, you were all over me." Accusation shone in her eyes, which shimmered with tears. "And now...now that I've come to you, you're brushing me off—"

He trapped her face in his hands and kissed her, silencing

her. "*I want you.* But I want you to want me when you're sober. I don't want you waking up in the morning with regret."

"All I have are regrets," she whispered brokenly.

The sound of her muffled sobs against his chest tore at him. He held her and let her cry. The scotch had done a number on her, and he felt guilt for having let her drink so much. He should put her in one of the other bedrooms, but he was worried she might wake up sick or try to flee. He would carry her if he could, but instead he wrapped his left arm around her and coaxed her into his bedroom. The covers were already pulled back from where he'd been sleeping.

"Move over, boy." Doug rose from the spot he had taken and moved to the far side of the king-size bed.

"Get in, honey."

Quinn wiped at her eyes and hiccupped. She wobbled as she unceremoniously pushed the oversized sweats down her hips and left them on the hardwood floor. He saw a flash of skimpy panties as she climbed onto the mattress. Thank God she'd left on the shirt, or he would have an even harder time getting to sleep. Carter nudged her over and got in beside her.

He could tell by the water running through the gutters that the rain was still coming down. Remaining clothed, he lay beside Quinn, who had turned on her side away from him. Her hair, spread over his pillow, smelled of tangerines and honey. Except for the occasional soft hiccup, her breathing soon evened, and she appeared to already be asleep.

Total power exchange. No safe words. No limits.

He swallowed in the darkness, anger again tightening his chest as he thought about Medero's latest stunt and what could've happened.

He had to put an end to this.

CHAPTER TWENTY-NINE

Quinn awoke to the room drenched in soft light, disoriented, a dull throb in her head. It took a moment for reality to crash in on her. This was Carter's bedroom. She was in his bed with its pillowed white duvet and silky, high-thread-count sheets. Sitting up, she pressed a hand to her face. Last night was murky, yet she recalled how she had kissed him, more than kissed him. She had practically dry-humped him.

Oh, no. She reached for Carter's wristwatch that lay on the nightstand. Ten forty-five a.m. Had she really slept that late? Replacing the watch, Quinn felt the sway of her naked breasts under his shirt she wore, its cotton hitched up around her waist.

The half-closed door to the room opened, and Doug trotted inside, tail wagging. Carter followed, holding an earthenware mug. "Well, you're alive."

"Barely." Embarrassed, she raked a hand through her hair, then looked up as he handed her the mug.

"Green tea."

"Thanks."

"I wanted to make sure you're up. We have the call with the attorney in about an hour." He wore the same clothes he'd had on last night. "How're you feeling?"

"Probably not as bad as I should." Holding the mug's warmth between her palms, she felt her face burn with the question. "Carter…did we…?"

"You mean you don't remember how good I was?" He feigned shock before the grooves of his dimples deepened. "Yeah, we slept together," he confirmed in a gentle voice. "But, no, nothing happened."

Not because she hadn't wanted it to. She had a blurry flashback of him being the one to cool the flames between them and her accusing him of playing with her feelings. Her sober self understood he was being a gentleman. Quinn wasn't a drinker, and the scotch had clearly won. Another wave of humiliation swept over her.

"Oh." He dipped into the back pocket of his jeans, extracting her cell phone. "While I was down letting Doug out, your phone rang. The screen said it was Nora. It looks like she's called a few times." He handed it to her, his mouth set in a hard line. "I considered not telling you."

"No, I should talk to her."

Even wearing yesterday's clothes, his hair sticking up in places, Carter managed to look casually handsome. Quinn could only imagine what she looked like. He turned to one of the dresser drawers, pulling out some clothes. Then he went into the adjoining master bathroom and returned with his shaving kit. "I'll give you some privacy to talk. I'll take a shower in one of the other bathrooms." Stopping in the doorway, he turned. "Quinn…don't let her make you feel like any of this is your fault. You're a victim in this, despite what you think."

His words soothed her. But as he departed with Doug following, that feeling soon receded. Quinn placed the mug on the nightstand. Taking a slow breath, she punched in Nora's number. She heard her mother's relief as she answered.

"Thank God, Quinn. I've been calling your cell all morning. When I couldn't reach you, I called the St. Clair and asked them to ring your room. They told me you never checked in."

"I'm sorry I didn't pick up."

"I was upset last night, understandably so..." Nora sounded regretful. "But I shouldn't have told you to go, not when who knows what kind of men saw that terrible ad. I'm sorry, Quinn. I didn't realize that you'd actually left until I went to your room this morning."

Her throat ached. "Are the police still there?"

"I took coffee out to them earlier. They...told me another man showed up overnight."

At the news, she rubbed her forehead. "Mom, after the guests leave today, I think you should find somewhere else to stay for a while."

"That's the other reason I've been trying to reach you. Considering things here, the Pickwells and Kents have invited me to go with them to the Keys. They're awfully nice people, and they've been so understanding about all this. I don't have any more guests booked until late March, but I don't want to leave you alone."

"It's a good idea. You should go." Quinn repressed a sigh, wanting to have complete honesty from now on. "And I'm not alone. I'm here with Carter. I stayed at his house last night."

"I thought you might've. Quinn, you're making another mistake—"

"He's done more to help me than anyone," she interjected. Things couldn't get much worse, so she figured she might as well tell her about the photos. "There's something else, and I want you to be prepared. The paparazzi took photos of Carter and me last weekend. They're going to publish them in a gossip magazine next week. The photos were taken out of context."

"What do you mean?"

"Carter knows all about Jake. He was trying to comfort me. The magazine's probably going to imply we're having an affair, maybe even that he's the reason for my divorce. These publications and websites thrive on salacious rumors—"

"*Are* you sleeping with him? Tell the truth. There's been enough lies."

Face hot, Quinn sat in Carter's bed, thinking of last night. "We haven't had sex," she managed.

"But you have feelings for him."

"Yes." Although her voice was barely audible, saying it aloud made it more real. Her heart hurt with the admission.

Nora sighed softly. "Oh, Quinn. I worry about you. Didn't you learn anything from Jake? You need to find a nice man with a stable job and an ordinary life."

She felt a stab of pain. Still, she said, "Have a good time in the Keys. I love you, Mom."

"I love you, too. I just wish you could've been honest with me from the beginning, Quinn."

Quinn disconnected. She sat there for several moments, trying to swallow the lump that lingered in her throat before noticing on the phone's screen that she had another missed call. Skipping over the messages from her mother, she listened to the voice mail left by the officer she had spoken with last night. He told her the website had taken down the ad and that both men who had gone to the B&B last night were fully cooperating with police, including turning over email correspondence. Quinn closed her eyes in gratitude.

Climbing from the bed, she looked for the sweatpants she vaguely recalled kicking off last night but couldn't find them. Instead, she straightened the shirt so it fell at midthigh. She started to reach for the mug of tea on the nightstand, but instead her eyes again fell to Carter's watch. It was a high-end designer brand, easily worth thousands. A year ago, he had been the face of the jeweler's ad campaign.

A reminder of the world he belonged to.

Her things were still outside in the car. Quinn went into the large adjoining bathroom that included a walk-in shower and vintage, claw-foot tub. Mascara smudged her eyes, making her look like a hungover raccoon, and she scrubbed it away. While she was there, she used Carter's brush to try to tame her hair, then looked for toothpaste but realized he must have taken it with him into the other bathroom. Rummaging in the cabinets, she found a brand-new tube and squirted some of the paste onto her finger, using it to brush her teeth, then cupped water in her hand and rinsed her mouth, spitting into the sink. She would shower after she went to the car for her things.

Leaving the bedroom, she nearly bumped into Carter in the hall. He still wore jeans but had changed into a Henley shirt, his hair damp.

"Sorry. I…uh…left my razor in my bathroom. I was coming back for it." He scratched at the sexy stubble on his face.

"How'd it go with Nora?"

"I told her about the photos. She took it rather well, actually." Aware of her bare legs and nudity under his shirt, she looked away, her voice weakening. "I guess after having your daughter advertising for a new dungeon master, the rest of it's pretty small beans."

Gently, he tipped up her chin. "You okay?"

Her lips parted. "Carter, about last night—"

"I wasn't rejecting you. I just wanted to be sure you felt the same way when you weren't blotted out of your mind."

Her skin prickled pleasurably from his nearness. Lost in his searching gaze, Quinn laid her fingers against his chest.

"I…still feel the same way," she murmured.

He lowered his mouth to hers then, his kiss slow and drugging. Her arms went up around his neck, and she pressed her body to his, aware of how much she wanted—needed—the physical comfort and distraction of him. Whether they were together for just another few weeks, whether he broke what was left of her heart when it was over, it didn't matter. Jake's treachery faded, replaced by an aching need as she leaned into Carter in the hall outside his bedroom. His hands had slipped to the hem of the shirt she wore, and she felt a shuddering sensation as he cupped her bottom, pulling her closer.

His mouth searched hers more hungrily. Like her, he tasted faintly of minty toothpaste. His hands moved to her lower back under her shirt.

"Wait…" She pushed lightly against his chest, breaking their kiss. He released a shaky breath. His lung capacity and strength had improved dramatically, but she had to ask. "Are you sure you're ready?"

"I think so." He traced a finger over her cheekbone. "But as much as I'd like to do something romantic like sweep you into my arms and carry you to bed, I'm pretty sure my shoulder's not up to it."

She smiled softly. A tingling in her stomach, she took his hand and led him into the bedroom.

"Sorry, boy." Carter closed the door with his heel, leaving Doug in the hall. "No voyeurs."

As they stood beside the bed facing each other, he began to unbutton the shirt she wore. His dexterity was better, but she helped him with the remaining buttons, unable to wait. The whole world would think they were lovers soon. They might as well be, some wild part of her reasoned. He slid the shirt down her shoulders, and it dropped to the floor.

"God, Quinn," he whispered. He filled his hands with her breasts, lightly squeezing them, brushing his thumbs over their hardened peaks. Quinn thrilled at his touch. Eyes closed, she felt his lips brush her brow.

Looking up at him, she eased down onto the bed, her heart thumping and throat dry. She lay back as Carter carefully pulled his shirt over his head. He had gained more weight, his body filling out, the raised scars nestled in the light matting of chest hair. She accepted those imperfections as she did the riveting blue of his eyes and masculine structure of his face. He lay down on his side next to her. Propped on his left elbow, his right hand encircled the mound of one of her breasts. Then his head dipped downward, his tongue tantalizing her nipple before he covered it with his hot mouth. The stubble on his face scratched her skin, sending an erotic shiver through her. Quinn threaded her fingers through his thick hair as he suckled her, drawing the sensitive bud into his mouth with a hard pull. She groaned at the pleasure of it. Her fingers glided down his stomach, trailing past his navel and through the narrow line of coarse hair that disappeared at the waist of his jeans. As she lightly stroked his hardened manhood through the denim, he nipped at her breast, sending fire through her. Soon, he was pushing impatiently at the waistband of her panties. She helped him, shimmying them down her hips. Her breath caught as he slid a finger expertly up and down the desire-wet lips of her sex before sinking it deep into her body.

"*Oh, God.*" Her back arched, her mouth falling open as her walls clenched around him. Quinn was vaguely aware of her uneven breathing as he spoke to her in low tones, words of encouragement that sent her flying closer to the edge. Fingers slicked with her juices, he pumped in and out of her, his thumb massaging in slow circles until she came in an exploding orgasm. He silenced her cry with his mouth. Then he gathered her into his arms and rolled her on top of him.

"Careful…your shoulder," she cautioned, panting, her hands on his chest. His face was flushed, and he, too, was breathing hard. His hand went up to fist in the waves of her hair, pulling just hard enough to elicit another moan.

"I want to be inside you, Quinn," he said softly. "I want to make love to you."

Looking into his eyes, she saw his need as well as his vulnerability.

"We need protection," he murmured. "I'm not sure, but there might be a condom in my shaving kit—"

"I'm on the pill." She had been, as well, when she had conceived, but she knew it was a rare occurrence. Hesitantly, she added, "And I got tested…after I left Jake."

She saw sympathy on his features. They worked together to free him from his jeans and boxers, both of them smiling at the momentary awkwardness his shoulder injury necessitated. But their levity faded as Quinn straddled him just as she had last night, although this time he was on his back. Guiding him into her, she sank down onto his hard length, eyes closed and hissing softly as her body stretched to accommodate him. His breath shuddered. She braced her hands on his collarbones and began to slowly ride him. Carter's hands slid to the swell of her hips. For a long time, the frictionless glide of their bodies felt like liquid heat as she ascended and descended, again and again. He watched her, a hungered passion in his eyes. Her breath began to grow ragged as her urgency increased, his hips rising under her to match her rhythm.

He groaned a short time later, coming inside her.

Minutes later, she still lay atop him, her cheek against his chest. Neither spoke as Carter stroked her lower back. She didn't want this to end. She wanted to just lie here in this quiet room with only their joined breathing. Regretfully, she disentangled herself and lay on her side facing him. Turning toward her, he threaded a hand through her hair.

"Welcome back to vanilla," he said softly, although his eyes were serious and searching.

He was comparing their lovemaking to what she'd had with Jake. But what she needed, wanted, right now, was a feeling of safety and trust. She felt traumatized by the things she had allowed Jake to do to her. She thought of the verbal abuse and humiliation. Quinn swallowed down the shame the unwanted memory caused.

"There's nothing wrong with vanilla," she assured him,

touching his face.

"You have to tell me what you want. I can't...I won't do anything to actually hurt you, but—"

She hushed him with her fingers against his lips. "Jake and I were a mistake. I did those things with him because it was what he wanted, not what I wanted." Her throat tightened. "But this...it was mind-shattering."

His hand stroked intimately up her thigh. "I *care* about you, Quinn."

A sadness kindled inside her. Still, she wrapped her fingers around his other wrist, kissed the inside of it. "I know."

But care wasn't love, and even if it were, she understood it wouldn't be strong enough to hold him once he returned to his former life. Quinn reminded herself she had made the decision to live in the *now* with him, to take what he offered to somehow begin to heal herself, emotionally and sexually. She needed Carter, as much as he had needed her during those first painful weeks of his therapy. He was growing stronger, and she would, too. They would continue helping each other, and then they would say good-bye.

"We should get up," she said with a resigned sigh. "The call's scheduled for noon."

"I'd rather stay here." He bent his head to kiss the top of her breast. They both grinned as Doug whined on the other side of the closed door, unhappy about being kept out.

"Stay with me, Quinn. You'll be safer here. It's the best solution." Carter pushed himself up in bed. Quinn followed suit, the sheets tucked around her. Reluctantly, she agreed, then looked out through the glass wall at the fragile, pale blue sky that had replaced the rain.

"I need a shower. But I need to bring in my things first.

I'll put them in the room across the hall."

"But you'll sleep here with me." It wasn't so much a question but a pronouncement.

Rising, Quinn picked up his shirt she'd worn and put it back on. As she did, she noticed the sweatpants she had been looking for earlier. They had been kicked under the bed skirt.

"After you talk with the attorney, I was thinking we'd take a late lunch at the St. Clair. Push therapy back until later today." Carter stepped into his jeans and, with some effort, zipped and fastened them. "I need to talk to Mark, and it's probably better if I do it in person."

"About the photos?"

"And other things." He released a breath. "We just made the conversation I've got to have with him even more complicated."

CHAPTER THIRTY

"So, when the photos were taken, you and Quinn weren't together, but now you are?"

At the censure in Mark's voice, Carter shifted in the wing chair in his brother's well-appointed office. Mark sat across from him, behind the massive mahogany desk that had once belonged to their father.

"This is *Quinn.* She's not someone you can just screw around with, and then—"

"It's not like that." Carter needed him to understand. "I care about her. And you've said yourself I've changed. Hurting Quinn is the last thing I'd want to do."

Mark frowned. "I believe you're sincere. *I do.* And you *have* changed, Carter. But you lead a big life. I don't know if it can support an ordinary, lasting relationship. I don't want Quinn being a casualty."

Carter stood and went to look at the framed family photos that sat on a shelf in the barrister bookcase. He had felt confident and strong enough today to come into the sprawling hotel without even bringing his cane. Just this morning, he had made love. The bouts of breathlessness, the chest pain...they were gone. Quinn was responsible for that. He owed her so much. He was disappointed in Mark's lack of faith in him, but not surprised. Who he was, his track record with women—it didn't exactly instill confidence. He wanted Mark's approval, but not getting it didn't change anything. He turned to him. "Regardless, I wanted you to know. I wanted to prepare you for the photos and be up front with you about this."

Mark sighed. "You're both adults. It's not like I can stop you. And I'd be lying if I said I haven't noticed something between you. I'd just hoped you wouldn't act on it. Quinn doesn't need another heartbreak—"

"She's moving into the beach house," Carter stated firmly. "It just makes sense for her to stay there. The gate's being repaired today, and the house has a state-of-the-art security system. At the least, it eliminates her traveling back and forth."

"Has something else happened?"

Carter knew Quinn wouldn't want Mark to know about the online ad, or the truth behind her divorce. Those things could come out if Medero wanted to further humiliate her, but that would also mean exposing himself. "There's been another issue with Medero. That's all I can say, so don't ask me more. Quinn doesn't want me talking about it, not even to you."

Mark frowned harder. "Where's she now?"

"Waiting for me on the boardwalk."

He got up from his chair, but Carter raised his palm in a halting gesture. "Mark, please. You have to trust me when I say she doesn't want to talk about it. I've got it under control, all right?"

Their eyes held until he finally nodded. "Don't let me down, Carter. On any of this."

A short time later, Carter went out through the hotel's rear doors, hoping to bypass the staff and smaller number of winter guests. He had requested one of the quieter alcoves in the St. Clair's restaurant, and he and Quinn had enjoyed a relatively undisturbed lunch, with only a few patrons noticing them and coming over. As he slid on his sunglasses, the crisp breeze ruffling his hair, he spotted Quinn standing alone on the boardwalk and watching the ocean. It was late February and another mild winter day. The water stretched across the horizon under a powder-blue sky. Reaching her, he faced the water, as well, placing his hands on the sun-weathered rail.

"How'd it go?" she asked nervously.

"He knows about the photos the paps took, and he knows about us now. Needless to say, he isn't happy."

Quinn released a soft breath. "Mark's been like a big brother to me. I know he worries."

They had turned to face each other, and she raised her face to his for a slow kiss. Then, palms against his chest, she said worriedly, "What if someone sees us?"

"The cat's out of the bag. At least it will be when the magazine hits."

He sensed the duress inside her. Carter had grown used to—or at least accepting of—his life in a fishbowl. It was a trade-off for his success. But such scrutiny would be new to Quinn. In fact, even as the wife of a professional athlete, it seemed she had gone out of her way to avoid the public eye. He couldn't protect her from the attention and possible criticism she would face because of their relationship. If it had been up to him, he would have kept it secret for as long as possible. But Medero had pushed them into the open.

His cell phone rang, and he reached into his jacket for it. The screen read Los Angeles County Police.

"I better take this," he said before answering. At what he was told, a coldness passed through him. There was concern in Quinn's eyes as she watched his face, able to hear only his side of the conversation.

"When?" he asked.

A few moments later, he thanked the detective for the heads-up and disconnected, a mix of emotions warring inside him. "That was the LA police."

Quinn shoved several strands of her wind-blown hair from her face. "What's happened?"

It would be on the news soon.

"Kelsey Dobbins is dead. She killed herself this morning."

CHAPTER THIRTY-ONE

They had watched the news the previous evening. Kelsey Dobbins's death had been briefly noted, the news anchor stating only that suicide was suspected, although an autopsy had yet to be completed. Carter knew from Detective Warren that she had ripped up her bedsheets and fashioned a noose, hanging herself from a water pipe inside the mental institution. He had also been told she had left a note addressed to him. If he chose to accept it, it would be forwarded once the death investigation closed.

The note remained on his mind as he entered the airy kitchen where Quinn was preparing lunch after a long walk on the beach.

"The attorney just called," she said, sounding tense. "The judge signed the temporary restraining order until the formal hearing. It's set for March eleventh."

That was just around the corner. "They're sending a copy of the order to the court here?"

"He says they are." With a sigh, she passed a hand over her eyes before going back to chopping vegetables. "Jake's being served this afternoon."

"Quinn…" Taking the knife, he laid it on the cutting board and took her hands in his. "This *is* necessary."

She merely bit her lip and nodded. He knew how much she dreaded facing Medero in court. The supporting documentation they had already provided—the police report detailing the property damage and the misdemeanor assault charge here, as well as screen shots of the text messages he'd sent—had no doubt factored into the decision for the temporary order. But the truly dangerous acts Medero had committed were largely without teeth, since so far they were untraceable to him. Medero would have his own attorney at the hearing who would refute any statements Quinn made about the car crash or the website ad, proclaiming a lack of proof his client was involved. They had learned late yesterday that the e-Rendezvous incident had been passed on to the FBI, but they had also been forewarned of a backlog of cases.

"There's no telling what Jake will say about me in court." Worry tightened Quinn's features. "The last time, his attorney implied I was trying to defame him. That I'd trashed my own apartment so I could blame it on him. I'm linked to you because of the photos. I don't want this to affect your career."

"Don't worry about me. You're not alone in this, Quinn. I'll be with you in the courtroom."

"Maybe you shouldn't."

"I'm going to speak about what I've witnessed. I'm not afraid of getting involved. We'll take care of this in San Francisco, put it behind us and go to LA from there."

The press junket he was contractually obligated to do was scheduled for the week after the hearing. They had already discussed Quinn accompanying him for the time he would be in LA, then going with him to New York for the junket's

East Coast arm and movie premiere. She had been hesitant about going, but he had convinced her that he needed her to continue his therapy and to help with some personal matters. Mostly, though, he just didn't want to be without her.

"That reminds me." She went to the fridge. "Your publicist called while you were upstairs."

After their walk, Carter had left his phone on the kitchen counter to charge, and Quinn must have read the screen. Ariel had already left one voice mail. She was becoming as much of a nuisance as Elliott now that the film's promotions were coming up. She was wanting confirmations on the rounds of late-night and morning talk shows stipulated in his contract.

"Oh, shoot!" While taking items from the fridge for lunch, Quinn had knocked over a glass decanter of tomato juice on the top shelf. The carafe broke, sending red liquid down the shelves and across the floor. Carter stared at the mess, his skin tingling.

"Don't move," she warned. They had both removed their shoes after coming up from the beach, and she carefully sidestepped the puddle and shards of glass. She headed toward the closet where cleaning items were kept. "I can't believe I did that—"

"I slipped on the blood."

She turned to look at him. Carter swallowed dryly, the memory crystalizing. "I was going to get the phone to call for help, and I slipped on Bianca's blood on the bathroom floor. It was pooling around her."

Quinn returned to him, her face paling. "You remembered this just now?"

"Yeah," he rasped. He wanted to close his eyes against the image—the gruesome gash in Bianca's throat, her labored struggle for breath as she bled out in front of him.

"Do…you remember anything else?"

He reached for something more, but came up empty. "No."

Carter looked again at the spilled juice. He felt Quinn's hand touch his arm. "Don't let Doug anywhere near this."

She went to get the cleaning supplies.

***

After lunch, Quinn guided Carter through several restorative yoga poses that wouldn't put stress on his recuperating shoulder. The poses were simple, intended to relax him, to take his focus off the press junket, his impending return to LA and the movie he had agreed to star in that would begin production in the fall. All big steps after a life-altering injury.

There were also his fragments of memory that appeared to be slowly returning, like broken shells washed onto the sand after a storm. It bothered her that her personal problems added to his burden.

His eyes closed, Carter lay on his back on the yoga mat in *Shavasana.* Quinn had created a peaceful environment in the workout room, lowering the lights and playing quiet music in the background. Sitting on her heels, she leaned over him as she performed a neck massage using lavender essential oil. As she worked, she studied the elegant planes of his face, the sweep of thick lashes against high cheekbones, the attractively stubbled, strong jaw.

He must have sensed her scrutiny, because she found herself staring down into his midnight-blue eyes.

"Keep your eyes closed. Slow your breath and bring it deep from the belly," she reminded softly, continuing the knead of her fingers. She expected him to tell her he felt silly or make some sarcastic comment about what they were doing, but instead he lifted his hand and slowly threaded his fingers through her hair, then used it to pull her mouth down to his. His kiss was unhurried and thorough, making her want more. But they broke apart at the interruption of the ringing phone. It was his. Carter had brought it downstairs since he was expecting a call.

"Let it go to voice mail," he said huskily.

"You need to take this—"

"Elliott will get over it. Let it go." His thumb stroked languidly over her thigh.

She left the phone where it was. Finally, its shrill stopped. Quinn's pulse beat in her throat as they stared at each other.

"I want you." His eyes smoldered with desire.

She wanted him, too. Slowly, she pulled her top over her head, her sports bra next. Carter sat up and kissed her as he fondled her breasts, sending an ache straight to her sex.

"Sit on the sofa," he murmured, his breath warm against her earlobe. "Scoot your bottom to the cushion's edge."

Quinn rose shakily. He made no attempt to hide that he was watching her as she removed the remainder of her clothing. Pulling off his T-shirt, he came to kneel closely in front of her. His mouth moved demandingly over hers, sending a surge of heat through her. Then, spreading her knees farther apart, he drew down the waist of his sweatpants. Bracing her weight on her elbows on the cushions, she lay back slightly and adjusted her body. Quinn moaned softly as he sank into her, the position allowing for deep penetration. Face flushed, Carter released a rough breath at the feel of it, too. Then he began to thrust, his pace slow and deliberate as his hands explored the soft lines of her hips, her waist. Mouth open,

Quinn arched her neck, and he sucked and bit lightly at her there, eliciting another moan.

For a long time, their bodies moved in perfect rhythm, their ragged breathing in unison. Then his jaw squared as his thrusts become shorter and more forceful.

"Quinn…" he panted. She cried out as she came, her walls clenching around him. He released into her with a groan.

Sometime later, they showered upstairs in the master bathroom. Carter soaped her body, his hands sliding over her slick curves.

"I think we scared off Doug downstairs," she said, feeling Carter's chuckle low in his chest.

"I like this new form of cardio."

She smiled softly. "Mmmm. Me, too. That was a creative position." She pressed a kiss against his still-healing shoulder. "I guess it's true necessity *is* the mother of invention."

He tipped her face up to his.

"You're under my skin." His eyes were serious. "I can't get enough of you."

He lowered his mouth to hers, his kiss sending a new spiral of need through her. Then, her hands trailing down his sides, Quinn looked up at him as she sank to her knees on the tile floor. She used her mouth on him until his body shuddered. One hand gripping the shower wall, the other fisted in her hair, he came again with a hoarse cry.

***

Although it was midafternoon, Quinn lounged in bed. A towel wrapped around his waist, Carter sat on the mattress's edge and talked on his cell phone with one of the military veterans they had met at the hospital in Charleston. The man had left a voice mail while they had been in the shower, and Carter had returned his call.

"AJ and some of the guys have this idea for a recreation and fitness center—one adapted for vets with disabilities," Carter said once he had disconnected. She recalled AJ was the one who had lost his leg in a roadside bombing. "It's a tough situation. They've been through rehab, but afterward they're pretty much on their own. The center's just a dream at this point, but they're looking to do a feasibility study and, based on that, raise funds."

"And you want to help?"

Cupping the back of his neck, he nodded. "We're meeting next week to talk more. There's a large veteran population in Charleston that could benefit."

His phone rang again. As he answered, Quinn turned onto her side and ran her fingers over Doug's coat, who was curled against her.

"Elliott." Carter stood, the phone against his ear. "Sorry I couldn't take your call earlier."

Quinn knew they were planning to announce Carter's starring in *The Rainy Season* to distract from the photos that would go public next week. She didn't understand some of the cinema and financing terminology as Carter spoke with his agent, but she recognized the name of the film's director and the actors being considered for other roles, including one very beautiful ingénue. Deciding to give him privacy, she got up and moved to the bathroom to dry her hair. At the doorway, however, she turned to look at Carter as he paced the room, talking the business of Hollywood.

Although her heart lifted at how normal—how healthy—he looked, the realization was also a bittersweet one.

Already, his former life was beginning to reclaim him.

CHAPTER THIRTY-TWO

Carter St. Clair Gets Some Healing of the Sexual Kind

At the headline, Quinn released a tense breath. The gossip magazine was on the newsstands, its digital site also posting the photos overnight. Her stomach tight, she viewed the images on her iPad. Some were simply of Carter and her walking on the beach. But the ones taken while they had been seated at the lifeguard stand were more intimate. In them, he had his arm wrapped around her, and her head lay against his shoulder. A caption accompanied the photos.

Carter St. Clair looks to be recuperating nicely with the help of his physical therapist, Quinn Reese-Medero, estranged wife of San Francisco Breakers running back Jake Medero. Did the hunky A-list actor play the lead role in their breakup?

Setting the iPad aside, Quinn rose from the sofa and paced. "They make it sound like I cheated on him. They don't mention we were legally separated before I even started working with you. And I never took his last name—"

"Hey." Carter came to stand in front of her. Gently, he clasped her upper arms. "We expected this, remember? And *we* know the truth. No one else matters."

She nodded mutely.

"There're three cars of 'em parked on the road," Jolene fussed as she entered through the front door. Quinn knew Carter had called her to forewarn her of the possible paparazzi. Now that the photos the magazine had paid for as an exclusive were out, it was likely the agency responsible for them had sold information on Carter's whereabouts to others in their business.

"It's not right." Jolene struggled angrily out of her coat. "It's an invasion of privacy!"

"But it's not illegal," Carter told her. "As long as they stay off the property, there's nothing we can do. Remember what we talked about. If they try to stop you when you leave—"

"I'll run the damn fools over!"

Despite the situation, he suppressed a smile. "I appreciate that, Jo, but just don't, okay? Don't engage them."

"You take all the fun out of it," she huffed. But her eyes softened as she looked at them. "Have to admit I'm thrilled with the two of you gettin' together. Been wonderin' when it would happen—I got a real sense about these things."

Still grumbling about the photographers, she bustled off to the kitchen. Carter turned his attention back to Quinn.

"There'll be some heat on us for a while, at least until some other scandal draws their attention." His gaze held concern. "We should probably stay off the beach for now."

It was a gray day, anyway, the morning sunlight feeble as it attempted to fight its way through the clouds that had rolled in overnight. Even the beach appeared colorless. Quinn forced herself to focus on something else. "We'll use the treadmill. We'll also ramp up your shoulder work now that Dr. Patel has given us the all clear."

"I need to make a couple of calls. I'll meet you downstairs in twenty?"

She gave a faint nod.

"Do me a favor? Don't read any of the comments online."

He went upstairs.

When she had been with Jake, she had seen some of the things being said online about him, especially when the Breakers lost a game. The comments, even from self-proclaimed fans, could be scathing. She would abide by Carter's request to avoid social media. But she couldn't help wondering what was being said about her.

***

By the end of the week, the paparazzi who had been camped in front of the home had thinned, with only one car now visible outside the gate. Peering at it between the slats of the plantation shutters, Carter stood in the living area with his phone to his ear.

"*Variety* and *Entertainment Weekly* are planning cover stories," Ariel Carrington, his publicist, enthused. "We'll be doing the interviews and photo shoots while you're here. You're going to need your stamina to keep the schedule I'm setting. I hope that *physical therapist* has been doing more than just sexing you up."

He ignored her comment. "I'll be ready."

"You looked good in those photos, so I suppose she *is* doing her job. But if you don't mind me saying so, she isn't quite up to par with your usual tastes, is she? What is it about her that's attracted a pro football player and now you?"

Irritation flickered through him. Although she was now in her early-forties, Ariel had been a runway model before moving to the business side of the industry. She had also unsuccessfully propositioned him on more than one occasion. He would consider getting a new publicist, but she was closely aligned with Elliott's agency and had been instrumental in Carter's rise to stardom. Still, he had his limits.

"I do mind. Watch it, Ariel."

She gave a throaty laugh. "Oh, my. You really *are* smitten, aren't you? Anyway, I've been coordinating your time for while you're here. In addition to the cover shoots, you'll be doing Kimmel on Thursday and Ellen on Friday. They both tape around four, so we'll need to go directly from the junket on those days. Also, I don't know if Elliott's told you, but they want you to present at the Silver Screen Institute's salute to Norman Weintraub on Saturday night."

"I'd rather not."

"Carter, it's *Norman.* It'll mean so much to him. When they found out you were going to be in town, they practically begged."

Norman Weintraub had been the director of one of Carter's movies. He was also eighty and finally retiring after a long and illustrious career.

"All right," he said, repressing a sigh.

"Elliott will be attending with you."

"Let them know I'll be bringing someone else, as well." Quinn was going to LA with him at his insistence. He could see from the schedule being set for him that she would be spending much of the time during the week alone. He wouldn't let that happen on Saturday night, too.

A tense silence filled the airwaves. Then, "Of course I'll arrange for another seat," Ariel replied coolly.

"Let's get back to the junket. I won't be answering any questions about the attack. Or my personal life."

"I'll make sure everyone's aware you're there to discuss the film only, but you're going to be asked questions. You're bigger news than the movie, Carter." What sounded like emotion entered her voice. "I want you to know, I've missed you. I've thought about you so much while you've been gone."

As she gave a rundown on which journalists she expected to attend, Quinn entered the room. After their therapy session that morning, she had run on the treadmill, then gone through an extended yoga practice behind the closed glass doors of the sunroom. Nervous energy, he supposed. She now wore a simple wrap dress, her russet hair pulled back.

"I've got to go, Ariel. Send me the itinerary once it's finalized." He bid her good-bye and disconnected. To Quinn, he said, "You're sure you want to go out?"

"You have AJ and the others coming by."

Carter had invited the vets over to talk about the center, figuring it was easier than meeting them somewhere in public. "That doesn't mean you have to leave."

"I know. But Samantha and I made plans for lunch before all this started. I don't want to cancel. And the truth is, I've got cabin fever. I need to get out."

They had sequestered themselves since the news about them had gone viral. It had been nice, the two of them tucked away from the world. Carter had done his best to keep Quinn occupied, to keep her away from the Internet and the celebrity news segments on television. Interest in her had peaked since the photos had come out. He walked to where she stood and took her hands in his. "You look great."

She gave a smile of appreciation. "It's nice to remember I own a few things besides yoga pants."

"I like you in those, too. Speaking of clothes, I'd like you to attend an event with me while we're in LA. It's black tie."

Anxiety filled her eyes, and she shook her head. "I don't own anything for something like that. The best I have is the dress I wore to Olivia's engagement party—"

"I have a stylist I work with in LA. She'll take care of everything." When she still appeared uncertain, he said, "I *need* you with me, Quinn. Getting back to my life after all this…it's a little overwhelming."

At his admission, she stared down at their fingers tangled together, then gave a small nod.

"The paps are outside. They're going to follow you."

"I know." She sounded nervous but resolved. "We've talked about this—I can't hide here forever. Samantha and I are having lunch at Café Bella. If anyone bothers us, she says she'll toss them out."

"Call me when you get there and again before you leave."

A short time later, he watched from the window as the Mercedes departed. As expected, the lone car that sat at the top of the road pulled out behind it. Resentment tightened his mouth. Carter thought of his call with Ariel. It had brought back to him just how frenetic his life had been, how different from the solace he'd had here.

With Quinn out of the house, he had a call to return before the vets arrived. Frank Holloway was a retired FBI agent who had served as a consultant on one of his films. Carter had played an agent, and the two had gotten to know each other. Frank still had contacts within the Bureau, and Carter had asked him several days ago if he could do anything to get Quinn's situation moved up. He had waited until her departure to call Frank back. He didn't want to upset her with what he was doing.

"I've got an update for you," Frank said upon answering Carter's call. "First, the good news—I was able to get someone in the Internet Crimes Unit to bump things up and trace the emails' originating IP address. You were right, the emails came from San Francisco, but not from Medero's home. They came from a coffee shop about a half hour away. It's not impossible, but the public Wi-Fi makes tying the emails to a specific computer more difficult. That's your bad news."

Carter frowned. He had hoped Medero had been stupid enough to send the emails from his house. "But if the shop has a security camera, wouldn't there at least be footage that coincides with the date and times the emails were sent? We might be able to see if he was in there."

"Maybe. It'd also depend on how far back they keep their recordings—that stuff eventually gets erased to save on storage space. But as far as the feds doing something like that goes, it'd require man-hours, including obtaining a search warrant. Same goes for getting information from the website about who set up that personal ad, or getting access to Medero's laptop. Since she wasn't physically harmed by this jerk-off's prank, I doubt they'll make it a priority over cases where real violence occurred. It looks like your friend will have to wait in the queue. I'm sorry I'm not able to be more help."

Carter tamped down his disappointment. "Thanks, anyway, Frank. I owe you dinner next time you're in LA."

He said good-bye and disconnected, his lips set tight. Still, Carter wasn't ready to give up. Medero had exploited Quinn. He had used her, put her in danger too many times.

They would be headed to San Francisco next week for the hearing. Maybe there *was* something he could do.

CHAPTER THIRTY-THREE

San Francisco, California

"Mr. St. Clair! Look over here!"

"Carter, are you in town for the hearing?"

The flashes from the paparazzi's cameras were blinding, as obtrusive as the questions being shouted at them. Still, Quinn kept her eyes on Carter's back as she followed him through the terminal at the San Francisco International Airport. He had been instantly recognized as soon as they had deplaned.

"You look healthy. How're you feeling, Carter?"

A backpack slung over his left shoulder, he maintained a steady stride, making her thankful for the hard work they had put in.

"Miss Reese, are you worried about seeing Jake in court?"

Her face grew hot as the photographers' questions shifted to her. But she schooled her features and kept going, rolling her carry-on behind her. Relief filtered through her when they finally reached the terminal's sliding electronic doors and were ushered into a waiting limousine by a chauffeur. It was still morning here, the sky gray and a chilly drizzle wetting the asphalt—typical weather for San Francisco in March.

"We have someone claiming the rest of your luggage from

the carousel. They'll bring it in another car," the chauffeur told them once they were settled. He closed the door, shutting out the din of activity around the vehicle.

"You all right?" Carter asked her as the driver went around to the other side and got in.

Rattled, she blew out a small breath. "How do you do this?"

"You get used to it." There was a grim twist to his mouth, however. "I'd been expecting this in LA, but not here."

But the media had been covering them since the photos had come out early last week. The temporary restraining order against Jake had been a matter of public record—it didn't surprise her that the media had found out about it and the hearing. It only further sensationalized the story.

They rode in silence as the limo left the airport and took the expressway north to the city. Then, as if to ease the tension, Carter asked, "What do you think Doug's doing right now?"

Quinn couldn't help but smile. "Probably being run ragged by Emily and Ethan."

He chuckled, his fingers intertwining with hers. They had left Doug in the care of Mark and Samantha, taking him to the bungalow last night.

Fortunately, their arrival at the hotel was more discreet than at the airport. The four-star hotel was lavishly decorated and featured views of the Embarcadero waterfront. Wrapped in a sweater to ward off the chill, Quinn could see the San Francisco-Oakland Bay Bridge, cloaked in an iron-gray mist, from their private balcony. It felt strange to be back in the city she had called home since her freshman year in college. She thought of her friends from school, her Mission District apartment, the job she'd loved. But knowing Jake's villa was also a short drive away aroused a sick feeling.

"We'll have a killer view of the Bay Lights tonight." Carter had walked onto the balcony and now stood beside her. He squinted at a ferry gliding across the ashen waters.

"This is a beautiful hotel." Quinn couldn't imagine what the top-floor suite had cost. It was nearly as elegant as the lobby, filled with antiques, fresh-cut flowers and art.

"Elliott recommended it. They're big on guest privacy."

A knock came from outside the suite, and they both went inside. Carter opened the door to a white-uniformed waiter, who rolled in a cart that held a sterling-silver coffee service and two lidded silver trays. He placed all of it on a handsome wood pedestal table.

"I ordered brunch," Carter said once he'd tipped the waiter at the door. Returning, he removed the lids from the trays. One contained a decadent-looking sourdough French toast, the other a savory mushroom and spinach omelet with fried potatoes. They had taken an early flight from Charleston, and with the time change, it was only midmorning here.

She shook her head. "I can't eat."

"Try." Carter touched her face. "You barely ate anything last night and turned down food service on the plane. Tomorrow's going to be a long day. You need to keep up your strength."

The reminder jangled her nerves. They were meeting with the attorney tomorrow morning to go over her statement and prepare for questions. The hearing itself would be at four p.m. Quinn sighed softly. "It wasn't long ago I was trying to convince *you* to eat."

"I'm trying to take care of you. Just like you've taken care of me."

Giving in, she sat on one of the slip-covered chairs at the table. Dutifully, she speared a potato with a fork and, putting it in her mouth, began chewing. Despite the tension in her stomach, the food was delicious. Carter poured her tea from the shorter of the two pots that had been delivered. Then, making a cup of coffee for himself, he leaned against a mahogany sideboard that sat in front of floor-to-ceiling windows framed by silk drapes.

"You're not eating?" Quinn asked around a mouthful of omelet.

"I'll get around to it." He sipped his coffee. "But as long as we're discussing the theme for the day—*me taking care of you*—I have a gift."

Swallowing, she put down her fork and touched her napkin to her lips. "That's not necessary."

"Too late." He winked at her over the rim of his china cup. "When you're finished eating, the limo's waiting. It's taking you to Devine Bliss."

Her chest fluttered in surprise. She knew of the exclusive wellness spa in the city's tony Pacific Heights neighborhood, but had never been there. She began to protest, but Carter pulled a chair up beside her. "You're stressed about the hearing, Quinn. I know I pushed you into it. I just didn't expect the media attention surrounding us. It's made things worse for you." He placed his hand over hers on the table and squeezed lightly. "Do this for me? I've got the day planned for you, including a masseuse and your own rooftop soaking tub. They also have a yoga studio. I booked you private time with a master instructor—maybe you can learn some new things." His gaze held hers. "I want to give you a day of peace where none of this can touch you. Let me do this for you?"

Her throat tightened at his thoughtfulness. "You're not coming with me?"

He shrugged. "A spa day isn't my thing. I get fussed over enough by Hair and Makeup."

"What will you do all day?"

"Ariel's got me on some phone interviews with reporters this afternoon. I'm also a little tired from the trip. I'll probably take a nap." Standing, he leaned over her and kissed the top of her head. "I'll see you back here for dinner tonight."

Picking up a slice of the French toast with his fingers, he bit into it and, still chewing, walked with it into the bedroom.

***

Carter entered the busy coffee shop sandwiched between an independent bookstore and an organic dry cleaner, typical of this section of the Nob Hill neighborhood. The aroma of coffee hung in the air, as did the sound of conversation. The shop catered to a diverse group, from young urban professionals to hipsters, and featured eclectic furniture, local artwork for sale and hanging red velvet lamps. As he walked up to the counter, he noticed the prevalence of laptops and other mobile devices in use by the shop's patrons.

"I'll have a macchiato," he said to the barista, a thin-faced girl with a nose ring and a bored expression.

"Which one? We have two specialties…" She halted, her eyes widening in recognition. "Oh, my God. You're Carter St. Clair!"

He smiled, but remained low-key. "What are the specialties?"

"Caramel and hazelnut. Wes, you have to come out here

now!" she yelled to someone in the shop's rear.

"Caramel," Carter decided as a slender male in his forties with dark hair and a goatee emerged from the back room.

"Heather, I told you to get those boxes out of the hall. They're a fire hazard, and if the inspector comes by, we're screwed." Based on his authoritative tone, Wes appeared to be the shop's proprietor, or at least the one in charge. Upon seeing Carter, his mouth dropped open, and he placed a hand over his heart in a dramatic gesture. "Someone catch me. I'm going to faint!"

"Don't do that," Carter responded with a smile. Wes reached across the counter and shook his hand.

"Carter St. Clair, here in my shop! I'm a big fan."

"Thanks."

"Are you filming a movie around here?"

"No, I'm here for a different reason." Carter had already noted the security cameras mounted to the shop's ceiling—one was trained on the front door, the other on the counter.

"Well, despite your recent troubles, you look as good as you do on film. And so tall, too. So many actors turn out to be short in real life." He continued to look Carter over appraisingly. "If my partner were here, he'd confirm it—you're at the top of my free-pass list."

Carter knew what he meant. It was a thing where people, mostly jokingly, created lists of celebrities they would be allowed to have sex with, if given the chance, without their significant other getting upset. Wes gave a taut laugh. "That was TMI, wasn't it? I run off at the mouth when I'm nervous. I hope I didn't offend you."

Carter chuckled. "Hardly. I'm flattered."

He was aware customers had since looked up from their

screens and were staring openly. The barista who had taken his order delivered the drink she had prepared, spilling some of it on the counter as she set it in front of him.

"Sorry." Coloring fiercely, she grabbed for a napkin.

"No worries." He reached into his back pocket for his wallet.

"On the house," Wes insisted. Carter thanked him, put a large bill in the tip jar, anyway, then picked up his drink.

"About that reason I'm here." Looking at Wes, he lowered his voice. "Believe it or not, it relates to your shop."

Wes lifted his eyebrows. "Do tell."

"Could we talk somewhere in private?"

He was ushered to the shop's rear, where Wes had a surprisingly homey office, complete with a futon and rag rug.

Some two hours later, Carter exited the shop, a cool mist falling around him on the hilly San Francisco street. He felt no guilt using his celebrity—he'd signed autographs, posed for selfies with customers and staff and even video-chatted with Wes's partner, who was a stockbroker in the financial district. But he had gotten what he wanted: access to the security footage. Frank Holloway hadn't been able to get the FBI to move faster, but he did get Carter the location of the coffee shop the emails had originated from, as well as the date and times they were sent.

He had gotten lucky the footage hadn't yet been erased and that the shop's proprietor was a fan and eager to help him out once he'd explained the situation—no search warrant required. Luckier still, Medero hadn't used someone else to do his bidding this time. But Carter's gut had told him the emails' explicit, sadomasochistic nature was something Medero would get off on.

It had simply been a matter of patience and fast-forwarding on the computer screen in the shop owner's office. The digital footage was dark and grainy, and Medero had worn a hoodie and sunglasses while inside. And although he had sat out of range of the cameras, it *was* him coming into the shop, Carter was certain of it. His entries and exits coincided with the timestamps on the emails.

The shop owner had offered to email the footage to Carter. In turn, Carter had forwarded it to Quinn's attorney from his cell phone.

He had lied to Quinn about his plans for the day, but it had been for a noble cause.

Hailing a cab, he felt a quiet victory.

CHAPTER THIRTY-FOUR

"You did this, didn't you?"

Quinn stood with Carter in the stately corridor outside the courtroom. The judge presiding over the hearing was in his chambers, reviewing the security footage from the coffee shop. A surprise to Quinn, it had been submitted by her counsel in support of her statement about the e-Rendezvous incident. While Jake's attorney had raised objections to the last-minute evidence, the judge had pointed out that this was a hearing, not a trial, that no one's liberty was at stake. He would view the footage before deciding on its admissibility.

"I had to do something." Carter appeared handsome in the same suit he had bought for Olivia's engagement dinner. "The FBI wasn't going to come through in time for this."

"Why didn't you tell me?"

"I didn't want to get your hopes up. I didn't even know if the coffee shop had security cameras, and if they did, whether they would give me access. The footage also wasn't that clear. David's had a digital specialist working to enhance it until just a half hour ago."

David Geller was Quinn's attorney. At the moment, he

was seated on a nearby bench, briefcase on his lap, going over his notes. Quinn imagined Carter charming his way into possession of the security footage. He'd done it, no doubt, while she had been at the spa. If the judge ruled the footage admissible, it would disprove Jake's statement that he'd had no involvement.

"I'm not letting him get away with the things he's done to you." Jaw squared, Carter pitched his voice low. "Not this time."

Quinn had the feeling there was more he was protecting her from. "What else don't I know about?"

His mouth hardened. "The attorney firm has a private investigator on retainer. He's looking for the banger who crashed into you and assaulted you on the beach. I've offered a reward for information leading to him. We're hoping it might entice someone to give him up."

Quinn searched his face, a thickness in her throat. "How much are you offering?"

"It doesn't matter—"

"It *does* to me. How much?"

"One hundred thousand."

Her head spun as she saw her debt mounting to him—the attorney fees and now the reward money. "I didn't ask you to take it this far. Why're you doing this?"

The faint lines at the corners of his eyes deepened. "Because I *care* about you, Quinn. Because I want you to be *free*."

A court officer swung open the double doors to the courtroom. "Case number three-nineteen is back in session," he announced into the hall.

Her attorney closed his briefcase and stood. "Let's go. I've got a good feeling about this."

Carter's hand at the small of her back, Quinn walked toward the courtroom. But she halted as Jake turned the corner with his own attorney. She felt the blood drain from her face. But as he passed to enter the courtroom first, she realized his lethal glare was focused more on Carter than on her.

***

The restraining order was granted for a period of five years.

The hearing now over, Carter had gone into the men's restroom, leaving Quinn and her attorney in the clerk's office, where they were awaiting papers. But as he washed his hands, his chest tingled as Medero's reflection appeared in the mirror over the basin. He stood about six feet behind him. They were the only two in the room.

Refusing to be intimidated, Carter finished what he was doing and reached for a paper towel from the dispenser.

"That order might keep me away from *her.*" Medero's voice was a low growl as he approached. "But it doesn't say a goddamn thing about you."

Wadding the towel and throwing it away, Carter turned to him, his posture rigid. "You want to try to kick my ass—go for it. This is as good a place as any."

Scowling, Medero took another step closer, until they stood nearly nose to nose. "Someone who makes a fortune off that pretty-boy face ought to be more concerned about getting it messed up."

Carter didn't flinch under his glare. Medero's lips slowly thinned into a cold smile.

"You know what? As much as I'd enjoy dropping you, you're not worth the trouble it'd bring me. You got your restraining order, St. Clair. I know you paid for that big-name lawyer. You might think you've won, but think about it. All you got are my sloppy seconds. Remember that every time you *fuck* her."

Carter's hands clenched at his sides. His hatred for Medero burned in his stomach like acid. He itched to tangle with him, no matter the consequences to his health. In his current condition, it wouldn't be a fair fight, but Carter figured he could get in at least one good hit. But a public scene, the media coverage...they were things neither he nor Quinn needed. Even now, the paps were outside the courthouse. Carter forced himself to remain still as Medero leaned closer.

"I used her in ways you can't imagine. She's damaged goods—"

"Go to hell."

Smirking, Medero took a step back. "Enjoy her." He reached for the door handle, but Carter's words halted him.

"Just so you know, the restraining order isn't my end game. It's just gravy."

Medero turned back to him.

"That footage from the coffee shop? Yeah, I handled getting that personally. It sealed the deal today, but it's got legs way beyond that." Carter raised his chin, his blood hot in his veins. "It's going to the FBI and to the Charleston County DA's office. You screwed up by cyberstalking her across state lines—it makes all this a much bigger deal. I'm not letting up until one of them pursues criminal felony charges. I'm making it my personal mission to destroy you."

He took pleasure in the spark of unease he saw in Medero's eyes before it was choked out by a growing rage, his face reddening and the cords in his thick neck standing out against the collar of his dress shirt. Medero took a step toward him, but halted as the door opened and two uniformed officers entered. They were in conversation with each other, oblivious to what they had walked in on.

With a seething look at Carter, Medero stormed out.

***

It was nearly midnight, yet Quinn lay awake in the hotel suite. Carter slept beside her, their legs tangled together under the silken sheets. He had taken her with an intense, unfettered possessiveness. Likewise, she had given her body to him willingly, wantonly, just as she had now for so many nights.

Turned onto her side facing him, she listened to his quiet breathing and studied his even features.

I want you to be free.

She understood what he had meant outside the courtroom. Carter wanted to give her freedom—from fear, from Jake's intimidations. But his words had also driven to the heart of her insecurity about their future, about what would happen when he fully belonged to Hollywood once again. She would be free to go her own way.

A lump forming in her throat, she vowed to be thankful for all he had done for her, but to also be wise and self-protective. To be strong enough to let go when the time came. She had lost so much of her dignity to Jake. She wouldn't lose more of it.

But lying in the darkness, Quinn admitted to herself that *freedom* was not what her heart wanted.

CHAPTER THIRTY-FIVE

Los Angeles, California

He wasn't certain what he had expected—fading crime-scene tape, smudges of fingerprint-powder residue—but everything appeared normal, a testament to the cleaning crew Mark had hired. Having disarmed the security system, Carter stood in the dramatic, two-story foyer with Quinn. Although they would be staying in the smaller guest cottage on the property, he had felt compelled to come here first.

Moving to the wall, he flipped on the crystal chandelier, half surprised when it glimmered to life, although he'd known the utilities, phone and other bills were paid while he was away. Looking up at the curved staircase, his stomach fluttering, he had an image of Bianca ascending the steps that night, one hand on the wrought-iron banister.

"Are you sure you want to stay here?" Quinn asked. "We could still get a hotel room."

They had already discussed his intentions. He planned to put the property on the market. He didn't want to live here anymore. But this had been his primary residence for the past three years, the place he had called home when he wasn't filming on location or traveling to promote a film.

"We'll be fine at the cottage. It's just weird being back here, is all."

He traveled with her into the vast formal living area with its coffered ceiling and high, arched windows that overlooked the canyon. The home had been built in the 1920s by one of the stars of the silent screen. Since then, it had changed hands multiple times before Carter had purchased it. He'd had renovations done throughout.

"It's beautiful." Quinn looked around the space. "If you're sure you want to sell, I'll handle finding a Realtor." She walked to the doors leading out to the terrace, her gaze on the infinity edge pool. Carter joined her, noting the brown leaves floating on the stagnant-looking water. "I'll get someone here for pool maintenance, too," she said.

"You don't need to do all that."

"Didn't you bring me here to help out? I'm in your employ. What else should I be doing?"

"Quinn…" He shook his head, not wanting to think of her in that manner anymore. If he'd ever thought of her that way.

"You're going to be crazy busy, and it'll give me something to do. I'm not much for shopping on Rodeo Drive or taking tours of movie studios."

She started to turn away, but he caught her delicate hands in his. He lifted one to his mouth and kissed the back of it. "You know you're much more to me than that, don't you?"

Despite her soft smile, he detected a distance in her eyes. The passion between them remained strong—they were both sexually charged people—but during their time in San Francisco, he'd also felt something had changed. He had hoped getting the restraining order against Medero would buoy her, but if anything, Quinn had become at times withdrawn, seeming to avoid any attempt Carter made to articulate his feelings for her. She had become his best friend, his lover. He might very well *be* in love with her, although he didn't want to tell her that in this house. Not after what had happened here.

"I suppose I should give you the full tour if you're insisting on working," he said.

They started with the expansive living areas on the main floor that included a gourmet kitchen, a dining room that seated twelve and a media room. Next, they moved to the recently added rear wing, which included a wine cellar and home gym, complete with a custom-built infrared sauna and European shower. There was also a garage that contained several cars and motorcycles. Quinn ran her fingers over one of the bike's leather seats, and he wondered if she was thinking of his late-night rides through the canyon.

"The batteries are probably dead." He kicked at one of the Aston Martin's tires, which had gone flat from disuse. He had battery maintainers for when he was out of town for long periods of time, but they hadn't been used. After the attack, no one had been thinking about practicalities. At least they had the rental car they had gotten at LAX.

"If you give me the phone number for your mechanic, I'll have them towed there so they can work on them," Quinn suggested.

"I don't feel right about you doing all this," he said again.

But she had turned her back to him and was looking at a leather weekender bag that sat on a workbench behind his Range Rover. Carter was aware of what the bag contained. It was unzipped and open, revealing a red, heart-shaped pillow among his things. It was something the hospital gave patients after open-heart surgery, instructing them to hold it against their chests to alleviate pain when coughing or moving. There were also pajamas, a bathrobe, slippers and toiletries inside the bag. Mark had taken it from the hospital for him and must have forgotten it in the garage. Carter picked up the pillow.

"I was told they did two rounds of CPR. One for over ten minutes in the ambulance," he said in quiet reflection. "I was technically dead for a while."

He recalled how weak he had been after surgery. How much pain he'd been in.

Quinn touched his arm. He returned the pillow to the bag. Then, his hand at her waist, he guided her back to the foyer where the staircase was located.

They might as well get this over with.

***

Entering his bedroom on the second floor, Carter felt the beat of his heart. His eyes were drawn to the brownish stains that had set into the hardwood flooring, something the cleaning crew hadn't been able to fully get rid of. A sour tang in his throat, he noticed they resembled shoeprints—most likely his since they led from the bathroom to the nightstand, where he had apparently retrieved the telephone to call 911. Standing beside him, her arms clasped around herself, Quinn remained silent.

He moved to the bathroom's threshold. The key was still in the door's lock as the detective had confirmed. Flipping a switch to illuminate the chandelier that hung from the high ceiling, he stepped inside. A tufted ottoman sat in the room's center and, beyond it, the large shower and entrance to his cedar-lined, walk-in closet. The bathroom was pristine, the events that had taken place here scoured away except for the brown stains in the grout of the Italian marble-tile floor. An image of Bianca, bleeding out, made his skin prickle. Dropping onto his haunches, he laid his fingers on the cool tile. He had been in this room, stabbed and bleeding, too. But he could still remember nothing of the attack on him.

"Are you all right?" Quinn asked.

He had nearly forgotten her presence. He found his voice. "Yeah."

***

"Of course, we're having a drink to celebrate your return." Elliott winked at Quinn as he popped the cork from one of the two bottles of champagne he and Ariel Carrington had brought with them to the cottage. "1990 Moët & Chandon Dom Pérignon," he announced as he began filling the champagne flutes Quinn had retrieved from the kitchen. He raised his glass to Carter. "Only the best to usher in your return."

They stood in the cottage's living area that featured a brick fireplace and sliding glass doors all around that could be opened in summer to catch the breeze. As she sipped the champagne, Quinn recalled Carter telling her that his agent had spent time not long ago in rehab.

"Relax," Elliott chided at Carter's critical expression. "It's just champagne. It's not like I'm drinking hooch from a paper bag and lying in the gutter."

"Champagne's practically water around here. Cheers." Ariel sipped from her glass, as well. She and Elliott had arrived unexpectedly a short time ago. Ariel was exotically attractive—tall and lithe, with almond-shaped hazel eyes and dark hair that fell to her shoulders. She was also well dressed in a short tweed skirt, cashmere turtleneck sweater and designer jewelry. She laid her hand on Carter's arm. "You should've taken my advice and stayed at The Four Seasons, darling. It would be so much more convenient since the interviews are being held there." She smiled at Quinn, a gesture that didn't quite reach her eyes.

"Ariel's right. I worry about you being here, Carter." Elliott grew somber. "This place, what happened here. It isn't healthy for your state of mind."

"That's why we're staying in the cottage," Carter said. They were still attracting the paparazzi's attention, and he had told Quinn he thought they would have more privacy behind the closed gates of his property than at a hotel.

"Quinn, would you be a dear and get some napkins?"

It wasn't the first task Ariel had given her since she and Elliott had arrived. Quinn didn't mind, but she got the feeling it was a power game. She hadn't been able to help but notice that since their arrival, Ariel had been openly flirtatious with Carter, who in turn had been polite but unaffected.

Quinn returned with napkins from the kitchen. She noted that although Ariel had been the one to request them, she made no move to take one from the table where they had been placed. Ariel and Carter were now seated on the overstuffed couch, her hand intermittently touching his knee as she briefed him on the interviews that would take place tomorrow, the first day of the junket. Meanwhile, Elliott had refilled his flute and now stood looking out through the glass doors toward the main house.

Feeling out of place, Quinn excused herself a short time later and went into the kitchen. She had already shopped for groceries and made dinner, and she began emptying the dishwasher she had run afterward. She was midway through the task when a voice caused her to look up.

"So you're the physical therapist who's turned out to be so much more." Ariel had the same bland smile on her face. "He looks good. So good, in fact, you must be worried you'll be out of a job soon."

Ignoring the backhanded barb, Quinn placed a dish in one of the cabinets. She could hear Carter talking with Elliott in the other room. "He's still receiving therapy to strengthen his shoulder," she said. "We'll be using the gym at the house while we're here."

"You must have some kind of magic." Ariel came closer, her gaze coolly assessing. "First Jake Medero and now Carter. You really should leave some of the hot ones for the rest of us girls."

Quinn stiffened, but continued unloading the dishes.

"Did Jake start out as a patient, too?"

"As a client," she corrected, although she didn't want to discuss it. "I'm also a certified strength and conditioning specialist."

"The tabloids said Carter went with you to San Francisco for the hearing. That's very protective of him. A restraining order means your husband was abusive to you, doesn't it?"

"I'd rather not talk about—"

Elliott appeared on the kitchen's threshold. "Ariel, it's time we got out of here and left these two alone. Carter's going to belong to you for the next couple of weeks. Let Quinn have him for tonight."

He walked to Quinn and warmly clasped her shoulders. "It's a pleasure to meet you, my dear. You've done a fabulous job patching him up for us."

Forcing a smile, she thanked him, then followed them into

the living room where Carter stood.

"Let Ariel drive," Carter advised.

Elliott made a face. "I'm fine—"

"Just do it, all right?"

With a put-upon sigh, Elliott handed Ariel the keys to the black Jaguar parked in front of the cottage. Ariel kissed Carter's cheek and told him a limousine would arrive for him at nine the next morning. Hands shoved into the pockets of his trousers, he stood at the window and watched them depart. Quinn went around the room picking up the glasses and champagne bottles—one empty, the other nearly so—and placed them on a tray to carry back to the kitchen.

Carter nodded to the bottles. "He finished most of that himself. I just hope he's staying away from the cocaine."

"How big a problem did he have?"

"Big enough. He kept it together for work, but he had a couple of embarrassing public incidents that cost him clients. His wife—his third—also left him."

"But you didn't." Quinn admired his loyalty.

"Elliott's been a good agent and a good friend."

She couldn't stop herself from asking. "And Ariel? Has she been a good friend, too?"

He sighed softly. "I saw her slip into the kitchen. I figured she was raking you over the coals, which is why I suggested to Elliott they get going."

"She's interested in you."

She could tell her statement didn't come as a surprise. Carter walked to where she stood. He gently pushed her hair behind her shoulder. "Ariel's my *publicist.* That's all she's ever been. I'm sorry they stopped by."

"It's okay. They're excited you're back."

Outside, night had fallen, the shadows deepening in the cluster of trees the cottage was situated in.

"It's still early," he pointed out. "It's just us now."

His nearness and the cadence of his voice brought her senses to life. He brushed his lips over hers.

"I'm going to get a shower," he said.

"I'm just going to finish picking up a few things."

Checking the door to ensure it was locked, Carter lowered the lights in the living area and then departed to the cottage's rear while Quinn carried the tray with the glasses and bottles into the kitchen. But as she returned, her eyes were drawn to the larger residence through the glass doors. The house stood in shadow.

Despite the cottage's warmth, Quinn felt a small chill. She tried not to think of what had happened there in November.

CHAPTER THIRTY-SIX

"That's all for now, Jared. I'm afraid Carter doesn't have time for more questions."

Carter heard Ariel's apology to the journalist as he left the room. He entered the luxury suite adjacent to where the interviews were taking place and closed the door behind him. Irritated, he stared at a massive, fresh-cut floral arrangement, then rubbed his fingers over his closed eyelids.

"*Bode* is an important publication," Ariel scolded as she entered a few minutes later. "Its circulation is over three million—"

"I don't care. The guy was briefed on what's allowed. He refused to stay on topic."

"We talked about this, Carter."

It was barely two o'clock, and already he had given a dozen interviews, half of them on camera. Despite his wishes, he had been asked questions about his health and emotional state, about Kelsey Dobbins and how he felt about Bianca's murder. He had done his best to be polite, but the last reporter had pushed especially hard, even with Ariel's reminders. He had inquired repeatedly about his relationship with Quinn and the restraining order she had been granted. Carter felt the reporter was baiting him, trying to get him to say something negative about Medero.

"You knew you'd be asked these kinds of questions," Ariel reminded.

He rubbed at the stiffness in his neck. "I'm contracted to promote the movie and that's all."

"Walking out of an interview isn't going to win you fans. Rub these reporters and bloggers the wrong way and they'll paint you as petulant and sullen. Have you forgotten the hatchet job they did on Heath Burke last year?" Ariel sighed sympathetically and touched his arm. "It's been a long day already. You're tired, and you're out of practice. Your next interview is in ten minutes, but I can stall it. Why don't you relax and have something to eat?"

Carter paced a few steps, then sat in one of the wing chairs. Ariel handed him a bottled water from a table that held refreshments, then went around behind the chair. As he took a sip from the bottle, she began to massage his neck. He wanted to ask her to stop, but instead, after a moment, he rose and walked to the table, feigning interest in the food to put some distance between them.

"You really shouldn't be so upset that they're asking about her." Ariel moved closer. "They're curious about the new woman in your life. I know *I* am."

Carter said nothing.

She pressed her lips together. "I'll go brief the blogger from *Celeb Weekly*. Before you join us, try to find some of that Southern charm you're so famous for?"

As she left the suite, Carter dragged a hand through his hair. Ariel was right. This was all part of the job. He worried his contractual obligations had forced him to return too soon or, worse, his heart wasn't in this anymore. He wanted to be back at the beach house in Rarity Cove, just Quinn and him.

Admittedly, he *was* tired. He hadn't slept well last night, partly due to dread about today and partly because he'd had a repeated dream, something no doubt fueled by his return to his home. In it, he had been in his bathroom, kneeling over Bianca's body and trying to help her as she lay bleeding and gasping for breath. Each time he'd had the dream, a feeling of his own impending doom had startled him awake.

A knock sounded on the closed door to the suite. Then it opened. Upon seeing the African-American male who stepped inside, recognition settled over Carter. Although he had spoken with Detective Warren on the phone several times, he had seen him only once, when he had been questioned about the attack while hospitalized.

"Mr. St. Clair, I'm—"

"Hello, Detective Warren." Carter stepped forward and shook his hand.

"They told me at the front desk where to find you." He indicated the gold badge at his waist. "This gets me into a lot of places, including past the studio's security out front."

"How'd you know I was here?"

"At The Four Seasons? Twitter, believe it or not. You're trending—your return to LA is a big deal. I was in the area, so I thought I'd drop this by, if you still want it. Save myself a drive up the canyon."

Carter's stomach fluttered as the detective withdrew an envelope from the pocket of his suit coat and handed it to him. "The death investigation's closed. We knew it was a suicide, but we still had to follow protocol."

"I understand."

"I don't think you're going to learn much from it—we didn't—but as you know, it was addressed to you. It's yours."

They spoke for another few minutes, the detective inquiring about his health. He also asked Carter to take a selfie with him. Carter complied, and the detective bid him good-bye and left.

The envelope felt heavy in Carter's hand. He knew Ariel was expecting him, but he felt compelled to read whatever Kelsey Dobbins had needed to say to him. He opened the envelope and slid out several sheets of ruled notebook paper, folded in half. His name was written in pencil on the outside. With a tight breath, Carter unfolded the letter and began to read.

Detective Warren had been right. The letter was cryptic, even nonsensical in places, a long, rambling profession of Dobbins's love for him, as well as her insistence they were meant to be together—things she had said in her previous letters. Toward the end, however, Carter's throat dried.

You were so pale in my arms, but so beautiful.

They told me I hurt you, that I hurt you both, but I can't believe that.

They don't understand.

I would die for you.

CHAPTER THIRTY-SEVEN

The week had gone as expected. Quinn had been with Carter each morning for therapy, then hadn't seen him again until the studio limousine dropped him off, typically in the early evening. She had filled her time with the projects she had offered to handle and spent the remaining hours at the guest cottage.

Yesterday, she had also selected an evening gown from the ones Carter's stylist—an ultra-thin blonde named Mandy—had brought over for her to try on after learning her measurements. It was for the event she would attend with Carter tomorrow night. She worried the designer gown had cost a small fortune, but Mandy would tell her only that Carter was taking care of it.

Quinn was now at the property's main residence, awaiting the pool-service technician, who was scheduled to replace a broken pump. As she waited, she wandered through the main floor, taking in the artwork and numerous framed photos. While many were of the St. Clair family, there were also ones of Carter with other actors and even a past president of the United States.

She paused at the sofa table, noting the blinking light on the phone console. When they had first arrived in LA, there had been more than twenty voice-mail messages, many dating months back. Carter had asked her to check them in case any were important. Most weren't, since the majority of people who needed access to him had his cell phone number. Instead, they had been the types of messages regular people received—robocalls from telemarketers, dental-appointment reminders, nonprofits seeking end-of-year donations. Quinn listened to the latest message, which had been left since she had been here the day before. It, too, was nothing out of the ordinary.

With a tense sigh, she crossed her arms against her chest. As beautiful as the house was, being here alone was a bit disconcerting. She had gone back upstairs only with the real estate agents vying to list the property.

There was still no buzz from the front gate signaling that someone was requesting entrance. She checked her wristwatch, hoping the pool technician would arrive soon.

***

Saturday night had begun with a limousine ride to the Berman Auditorium in Beverly Hills, then Quinn watching as Carter posed for photo ops on the red carpet in the lobby. He had appeared poised and relaxed, turning toward the various cameras pointed at him as photographers called his name.

Quinn now sat at a linen-covered table between Elliott Kaplan and the chair Carter had vacated. The table was one of dozens inside the elegant ballroom overflowing with the Hollywood elite. Anywhere she looked, she recognized faces that previously she had seen only in magazines or on-screen.

Elliott leaned closer, his arm around the back of her chair.

"You do look lovely tonight, my dear."

The salute honoring Norman Weintraub was in intermission, and Carter had gone backstage in preparation for the presentation he would be giving next—an introduction to a film clip of *Paper Hearts*, a romantic comedy he starred in and Weintraub directed.

Quinn thanked Elliott for the compliment. The dark blue evening gown she wore was simple yet sophisticated, and her hair was swept into an updo as the stylist had suggested. Around them, the room buzzed with conversation as waiters went about removing the fine china and silver from the tables, the dinner portion of the night over.

"So how is he, really?" Elliott inquired in a low tone since they shared the table with others. "I'm asking because you know better than anyone."

Quinn wondered whether he meant because she was Carter's physical therapist or his current lover. She looked up to the stage, which remained empty.

"He's doing well," she assured him. "He was in excellent physical condition previously, which has helped his progress." Elliott was Carter's friend, so she didn't think she was breaking a confidence. "It was mostly a matter of getting him in the right head space to want to get better."

"Well, if you're responsible for that, you have my eternal gratitude. I visited him in South Carolina, you know. He wasn't in great shape, mentally or physically." Elliott appeared pensive as he took a long sip from his vodka tonic, his second that night. "It's good to have him back and with a project on deck. Maybe you could convince him to buy a home in Malibu or Pacific Palisades. A place on the water might stop him from pining for that little Southern beach town."

The comment reminded her that the house in Rarity Cove was only a rental. As he resumed his career, Carter would be returning permanently to LA. Quinn had made a decision. She knew she would have to speak with him soon, her heart heavy. But as she had watched him pose for the photographers, as she had waited while his fellow actors and others had come over to greet him with such warm regard, she knew he belonged here.

Music started and the chandelier lights lowered, signaling the night's events were about to resume. Along with the others at their table, Quinn and Elliott turned their attention to the stage. Carter walked onto it, handsome in a classic black tuxedo. He tried to speak, but the applause continued as the entire ballroom came to their feet. A lump formed in Quinn's throat. She could see Carter had been caught off guard by this show of affection and, for a moment, it appeared as though his eyes had grown wet. But as the audience finally seated themselves, he pulled himself together. Clearing his throat, he gave a sincere thank-you for the welcome, spoke eloquently about Weintraub and introduced the clip.

***

Morning light outside the bedroom window awakened Carter. The space in bed beside him was unoccupied, however, and he rolled over to squint at the clock on the nightstand. It was relatively early for a Sunday. It was also the first day he didn't have somewhere he had to be since they had arrived in LA.

"Quinn?" He received no response.

For a moment, he laid his head back on the pillow and reflected on last night. After all that had happened, it had been difficult to walk onto that stage, to attempt to step back into his life *before.*

Although he knew Quinn had been reluctant to attend, she had been a grounding presence. The gown she had worn now lay carefully arranged over an upholstered chair in the corner. Carter had been more than happy to help her undress when they had returned here. He savored the memory—Quinn at the full-length mirror, watching as he stood behind her, unzipping the gown and slowly lowering it from her shoulders. He had taken down the glorious mass of her hair, as well, removing the pins and then sliding his fingers through its silk before she had turned to him and lifted her mouth to his.

Rising from bed, he pulled on sweatpants and a T-shirt to go in search of her. He felt disappointment upon finding her in the kitchen, scrambling eggs in a skillet at the stove.

"I wanted to take you out for breakfast, remember?"

"I thought this would be better. No one hounding you for autographs and selfies." She pushed the lever on the toaster, lowering two slices of bread. Quinn wore yoga pants and a long-sleeved athletic top, her wavy hair pulled back into a ponytail. Carter wondered how long she had been up. He figured she had already done her yoga practice on the patio. He had seen her out there before, going through the sun salutations that often started her mornings.

"Sit down." She pressed a mug of coffee into his hands. Carter sat at the table in front of the window that provided a view of the clematis-hung trellis that separated the guest house from the main property. A moment later, Quinn placed a plate of eggs and whole-grain toast in front of him.

"You're not eating?" he asked, reaching for the pepper.

"I'm not that hungry. I'm just having toast."

Carrying her plate and a mug of tea, she sat across from him. As Carter ate, they talked about last night's event. She also updated him on her progress in getting the house listed on the market.

"It's a high-end property, obviously. The Realtors have all told me the same thing—it'll take a while to sell, especially considering things." Her hands fidgeted on the table. "The flooring in the bedroom will have to be sanded and restained, and the tile in the bathroom regrouted before it can be shown, which we already knew. I'm trying to get an estimate from a flooring contractor one of the agents recommended. He specializes in high-end homes."

Carter again felt guilt for her handling such a grim task. He had also noticed she hadn't touched the toast or her tea. She seemed distracted, absently twisting a silver ring on her finger. He laid his fork on his plate. "You okay?"

She frowned, picking at the woven tablemat. "There's something else I need to talk to you about. When you leave for New York later this week…I'm thinking of going back to Rarity Cove."

Surprise made his stomach drop. "Why?"

She shook her head, her eyes not meeting his. "I really don't have any reason to be in New York. There've been jobs around here to keep me busy, but there…"

He couldn't help it. He felt thrown by her decision, as well as hurt. "I don't understand why you want to leave."

She gave a halfhearted shrug. "You're so much better, Carter. You really don't need a PT anymore. You can self-manage exercises for your shoulder at this point. I know your strength in it isn't back one hundred percent yet, but you should be okay to drive—"

"I'm not talking about therapy." His throat ached at her detached rationalization. "What about *us*?"

Her lips parted as she looked at him, unable to hide the insecurity in her eyes. She stood from the table and took several steps away, her back to him, rearranging items on the counter. "We've been kidding ourselves. I don't fit into your life. Not here and not in New York. It worked when it was just us in Rarity Cove, but now…"

Brows furrowed, Carter rose and traced her steps, turning her to face him, his hands gentle on her upper arms. "Did I do something wrong?"

"No."

"I don't know where this is coming from, then. Quinn, we're supposed to be *together*." He felt a tightness in his chest. "After these last few weeks, how can you even question that?"

Her features pained, she spoke in a suffocated whisper. "I can't just be here to have sex with you."

Was that all she thought this was? He continued holding on to her.

"Is that what you think of me? That I just want someone in my bed?" He stared at her, his heart seeming to stall inside him. "Quinn, I'm *in love* with you."

She closed her eyes as if trying to put her emotions in order. "Don't say that—"

"Screw that. I *will* say it." He cradled her face in his hands, forcing her to look at him. "I love you, Quinn."

She wrangled free, breathing shallowly. "This won't work. I'm not some actress or supermodel. I…I'm not even Shelley."

He nearly flinched.

But despite the arrow she had shot into him, hurt as well as longing lay naked in her eyes. Then she turned away again. She was deliberately trying to injure him, trying to create some unfixable fissure between them so he would just let her go. She began to walk away, but Carter's words stopped her.

"What are you so afraid of? Of getting hurt again? That my head will be turned by the first actress I share a screen with?" Emotion roughened his voice. "Because even *thinking* about leaving me is killing you. You can't hide that."

Her shoulders rigid, she remained motionless. Carter strode to where she stood, blocking her exit, his face hot, his voice hard. "Or is it that you're afraid of being with someone who actually *wants* to be good to you? Who doesn't get off on hurting and humiliating you?"

Appearing stricken, she bowed her head. He cursed himself, instantly regretting how viciously he'd spoken. Anger and frustration had gotten the best of him.

"I'm sorry. I didn't mean that," he said unsteadily.

He thought she might walk out, but instead she leaned into him and pressed her face against his chest. The fear he was going to lose her sent a tremor through him. Last week had been a jarring return to reality for them both. He simply held her, a heaviness inside him. They remained like that until his cell phone sprang to life on the counter nearby, causing Quinn to step back and wipe her eyes.

He planned to let the call go to voice mail, but he could see the name of a local hospital on the screen. He picked it up, a moment later receiving another gut punch. Closing his eyes, pinching the bridge of his nose as he listened, he said, "Just keep him there. I'll be there, or I'll send someone."

As he disconnected, Quinn's gaze was questioning.

"Elliott was brought into the ER last night by ambulance," he said hoarsely. "Cocaine overdose."

"God." Quinn paled. "Is he going to be okay?"

"They think so." In disbelief, he passed a hand over his eyes. "The treating physician said they didn't bring in the police. When Elliott finally came down enough to communicate, he gave Kathy, his ex-wife, as his emergency contact. But when they reached her, she refused to come to the hospital. She gave them my cell number."

Quinn wrapped her arms around herself. "You need to go to him, Carter."

He looked at her, feeling torn. "I'm not letting you leave. Promise me you'll be here when I get back."

She appeared as wounded as he. Still, she gave a small nod.

CHAPTER THIRTY-EIGHT

Elliott sat hunched in the passenger seat, Carter behind the wheel. Since his mechanic had gotten the vehicles running again, he'd decided to test Quinn's theory that he was okay to drive and had taken the Range Rover to the hospital. Glancing at Elliott, he was surprised they had let him leave. He appeared pale and shaky.

"How long has this been going on?" Carter couldn't tamp down his irritation. "You were hitting the booze hard last night, too. Are you trying to kill yourself?"

Elliott sighed tiredly, elbow propped against the window, his fingers rubbing his forehead. As they traveled along the palm-tree-lined coastal highway, Carter had a déjà vu of escorting him to rehab once before. The ER physician had told him Elliott had become agitated and combative—not unusual for someone who had done too much blow times ten. The hospital had had no choice but to restrain him.

"Your heart rate and blood pressure were through the roof. You could've died—"

"I don't need a lecture. My head's killing me," Elliott mumbled. "I don't remember anything after I left you last night."

"Were you high when you came to see me in South Carolina?"

He didn't answer, instead raking a hand through his disheveled salt-and-pepper hair. Guilt thickened Carter's throat. He had known Elliott was drinking again, but he had been too caught up in his own health problems to press the issue.

"Maybe you were right." Elliott stared morosely out the windshield. Sunlight illuminated the gray stubble on his face, as well as the deepening lines. "Maybe you should've stayed away from here. This business eats you alive. It screws with you until you don't know who you are or what you're doing anymore."

Carter pressed his lips together, frustration and sympathy warring inside him. He was reminded of how easily he could have gotten caught up in a similar hell with the pain medication. *There but for the grace of God...* He released a small breath. "It's going to be okay, Elliott. You're not the first who's had to do this more than once before it sticks."

A short time later, they passed through the gate at New Beginnings. The residential treatment facility catered to the rich and famous. It was tranquil, spread out over twelve acres, with resort-like facilities and views of the Pacific. It looked like a place where one might go to vacation, not detox. Carter had called the center while Elliott was being discharged. Elliott had asked him to, to his credit.

Carter stopped the SUV under the columned portico in front of the lobby. A staff member waited to take the bag Elliott had packed at his place after they had left the hospital.

"I didn't ask them to call you," Elliott said.

"I know. Do you want me to go in with you?"

"I'll do the walk of shame by myself." He attempted a weak smile, his eyes hidden behind the dark tint of his sunglasses. "You've got a good girl, by the way. Quinn...she's real. She might be the one to keep you sane around all this." He cleared his throat. "I love you, Carter, you know that? I'm sorry for leaving you in the lurch. I'll call you every morning—"

"Just focus on getting better."

"I'm still your agent. I'll stay in touch."

He patted Carter's knee, then got out. His heart hurting, Carter watched as he handed over his bag to the staff member and walked inside.

***

It was well into the afternoon by the time Carter returned. As he entered the cottage, Quinn put down the magazine she had been reading on the sofa. "How is he?"

"Back in rehab." He sat next to Quinn, feeling beaten down. She wore slacks and a white wrap-sweater, her hair in a pretty French braid. He told her what he knew about the incident that had led to Elliott ending up in the ER. "Another resident in his building found him in the parking garage, car still running and him slumped over the steering wheel. He drove like that. It's a miracle he didn't kill himself or someone else."

"What about you?" she asked. "Are you all right?"

"Yeah." But this situation with Elliott had unsettled him. He thought of others he had known in this business who had self-imploded, victims of Hollywood's pressures and excesses. "I'm sorry I had to run out on you."

"I'm just glad you got him somewhere he can be taken care of." Hesitantly, she added, "I...also want to apologize."

Carter had sat forward, elbows on his thighs, but he turned his head to look at her.

"I know I blindsided you. This morning didn't go the way I intended." Her teeth worried the flesh of her lower lip. "And you were right. I'm afraid of the things you said—of getting hurt again, of making another mistake."

He turned to her on the sofa, swallowing down his pride. "Do you love me, Quinn?"

Her eyes were pained. "It's not that simple. Who you are—"

"Forget Hollywood." His throat ached. "Do you love *me*?"

"I...do love you," she admitted, a quaver in her voice. "But I'm afraid of not being enough for you. That your world is just too big for me, and we won't last. We've been living in a bubble, Carter—"

"You're *more* than enough for me." Earnest, he took her hands in his. "We can make this work."

Her gaze was liquid and uncertain. He squeezed her fingers, needing her to believe him. "It won't be as easy as other relationships, but it's possible if we want it badly enough. And I *do* want it, Quinn. I want a life with you, whether that's here or somewhere else. There're other actors who don't live here. They come here when they have to, they travel to wherever they're filming, but they have a home and a life away from LA." He thought again of Elliott. "I've been thinking lately maybe that's something I need."

She stared at him, her lips parted. "What're you saying? My divorce isn't even final yet."

"Then we take this one day at a time." Gently, he took her fingers and slipped them inside his button-up shirt so they touched the vertical scar on his chest. His voice was tinged with emotion. "*This* led me back to you, Quinn. Even with what I went through, I wouldn't change it, not if that meant never finding you again."

Her eyes misted.

"Just don't bail on me." His husky voice held a plea. "Don't go back to Rarity Cove yet, all right?"

When she nodded faintly, he caressed her lips with his.

"They've been running me ragged, but that's ending, at least until I get to New York." Looking into her eyes, he toyed with a loose strand of her hair. "I have a photo shoot late tomorrow afternoon in Santa Monica—it's the last thing on Ariel's itinerary here. But up until then, we'll spend the day together. You can go to the shoot with me. It's supposed to go into the evening."

She shook her head. "I'm okay being here without you—"

"I want to take you to the Santa Monica Pier. It's one of my favorite places. There's a great lunch spot, and they put me in a private room in back. We'll eat, have a look around and then we'll go to the shoot. They can be a lot of fun." He wanted to make up for the time she had been left alone.

She looked into his eyes and then released a small breath of acquiescence.

"We'll also go out to dinner tonight." He touched her cheekbone. "I do love you, Quinn. I don't take that word lightly."

She leaned into him. Carter held her, reveling in the feel of her relaxed against him. Then, placing a fingertip under her chin, he lifted her face to his, his lips again brushing hers.

"We still have hours before dinner. Is there anything you'd like to do right now? Somewhere you want to go?"

"This morning left me drained," she admitted softly. "I

was thinking maybe we could just lie down for a while?"

Standing, he held his hand out to her. Quinn's fingers clasped his as she rose and walked with him into the bedroom. Then, slowly, they undressed each other behind the window's closed shutters.

Afterward, they lay in bed, Quinn's head on his chest. Carter knew by her quiet, even breathing she had fallen asleep, sated and spent. Pensively, he watched the play of dappled sunlight that filtered between the shutter slats. Carter had never imagined he would find someone he wanted to share his life with. To have what his brother had been lucky enough to find twice. He had figured it was the trade-off for his stardom, for the wealth of opportunities he had been given.

Quinn stirred against him. Her hand slid over his stomach as she mumbled something he didn't understand. She talked in her sleep. It was a trait he had discovered once they had begun sharing a bed. Smiling softly, his lips brushed against her forehead.

A younger version of himself might have imagined getting bored with just one woman. But this…

Quinn had begun to feel like home.

CHAPTER THIRTY-NINE

They'd had a perfect day in Santa Monica with its rising sandstone bluffs and rocky shores. Although they had been detained at times by fans who recognized him even in his ball cap and sunglasses, Carter had still been able to show Quinn around the storied pier and amusement park.

It was now late afternoon, and they were at a private oceanfront home for the photo shoot, which was to accompany a feature article in an entertainment magazine. While Carter had been whisked away by hair and clothing stylists, the home's owner had graciously offered to take Quinn on a tour of the impressive Spanish Colonial-style residence that was just blocks from the pier.

As she returned to the rooftop terrace where the shoot was underway, she took a seat on a brown-and-tan-striped chaise, where she could watch while staying out of the way. The terrace was a beehive of activity, with nearly a dozen people working amid the mobile lights, reflectors and other photography equipment that had been set up by the pool. Around Carter, professionals adjusted lighting and instructed him on how to sit or stand. He appeared Old Hollywood handsome in a dark suit and silk tie.

"I've said it before—no one wears Tom Ford better than Carter St. Clair."

Quinn recognized Ariel Carrington's voice, although the woman wasn't talking to her but to one of the hair stylists. Both had their backs to her and were looking at Carter. Neither was aware she was within earshot, since a large reflector on a tripod partially hid the chaise where she sat.

"Have you met the new girlfriend?" the stylist asked.

"She's no big deal—average, at best. She won't last. Carter will have his fill of her, and he'll move on."

Quinn's face heated, but she remained frozen in place. If she got up and left, they would become aware of her presence and know she had overheard.

"I don't know, I think she's pretty." It was the stylist speaking again. "She *was* with Jake Medero. That's saying something."

"Too bad he didn't keep her," Ariel replied haughtily. "Carter could do miles better than that Italian bitch the studios set him up with, but this slut isn't even in *her* league."

Someone called the publicist over, and she walked away. Quinn startled as her phone sprang to life. She reached into her bag to try to mute it, but it got the attention of the stylist, who turned around, a flush creeping over her cheeks as she saw Quinn. Their eyes held for an awkward second, then Quinn got up and took the phone into the house so she could hear, relieved to escape. The caller was the flooring contractor she had left a message for over the weekend. He was finishing up a project at another home in the canyon and was wondering if he could drop by to get a look at the floors.

She glanced at her wristwatch. "I'm not there right now, but I could meet you in an hour?"

She gave him the address and disconnected. Quinn turned, caught off guard by the stylist who now stood in the hall. She had a platinum-blond pixie cut and tattoos on her arms. Quinn had met her earlier and recalled her name was Dove.

"I'm sorry you overheard us," she said, appearing upset.

Quinn felt her pulse in her throat, embarrassed. "It's all right."

"It isn't." She looked over her shoulder, no doubt checking to see where Ariel was on the terrace. "Don't take what she said personally. She's jealous. She's territorial about Carter and she doesn't like anyone he's ever been with. I really *am* sorry."

Quinn waved the incident off again, then changed the subject. "Would you mind doing something for me? Let Carter know I had to go to his house to meet a contractor? I'm going to take a taxi and leave the car here for him—he has the keys. Tell him I'll see him tonight at his guest house?"

Dove agreed, although she still looked worried, then turned and went back to the terrace. Quinn peered outside. She knew the shoot was supposed to continue into early evening, as nighttime shots had been planned. Carter would be disappointed she had left, but the contractor had come highly recommended. If she could secure his services before they left town, they would be a step closer to getting the house on the market.

Going back to the property would also let her avoid Ariel, who was talking to Carter as two stylists fussed with his clothes. They had removed his suit coat, and he stood with his tie undone and hanging loosely against his shirtfront, slim-hipped and tall, hair ruffled by the ocean breeze.

Quinn turned and went down the staircase, planning to take one of the taxis that had been parked at the pier's entrance.

***

"I wasn't going to say anything, but I thought she'd probably tell you when you got home." Dove appeared contrite. The photographer had called a short break, and she had taken Carter aside to give him Quinn's message. Hesitantly, she had also told him what Quinn had overheard. Irritated, Carter peered at Ariel as she conversed with the magazine's editorial director on the other side of the pool.

"Was she upset when she left?"

"I don't think so…I mean, I couldn't tell." Nervously, the stylist scraped her fingers through her short hair. "I get a lot of work from the magazine, Carter. Please don't get me in trouble."

"It's fine, Dove. I appreciate you telling me."

Briefly touching Dove's arm, he walked to where Ariel stood. Seeing him, she broke into a smile. "The layout's going to be fabulous, Carter. I saw the shots on-screen. Even unretouched, they're—"

"We need a word in private. Excuse us," he said to the man, then took Ariel by the arm and guided her to an unoccupied area in the terrace's corner. It was getting late, and overhead the vibrant blue sky had faded.

"You look so *intense*, darling. What's all this about?"

"I heard what you said about Quinn. Quinn heard it, too. She was sitting right behind you."

Ariel huffed. "And of course she went running to you."

"She didn't tell me. Someone else did." He leaned in closer, annoyance tightening his jaw. "Quinn's off-limits. You don't talk about her, and you treat her with courtesy. You're not the only publicist in town, Ariel."

Her shoulders rigid, she stared off to a line of waving palms near the beach. The photographer announced they were getting back to work. Having made his point, Carter began to walk off.

"From what I hear, Jake Medero is into some hard-core kink. Word is, he visits that sex dungeon in Mid-City whenever he's in town. Is your new girlfriend into that, too?"

Carter turned back to her. Her mouth was pinched, and her dark eyes glittered.

"You're fired," he bit out.

"You can't do that! We're leaving for New York in a couple of days. The premiere's next week—

"You won't be going. I'll rely on the studio publicists. And if you say another word about Quinn, I'll make sure you never work for any of Elliott's clients again."

Anger coursing through him, he turned and strode back to where the next shots would take place, counting down the time until he could go after Quinn.

***

Closing the door behind the departing contractor, Quinn walked from the foyer to the living area where she had placed her purse when she arrived. As she entered, her eyes were drawn to the windows that provided a view of the canyon, the shadows on the hillside lengthening as daylight began to recede. For a time, she simply stood looking out, thinking of what Ariel had said. Quinn's fingers toyed absently with the necklace she wore. She understood beautiful women would always be around Carter, and many would be attracted to him. If they had any chance at all of making this work, she would have to take that in stride.

Preparing to leave for the guest cottage, she picked up her purse and the house keys. But as she passed the sofa table, she noticed the blinking light on the phone console. Another message. She hadn't been here since late last week. She put down her things in case she needed to write down a name or number and pressed play.

I'm sorry. So damn sorry for everything…

Her stomach quivered at the distraught male voice on the recording. It sounded like Elliott Kaplan. Had he called here the night he had ended up in the ER? As he rambled on, some of it incoherent, Quinn felt as though she were invading his privacy by listening to what was a very personal message meant for Carter. She poised her finger over the button to stop the playback, then froze.

I saw you tonight on that stage and I finally knew you were going to be okay. That I hadn't ruined your life. It was the goddamn coke! You've got to understand. I was high!

He began to weep.

I'd give anything to take it back, but she just made me so damn mad! I-I should've just left, but I took the scissors from your desk, and I…oh, God. I-I tried to get away, but you were coming up the stairs…

Quinn's hand rushed to cover her mouth, her heart turning over even as her mind reeled. Kelsey Dobbins had been the attacker. But what Elliott was saying…

It sounded like a confession.

Movement in her peripheral vision made her whirl. She gasped, adrenaline tingling through her body. Elliott stood beside the hearth. He had a harried, wild appearance. She hadn't heard anyone come inside. How long had he been there? A weakness in her limbs, Quinn quickly stopped the recording.

"Elliott, I..." she stammered. She tried to appear calm, although she was also looking for a way out. The terrace doors behind her led to nothing but a thirty-foot drop into the ravine below. Her voice trembled. "I-I thought you were in rehab."

"I was. I left."

Quinn's heartbeat roared in her ears as he took a step closer, his tone somber.

"I was in group therapy when I got this flashback of making a really stupid, coked-up call. I'd hoped it was just my imagination, but according to my list of outgoing calls, it wasn't." His pained expression held regret. "It turns out I was so fried I dialed the wrong number, though. I called here instead of his cell, which explains why I'm still walking around a free man. I slipped out of the center and took an Uber here."

His gaze moved to the phone console. "I was hoping I could delete it before anyone heard. You're not supposed to be here, Quinn. I talked to Carter this morning, and he said you were going to the shoot with him."

She tried to swallow, but her throat had gone dry.

"I...can't let you tell him."

Electricity crackled in the air. Quinn's brain floundered. Elliott stood there, his shoulders slumped and skin bunched around his eyes.

"I like you, Quinn. I don't want to hurt you."

"*Listen* to me, all right?" Heart jumping, she took a step back. "You were high when you left that message, but you called Carter to *confess.* Don't you see?" She tried to appeal to any sense of morality he had. "Some part of you doesn't want to carry this burden anymore. It's eating you up inside. You did a horrible thing, but you weren't in control of—"

"I'm sorry." His voice roughened. "But I won't let you tell him."

He began to close the remaining distance between them. Quinn broke into a sprint toward the kitchen, hoping she could make it to the service door and get it open before he caught her. But Elliott was on her heels, grabbing at her, his hands snatching at her clothing. Racing through the butler's pantry and into the kitchen, she saw the knife block on the counter. She tried to get to it, but Elliott shoved her hard from behind. She stumbled and fell, her forehead glancing off the counter's edge.

Pain exploded in her skull.

A black mist closed over her.

CHAPTER FORTY

This couldn't be happening. Elliott propelled Quinn from behind, his arm braced over her chest, the knife he gripped in his other hand pressed against her throat. Fear swamped her.

"Through there. Go."

They were in the hall, headed toward the rear wing. Quinn felt dizzy, her head throbbing where she had hit it. When she had come to on the kitchen floor, Elliott had forced her up, threatening her with the knife.

As they entered the gym, she glimpsed the adjacent open door that led to the garage. It must have been how he had gotten in. She thought he might take her away from the property. But instead he pushed her past the treadmill and weight machines, past the shower. She bit back a cry at the sight of them in the mirrored walls. Then the blade left her throat as he released her. Quinn faced him, her limbs weak and chest heaving.

"Elliott, please." Her voice trembled. "You don't want to do this. Whatever you're planning—"

"He wasn't supposed to survive, you know." He studied

the glinting knife in his hand, seeming to be speaking mostly to himself. "He'd lost too much blood. They'd already prepared his family..."

Quinn stared at him, her heart beating erratically. There was so much she didn't understand—why he had been here that night, what Bianca had done to provoke him. How had he remained undiscovered and in Carter's confidence all this time? As he continued to ramble unsteadily, she attempted to glance around, looking for something to use to defend herself. But the blow to her head had made her vision sluggish. The room tilted, and she grabbed on to the stationary bike's handle for support.

"When they found his stalker here, I thought maybe God was giving me a second chance," Elliott murmured, his face lined. "The police just assumed Dobbins had done it—she had a history of mental illness, she was here in the house." He shook his head in seeming reflection. "I never saw her, so she must've come in after me. She was probably trying to help them."

Which was how Kelsey had gotten their blood on her. Her prints had been on the shears—had she pulled them from Carter's body after Elliott fled? Quinn's stomach clenched at the image. Still, she attempted to keep him talking to stall him.

"You…tried to keep Carter out of the bathroom, didn't you?" she asked carefully. "You locked the door. You were in there all along."

He lifted his chin, his gaze narrowing. "How'd you know the door was locked?"

She wouldn't divulge that fragments of Carter's memory were returning. That would put a target on his back, too. Instead, she said, "The police found a key in the lock. Carter told them he kept it in the nightstand. They figured he'd had to use it to get in."

At her explanation, his eyes grew distant. "When he came upstairs, I had no choice but to go back into the bathroom. I didn't know he had a key. I was trying to open the window to climb out, but when I heard the lock turning, I hid in the closet." Emotion thickened his voice. "He called 911. The police were on their way. I had to get out of there, and I couldn't let him identify me."

"You *had* to kill him," she prodded gently, as if understanding his plight. "But you didn't want to, did you?"

His eyes grew wet. "No."

"Elliott…I-I know you care about Carter. What you're doing right now will hurt him all over again." She held her hands out pleadingly. "If something happens to me—"

"You can't talk me out of this. Don't even try!" Scrubbing a hand over his face, he began to pace, his remorse replaced by a growing agitation. "I can't go to prison! I won't!"

She was losing him. The panic she was trying to keep at bay clawed at her.

"Take off your clothes."

Every muscle in her body tensed. Elliott pointed the knife's tip at her. "Do it now. Don't test me."

He opened the door to the sauna.

Oh, God. Her heart plummeted. Quinn suddenly understood why he hadn't taken her off the property. Elliott had been high the first time he had killed. But he was sober now and wanted to avoid such violence. Instead, he was going to try to make her death look like an accident, make it appear as though she had simply gone into the sauna and stayed too long. Her body tremored. She would die of heatstroke. She looked again at the knife he gripped in his fist, his stance unmoving. Even if he didn't want to, she had no doubt he would use it if she resisted.

"Do it!" Spittle flew from his lips.

Her hands shook as she peeled off her top and removed her khaki capris, clinging to the stationary bike for balance. He focused his gaze on the floor instead of looking at her.

"Your underwear, too."

The room tilted again. Unsteadily, she removed her bra and panties, a sense of doom pushing down on her. Elliott handed her a towel, and she wrapped it around herself.

"Get in. All the way to the back."

Her breath rasped out of her. Tears burned behind her eyes. "Elliott, what you did…it wasn't premeditated. But this…"

His chin quivered. But he moved forward, brandishing the knife at her until she backed clumsily inside. Following her in, he used the blade to pop the control panel from the sauna's interior wall, then disconnected it from its wires.

"You mentioned God before." Her voice shook with desperation. "Maybe you're being given a chance now to do the right thing, to make up for what you did before—"

She'd taken a tentative step closer, and he pointed the knife. "Get back!"

Quinn complied, her knees weak. "Elliott, you nearly OD'd! You can't live with this on your conscience anymore!"

"I'm sorry," he mumbled. Despite the anguish in his eyes, he again threatened her with the knife. "Stay put, or I…I swear to God I'll kill you."

Carrying the knife and control pad, he walked out and

closed the door. Quinn watched in panicked disbelief through the tempered glass window as he removed the plated weights from each side of a barbell and then slid its metal shaft through the door handle on the sauna's outside. Beeping noises told her he was setting the temperature on the exterior control panel.

She cried out and beat on the thick pane with her hands, terror consuming her. "Elliott, please!"

He turned away as she continued to scream and plead. Then he sank to the floor. Looking down through the glass, Quinn could see him. Head cradled in his hands, his shoulders shook as he sobbed, making deep, racking sounds.

"I know you don't want to kill anyone else! Please!"

He ignored her cries. Minutes passed before he climbed wearily back to his feet. Quinn's throat had grown raw from screaming. Her palms throbbed from beating on the glass. He didn't look at her again. Using his shirtsleeve, he wiped his nose and eyes. Then he picked her clothing up from the floor, folding them neatly and leaving them on a padded bench outside the sauna. He walked from the room with heavy steps, closing the door behind him.

Quinn's heart beat as though it might explode. She looked frantically around the sauna, searching for something to break the window's heavy glass. But there was nothing. Already, the temperature had risen, and a trickle of perspiration rolled down her back. She nearly keened as she thought of being slowly overcome by unrelenting heat. Quinn knew the signs of heatstroke, what she would experience. How long would it take for her to succumb? Thirty minutes? More?

Elliott would return after she had expired. He would remove the bar from the door and reconnect the control pad, and then he would leave.

Her lungs squeezed. Carter would never know the real cause of her death. He would never know his friend was a killer unless the whole of his memory returned. She listened to the sound of her too-rapid breathing. She was nearly hyperventilating.

Calm down. You have to.

Anxiety would only hasten the heat's effects. Still woozy from the blow to her head, Quinn sank onto one of the benches. Closing her eyes, she forced herself to slow down her breathing. She touched her forehead where she had hit it. It felt puffy and sore. It would look as though she had injured herself when she had been overcome by the heat and fainted. She would be the second of Carter's lovers to die in his home.

Perspiration began to sheen her body. The air she drew into her lungs grew heavier and hotter.

Terror choking her, she prayed.

CHAPTER FORTY-ONE

Carter made his way up the canyon road. Above him, the last vestiges of daylight had begun to fade, the sky visible through the Range Rover's sunroof a wash of eggplant and mauve. When he hadn't been able to reach Quinn by cell after several tries, he had ended the photo shoot early, much to the photographer's and magazine staff's consternation.

Quinn was already apprehensive about their relationship. He worried Ariel's harsh words had been the breaking point.

Heading through the gate, he drove past the main house and parked in front of the cottage, although it appeared dark inside. He went in, anyway, relief filtering through him upon seeing Quinn's clothing and luggage still there. Looking at the larger house through the glass doors, he noticed a light coming from a window. Was she up there? He had seen no van or pickup truck to suggest she was still with the workman.

Going outside, he walked under the trellis that separated the cottage from the main property, then went across the lawn until he stood under the porte cochere. Unlocking the front door, he entered. The security system wasn't on.

Although the foyer was dark, the light he had seen appeared to be coming from the kitchen. As he reached its entrance, surprise made his skin tingle. It was Elliott who sat at the granite island with his back to him, his head in his hands. He must not have heard him come in. Carter made his presence known. "What's going on?"

Elliott startled, standing quickly and whirling to face him. Carter frowned at the bottle of scotch and nearly empty glass on the island. "Why aren't you at New Beginnings?"

Elliott stared at him as if he were a ghost. "I…couldn't take it," he stammered finally. "I-I'm going to try to beat this on my own."

Carter nodded to the bottle. "You're off to a shit start."

"The photo shoot you told me about this morning," Elliott said, his voice taut, "I thought it'd still be going on—"

"I called it off early." He noticed Elliott seemed especially jittery. Disappointed and frustrated he hadn't given rehab a chance, Carter came farther into the kitchen. "If you don't care enough about yourself to try to get better, I can't make you. But why're you here?"

A tightness around his reddened eyes, he seemed to search for a response. "I…didn't want to face those judgmental pricks in my building. My ears have been burning since what happened Saturday night. I still have a spare key and the security code. I thought it'd be okay if I lay low here for a while."

Carter wanted to have it out with him about leaving rehab, but at the moment he wasn't his top priority. He drew in a breath. "Have you seen Quinn?"

"I-I thought she went with you to the shoot."

"She left. She was coming here to meet a contractor."

Elliott rubbed at the back of his neck. "I haven't seen her. She must've already come and gone."

"How long have you been here?"

"I don't know. Maybe forty-five minutes." He fidgeted, shifting his stance and passing a shaky hand over his brow. "Look, I'm sure she'll turn up eventually. Why don't you go to the cottage and wait for her? If she shows up here, I'll send her down."

Quinn's unexplained absence concerned Carter. It wasn't like her to just fall off the radar. He knew nothing of the workman she was supposed to have met here. There were situations in the news from time to time, cases where women had been attacked or abducted by men posing as service professionals. He recalled having seen the business card of the Realtor with whom Quinn planned to list the property back at the cottage. The agent had recommended the contractor, if he recalled correctly. He would give her a call to see what he could find out. There was also the taxi Quinn was supposed to have taken from the pier, although he had no idea which cab company it was from.

Maybe he was overreacting, but something just didn't feel right.

"We're going to talk about this later. You're a train wreck, Elliott. You need to go back to rehab." He walked from the kitchen. As he passed through the butler's pantry, however, a glimmer on the floor caught his eye. The necklace Quinn had been wearing today. Picking it up, he saw its delicate chain was broken.

"What's that?" Elliott asked from behind him.

Carter's mouth had gone dry. She had definitely made it here. It could've just gotten caught in her hair and she'd unknowingly broken the chain, he reasoned. *Don't think the worst.* Still, he loudly called her name, that same, undefinable unease growing inside him.

"Quinn!" he shouted again into the large house.

"I-I'm telling you, she isn't here!" Elliott insisted.

Returning to the foyer, Carter went up the curved staircase, but there was nothing in the master bedroom suite or bathroom where she and the contractor would have been. He checked his study and the other rooms before returning to the main floor. Elliott was still in the living area, pacing, dragging a hand through his unkempt hair and mumbling to himself. When Carter spoke his name, he stopped in his tracks, appearing even paler than before.

"Jesus, Elliott. How much have you had to drink?" Carter shook his head at him as he headed for the rear wing. "I'm worried about Quinn. Instead of just standing there, do you think you can help me? Check the library and media room for her, all right? I'll look in the gym."

Elliott's voice was strained. "Don't go back there."

Carter halted at the warning, the hair at his nape prickling. He turned to look at him.

"I mean, I-I just came through there earlier." He shrugged weakly. "No Quinn."

Carter's eyes fell on Quinn's purse beside the phone console. What the hell was going on? Ignoring Elliott, he went quickly down the long hall. Carter opened the door and entered the gym, his gaze sweeping the space.

His heart turned sideways as he saw the metal shaft lodged under the sauna's door handle.

He dashed to it and removed the shaft, tossing it to the floor. A wave of oven-like air rolled over him as he flung the door open. *Dear God.* Quinn lay motionless on one of the cedar benches, her eyes closed. A cry tore from his throat.

"Quinn!"

He sprinted inside, dropping onto his knees beside her. Terror sawed through him. Her skin was hot and dry as he tried to shake her awake. No response. Who'd done this? The man she'd met here? He called to Elliott for help. Cursing, fear squeezing his chest, Carter gathered her into his arms. He felt the strain in his shoulder as he half carried, half dragged her limp body out and into the shower. He had to get her temperature down. Turning on the cold water, he sank with her onto the tile floor.

"Wake up, honey. Please." Tears welled in his eyes as the frigid spray rained over them. Holding her, her neck and head cradled in the crook of his arm, he undid the towel wrapped around her body, letting the cold water make direct contact with her flushed skin. He laid his trembling fingers against the side of her throat, his heart dropping at the too-fast beat of her pulse.

Please, God. Please don't let her die.

He gasped in relief when she moaned a moment later, her eyes fluttering open, although her gaze was unfocused.

"I've got you, sweetheart. You're going to be okay." A knot in his throat, water running down his face, Carter examined the swollen, discolored area at her hairline. Confusion as well as a livid anger coursed through him. She'd been trapped in there. Why? He yelled for Elliott once more.

Quinn anchored her fingers in his sodden shirt, grabbing on to him as if she were trying to crawl into his skin. She struggled to tell him something, but her words were slurred and unintelligible. As he stroked a hand over her wet hair, her lashes fluttered closed, her body going limp again. "Quinn, stay with me!"

He had to get her to a hospital. He had to call for help. His cell phone was in his jeans pocket. He'd kept it on him in case she called. Carter rolled Quinn off his lap and onto her side so he could get to it, positioning her so she wouldn't inhale water. He got to his knees and removed it from his jeans pocket, water beading and bouncing on the screen. He began to punch in the numbers, but stopped.

Elliott stood in the doorway.

He held a large butcher knife.

Carter flashed on an image of Elliott on top of him, driving the shears into his chest. Shockwaves ran through his limbs. The ghost-pain of it made it hard to fill his lungs.

But Elliott remained frozen, his face haggard, the knife's handle gripped loosely in his fist. Blood roaring in his ears, Carter scrambled from the shower, putting himself between Elliott and Quinn. Water dripped from his clothes and hair as he picked up the steel shaft that had blocked the door. He held it in his left hand like a club, ready to defend himself, to protect Quinn at any cost. Emotion thickened his throat.

"It was *you*." Quinn must have discovered the truth. Carter's thoughts splintered as he tried to understand. His voice shook. "Why?"

"You were going to leave me! After all I've done for you!" Elliott's voice cracked, his face and neck reddening. "Don't try to deny it! You were at CTA's offices that morning. You were going to sign with Harvey Gold!"

He neared with slow, weighted steps. Carter remained poised to fight, clenching the steel shaft.

"I told Bianca I'd take a meeting with her agent to appease her, that's all. I wasn't going to leave you. And even if I had…Christ, Elliott…we're talking about murder!"

Elliott released a shuddering breath and stared down at the knife in his hand. Then he looked at Carter again with wounded eyes. "You were supposed to be at the afterparty that night. Both of you. I came here to look for the contract in your study, to see if it was really true. Bianca found me there. That piece of Eurotrash always looked down on me. She thought I wasn't a big enough name to rep you. It'd be a feather in her cap if she could bring you to CTA. She was so smug about it, taunting me, telling me I was through—"

Disbelief turned Carter's stomach. "You *killed* her for that?"

"I should've just let her go. I wish to God I had." Elliott's words were strangled. "But I was high and I was angry! The shears were on your desk. I took them and I went after her. She'd gone into the bathroom." He swallowed hard, his eyes filling. "Then you came upstairs."

Carter had been collateral damage. His lungs burned with the betrayal. He glanced quickly behind him to Quinn. She remained motionless on the shower floor. His heart raced, his throat dry. He raised the shaft, ready to swing it to keep Elliott away.

"What're you going to do?" he demanded, jaw squared, his throat tight with revulsion. "Stab me again? It won't be so fucking easy this time!"

An electric moment passed. Then, to Carter's shock, Elliott dropped the knife. It clattered to the floor.

"I'm tired. I…can't do this anymore," he whispered. His features collapsed. With a sob, he stumbled from the room.

Carter couldn't follow. He had to stay with Quinn, get her help. He returned to the shower and, kneeling beside her, he picked up his cell from where he had shoved it out of the water's way. As he dialed 911, he saw Quinn's eyes were open again, her chest still rising and falling shallowly. Carter heard the roar of the Aston Martin's powerful engine in the garage. Tires screeched as it pulled out.

A dispatcher spoke. "What's your emergency, sir?"

He gave the home's address. "I need help! I've got a woman in her early thirties. I think she's suffering from heat-stroke!"

"Is she breathing?"

"Yes, but she's in and out of consciousness." He touched Quinn's skin, which had cooled under the water stream. "I've got her in a cold shower, but—"

He ducked, startled by the boom that came from somewhere outside, nearly shaking the house.

"Sir, I heard a noise. Are you still there? We have paramedics en route."

"I'm still here." As he spoke, he got to his feet. He moved quickly to the gym's threshold and looked out through the open garage. The car was at the bottom of the rear driveway. He could see only its taillights and smoke rising through the boughs of an ancient black oak.

His muscles went weak. Elliott had driven into the tree at high speed.

"I have a second person who's injured." He passed a hand over his eyes as he returned to Quinn. "There's been a car accident on my property. No, I'm sorry, I don't know the driver's condition. I'm staying with the woman." He sank again to his knees beside Quinn, touching her face, his heart constricting. She moaned softly. "Please just tell me what to do to help her."

CHAPTER FORTY-TWO

Carter nodded somberly to the police officer stationed outside the hospital room before entering. Elliott lay in bed, covered with a blue blanket, his left wrist handcuffed to the bed's railing and his right leg in a cast. He had been staring absently out the window, but upon seeing Carter, he swallowed heavily.

While he had failed to kill himself, he had broken his leg and ruptured his spleen. The deployed airbag had left contusions on his face. He had been hospitalized for the past three days. Upon release, he would be in the custody of the LAPD.

"I'm surprised to see you," he said, subdued. "If the situation were reversed, I wouldn't be here."

Carter's jaw clenched. It had taken a lot for him to come here, but he needed answers. He had spoken with the police, trying to piece together what had really happened last November. But there were things only Elliot could tell him.

"How's Quinn?" Elliott inquired carefully. "Not that I have a right to be—"

"You don't." Tension tightened his body. Every time he thought of what Elliott had done to try to keep his secret, what he had nearly gotten away with, he felt sick. He thanked God he had found Quinn in time. "She was released yesterday," he said finally.

Elliott let go of a contrite breath. "What about you? Shouldn't you be in New York right now?"

"I'm doing the remainder of the junket via Skype. Considering what happened, the studio grew a heart." It was absurd that after everything, they were having a business discussion. "I'm escorting Quinn back to Rarity Cove this afternoon. I'll fly to New York next week for the premiere."

Elliott nodded, not making eye contact, instead staring at the IV line attached to the back of his tethered hand. A hollowness in his chest, Carter studied him, trying to see beyond the outward shell of the man he had thought he knew to the killer underneath. His heart hurt. It was still unbelievable Elliott had been capable of such violence and deception.

"There must be a reason you're here. I can't imagine you're concerned for my welfare. You probably hope I rot in prison." His voice thickened. "For what it's worth, I hope that, too."

Carter didn't respond. Instead, he dragged over a chair and sat beside the bed. "I've been talking to the detectives. Kelsey Dobbins told them she saw someone fleeing my house that night. But with her schizophrenia and history of stalking, they dismissed it."

Elliott had grown still. Carter knew he had told the detectives he had used the hidden drive in the rear of the property that night. He had parked there, which was why his car hadn't been visible when he and Bianca had arrived home. When asked how he had left no shoe prints at the scene, Elliott had confessed he had removed his shoes and used a towel to wipe his prints from the floor before fleeing, leaving only Carter's behind. He had carried the shoes and bloody towel out with him. During the time it had taken emergency responders to make it up the canyon road, Elliott had been able to leave the property. And while his fingerprints had been in multiple places in the house, including on the shears along with Kelsey's, the police had cleared him since he had been a frequent visitor. Carter gave a slow, disbelieving headshake. He felt disgust. "You were at the hospital with my family. You *comforted* them. You sat vigil with them in the ICU."

When Elliott finally spoke, his voice was halting. "You weren't supposed to *live*, Carter. Not after what I did to you. I was sure you were dead." Eyes watering, he appeared reflective. "I was freaking out. I went back to my condo and somehow managed to get inside it without being seen. I washed the blood off me and hid my clothes in the trash. While I was doing it, a doctor from the ER called. You had me listed as your emergency contact in your wallet. He told me you'd been brought in but your condition wasn't good and he doubted you'd make it. He advised me to get in touch with your family."

Carter tried to tamp down his hurt.

"I…decided to play it out," Elliott said quietly. "I had to make things appear normal. I called your brother, and then I went to the hospital."

"And when I *didn't* die?" He felt a pain in his throat. "I could've identified you at any time."

Elliott sighed. "When it started looking like you might make it, after all, I packed a bag and went to Mexico. I was down there for two weeks, living on tequila and blow, trying to come to terms with what I'd done. I was keeping up with things online. I knew you were out of the coma. But when the reports kept talking about Dobbins being the attacker, I knew something was up." He moved his hand, the cuff clinking against the bedrail. "I called your brother, told him I'd had to go out of town and was checking to see how you were. He told me about the memory loss and that the doctors believed, with the extent of your injuries, you'd never remember anything. They labeled it permanent retrograde amnesia."

"So you came back." Carter's eyebrows drew downward. "You accepted the risk that one day I'd remember."

Elliott shrugged. "I loved being an agent. When I landed you, things started getting even better. I couldn't believe you'd signed with me instead of one of the big agencies. I loved the money, being a part of the glamour." His voice hoarsened. "They were my other addictions."

Carter figured the cocaine and alcohol had become Elliott's coping mechanisms against the possibility he would be exposed should his memory ever return. But it still seemed crazy he had come back and waited in plain sight, never knowing if or when his world might implode.

"You were *more* than an agent to me." Carter couldn't help it. His voice quavered. "I…thought of you as a friend."

Elliott took a deep, pained breath and closed his eyes.

A thickness in his throat, Carter rose from the chair. "I hope you get the help you need in prison. Good-bye, Elliott."

He walked to the door, but Elliott spoke his name. He turned back to him.

"How do I live with this? With what I did?"

His heart heavy, Carter left the room.

***

"I'm taking it easy, I promise," Quinn assured her mother

over the phone. Nora had flown to California as soon as Carter had gotten hold of her to let her know what had happened, but she had returned home once Quinn was out of the woods.

"We're flying back to Charleston this afternoon, but with the time change, it'll be pretty late when we get there. I'm not supposed to drive for a while, but you can come see me tomorrow, if you want."

As she walked from the bedroom into the cottage's living area, her eyes met Carter's as he entered. He had been out all morning, attending to business before they left town. Quinn had been packing while she talked to her mother and hadn't heard his car pull up outside. "Mom, Carter's here now. I'm going to go…I will. I love you, too."

Once she disconnected, Carter leaned against the doorway and shoved his hands into his pockets. "Did Nora ask about me?"

She smiled at his humor. "She made a point of *not* mentioning you, actually."

His dimples deepened. "I'll win her over eventually." He grew more serious. "How're you feeling?"

"My headache's better, but the light's still bothering me a little." Quinn absently touched the bandage that covered the ugly bruise at her temple. In addition to mild heatstroke, she had suffered a concussion. Except for when he had stepped out of the room to speak to police, Carter had been at her side in the hospital the entire time. She recalled him at her bedside, teary-eyed and emotional. Once back on the East Coast, she would still have to go through some follow-up neurological testing.

"We really don't have to travel today if you're not up to

it," he said.

"I'm ready. I'll wear my sunglasses."

There wasn't much left to do. They were both packed. The flooring repairs in the main house were underway, and the property would go on the market once they were completed. Carter's furnishings and other belongings would remain in place until the estate sold.

"How's your shoulder?" she asked as he came closer. Quinn had learned he had carried her out of the sauna, a feat she wouldn't have thought his shoulder was ready for. But she supposed adrenaline had kicked in, and he'd done what he had to in order to save her.

"The ibuprofen and ice helped last night." Gently cupping her jaw, he lowered his mouth to hers for a slow kiss. When their lips parted, Quinn looked into his eyes and saw a somberness there. "What is it?"

He sighed softly. "I went to see him."

The admission made her chest tighten.

"I had to," he said. "I had questions, and I needed closure."

Quinn knew it couldn't have been easy. Seeming to want to change the subject, he took her hands in his. "I have some other news. I made an offer on the house in Rarity Cove."

Her eyes widened in surprise. "When?"

"Yesterday."

She thought of the beautiful beach home. "You just up and made an offer on the house? Like it was as simple as buying eggs or toothpaste?"

He shrugged, nonchalant.

"I didn't know it was even for sale," Quinn mused.

"It wasn't, but I made an offer, anyway—one the owner

couldn't refuse. It's ours."

For a moment, her voice failed. "Ours?"

"I know we talked about taking this one day at a time." His sapphire-blue gaze held hers. "But I *want* a life with you, Quinn, out of the spotlight as much as possible. I'm going to take steps to slow down this hamster wheel I've been on. I'll have to be away some. I'll still have to travel for filming and promotions, but Rarity Cove is going to be my home base from now on."

Her stomach fluttered.

"I'm not rushing you. I know you're waiting for the divorce to be finalized. I just want you to know how serious I am, and when you're ready, I'm ready, too. Buying the house might be an impulse move, but I thought it was the right thing. It was starting to feel like our home."

Hopefulness brimmed in his eyes. He stood there, tall and handsome, in front of her. Only a few months ago, she had thought of Carter as arrogant and spoiled, the grown-up, famous version of the teenager who had broken her heart. She couldn't have been more wrong. She knew him now for the man he had become. He was generous and protective, kind-hearted and compassionate. Qualities that transcended what the world saw on-screen.

And just as he had needed her to help him recuperate, she had needed him, too. She still did. Quinn felt a pang inside her. She dared to believe she always would.

They *could* do this, couldn't they? It would be crazy, but they at least deserved to try. Joy bubbled in her laugh. "I can't believe you bought the house."

His movie-star smile was dazzling.

EPILOGUE

Seven Months Later

"Uncle Carter!"

Entering the house, Carter dropped his suitcase and carry-on onto the foyer's floor as Emily and Ethan swarmed to greet him, a barking Doug on their heels. Surprised by their presence, he laughed and caught Ethan in his arms and hoisted him up as Emily excitedly told him about the jigsaw puzzle she and Quinn were working on in the kitchen.

"It's over three hundred pieces! Aunt Quinn says when we're done we can glue them onto a board so I can hang it in my bedroom like a picture."

As Emily talked, Carter's eyes met Quinn's as she appeared from the kitchen's arched entryway. Like it always did, his heart warmed upon seeing her, his mouth curving into a smile. He had been away for the last six weeks filming *The Rainy Season* in Vancouver, Canada.

"Hi," he said to Quinn.

She smiled as she came closer. "Hi, yourself."

He set Ethan back down. "Em, how about taking your brother into the kitchen? I want to talk to Quinn. We'll join you in there in a few minutes, okay?"

"Can I have a cookie?" Ethan asked as Emily led him away.

Quinn briefly laid her hand on the little boy's dark head as the children passed by. "Just one, Em. Dinner's in a few hours."

"You have cookies?" Carter's eyebrows raised once they were alone. "When I'm here, all you have are wheat grass and chia seeds."

"Funny. Samantha sent the treats. They came with the kids."

He walked to where Quinn stood. She looked beautiful in the fall sunlight filtering in through the wall of French doors. It had done nothing but rain in Vancouver, and he had missed the mild fall weather here.

He had missed Quinn more. She had flown up for two weekend visits while he had been filming, but it hadn't been enough. He spoke as his lips brushed hers. "Not that I don't love my niece and nephew, but what're they doing here? I was hoping to have you to myself."

"Samantha had something she needed to do, and with Olivia and Anders still in Europe, I offered to take the kids since I only had morning appointments." Quinn had opened a small, private physical therapy practice in town, just a few doors down from Café Bella. Being self-employed allowed her to set her own hours. "I didn't realize you had gotten an earlier flight."

"I wasn't sure what your schedule was like, so I arranged for the St. Clair limo. Besides, I wanted to surprise you."

"You did." She touched his chest. "We're having dinner at Mark and Samantha's, by the way. Mercer and Jonathan will be there, too. They came in for the weekend."

"I don't suppose we could just skip?" he suggested good-naturedly.

"You've been gone for six weeks. Everyone wants to see you."

"What about what *I* want?" His words were husky. "I want to take you to bed and make love to you."

Despite the sensual flare he saw in her eyes, Quinn hushed him, not wanting the children to overhear.

She turned to the kitchen, but Carter caught her hand, growing serious. "I talked to David this morning." He saw her tense at the San Francisco attorney's name. "He heard through the grapevine the trial's been set for November fourteenth. It'll probably make the news tomorrow."

It had been a long time coming, but Jake Medero had finally been indicted—in federal district court for felony interstate stalking, although the state's attorney here had decided not to pursue conspiracy attempted rape charges.

"There's more." He'd held off on telling her because he wanted to break the news in person. The bounty he had offered for information on the gang member who had crashed into Quinn and assaulted her on the beach had finally paid off. "They found the gangbanger in Atlanta. He's in police custody and being extradited here. He flipped on Medero—things are about to get worse for him." At her visible unease, he lowered his voice. "We're a step closer to putting this behind us, honey."

She gave a faint nod. Carter thought at times she would prefer to just have the whole matter dropped, that the restraining order was enough as long as Medero continued to obey it. But things were in the hands of law enforcement now. Unfortunately, media attention would surround the trial, putting Quinn back in the spotlight. But they would get through it together.

Emily called for Quinn from the kitchen.

"I'm glad you're home." Her eyes shone with affection. "I've missed you." She glanced down to the dog, who sat at Carter's feet, tail wagging. "So has Doug."

As she went into the kitchen, Carter walked to the foyer for his carry-on bag. He brought it to where Quinn and Emily sat at the island, puzzle pieces spread over its top. The puzzle was only a third completed, but he could tell the colorful image was of Charleston's Rainbow Row. Nearby, Ethan nibbled on a cookie, which had caught Doug's attention.

Unzipping the bag, Carter withdrew souvenirs from Vancouver—a snow globe for Emily and, for Ethan, a pint-size hockey stick and plastic puck imprinted with the logo of the Vancouver pro hockey team. Both children expressed their delight. His cookie forgotten, Ethan began knocking the puck around on the tiled floor with the stick.

Quinn smiled and shook her head. "Samantha's going to love you for that."

"This is for Nora." He extracted an exquisite jade bowl. "I bought it in an art gallery in British Columbia."

"Brownnoser," she teased. Over these last months, Carter had worked his charm on Nora. She also seemed pleased to have her daughter nearby, even if she still didn't approve of their living together.

Emily shook the snow globe, sending white and silver flakes over the miniature skyline of Vancouver. "What does Aunt Quinn get?"

Carter handed an elegant box about the size of a stick of butter to Quinn. "You might want to open that alone."

"Why?" Emily craned her head as Quinn lifted the box's lid just enough to peek inside. She closed it again, emotion passing over her face. His heart filled as their gazes held.

Emily continued to peer inquisitively at the box. "I want to see! What is it?"

"That's a secret for now," Carter told her.

***

"Do you think they'll ever come back?" Mercer asked jokingly, referring to Olivia and Anders's honeymoon trip that was well into its second month. She was in the kitchen with Samantha and Quinn, the three having cleaned up after dinner while the men had gone onto the porch. "They've had time to see about every square inch of Europe."

Samantha placed a glass-domed cover over the remains of the fluffy coconut cake she had served for dessert. "I think it's sweet. It's nice they're taking a trip like this while they're both still in good health."

"Which reminds me, do you have a date set for the move yet?" Quinn inquired of Samantha. With Olivia moving into Anders's home in Charleston, she had offered the Big House to Mark and his family.

"Not yet." Samantha wiped crumbs from the counter with a cloth. "Not until Olivia comes back, since we have to figure out what she's taking with her and what's staying or going to be sold. I'm really not in any hurry, to be honest. I love living here. But when Ethan came along, we started getting a little cramped. The move just makes sense."

Quinn thought of the white-columned home. It was elegant and spacious, but she could also understand Samantha's reluctance to leave the picturesque bungalow.

"I know you're happy to have Carter back. We all are."

Samantha added lightly, "Although I have a bone to pick with him about that puck and hockey stick."

Quinn merely smiled and took a sip of her herbal tea. Despite the time he had been away from Hollywood while he had been injured, Carter was taking another extended hiatus now that filming of *The Rainy Season* was completed. With the exception of being called to the West Coast for reshoots or post-production work, he wasn't committed to anything else film-wise until the following summer. While the new talent agent representing him had argued against it, Carter had passed on another highly anticipated movie slated to film in the spring.

Jonathan entered through the front door and headed into the kitchen. His cancer was now fully in remission. "Just coming in for another beer, ladies. Don't mind me."

Quinn liked the way his eyes crinkled when he smiled.

Mercer gasped and laughed when he unexpectedly swung her into his arms, pulling off a few steps of a Carolina shag before releasing her and heading to the refrigerator.

"We should cut you off," Mercer called as he retreated back outside, amber bottle in hand. She gave Quinn and Samantha an exasperated look, but she was also beaming. "Thank goodness I'd already put down my wineglass."

Children's play-filled shrieks, as well as barking, came from the home's rear. The dog wasn't Doug, who had been left at home, but a Lab mix the family had adopted from the local shelter several months ago.

"I better go check on that. We're about done in here, anyway." Samantha slipped down the hall. At nearly the same time, Mercer's cell phone rang. She took it from her purse on the counter and looked at the screen. "I need to take this," she said to Quinn. "Do you mind?"

"Of course not."

Phone to her ear, Mercer walked farther into the living area. Not wanting to eavesdrop, Quinn left her teacup on the counter and wandered onto the porch, where Mark and Jonathan were engaged in conversation. Carter wasn't with them. It was mid-October, but the nighttime air was still warm and held the invigorating scent of ocean brine.

"Quinn," Mark said upon seeing her. "Carter was just updating us on the center. I knew you were on its board, but I didn't realize how involved you've been with it."

She nodded. "I've been having some say on the facility."

It was one of the other things she'd done to occupy her time while Carter had been away. Construction on the fitness complex specially equipped for vets with disabilities would begin in February. Carter had given a million dollars to the cause and was also lending his time to a public fundraising campaign. The center was being built in Charleston, with hopes of opening others around the country if the concept took off. Carter's funding of the facility, as well as Quinn's physical therapy experience, were the reasons she had been given a seat on the board.

"Where *is* Carter?" Quinn asked.

Mark nodded to the sand dunes and the path that ran between them to the beach.

"Is he okay?"

"I think so. He just said he wanted to go down to the water."

Excusing herself, Quinn left her shoes on the porch and followed the path Carter had taken, a star-filled sky above her and cool sand between her toes. Upon seeing him at the shoreline, she quietly observed him as he watched the water. Her heart lifted. He looked so fit and strong. Over the last seven months, with the exception of the time he had been away, Quinn had gradually shifted her role from therapist to personal trainer. Other than the scars that remained on his body and a slight diminishment of the fine motor skills in the fingers of his right hand, he had fully recovered, at least physically. She worried Elliott Kaplan's betrayal had affected him much more deeply than he let on.

While they still had to face Jake's trial, there would be no such ordeal for Elliott. He had died of cardiac arrest just a few weeks after Carter's visit to him in the hospital. An autopsy had revealed a weakened heart. Whether it had been caused by his escalating alcohol and drug use, or the stress of living with what he had done, they would never know.

She made her presence known, walking up beside Carter and slipping her fingers inside his.

"What're you doing?" she asked, the wind whipping her hair. "You look lonely out here."

"Far from it." His profile was illuminated by the moonlight as he looked out. "I've got the fullest life of anyone I know. Sometimes I just need the quiet to appreciate it."

"That's one of the reasons I tried to teach you meditation."

He chuckled. "It didn't stick. Just being out here, though, gives me peace of mind. It's my own form of meditation."

Turning to her, he tenderly rested a hand on her stomach. "You're going to be showing soon."

Quinn thought of the gift Carter had brought her from Vancouver. It wasn't for her, really. It was a silver spoon for their baby. It was clichéd perhaps, but she knew Carter intended to give his child everything he or she could want. Quinn worried about another miscarriage, but she had made it much further with this pregnancy already. Going off birth control had been something they had discussed, although she had gotten pregnant much more quickly than she had expected. Her pregnancy, in fact, was the main reason Carter was taking more time off from Hollywood. He didn't want to miss any of it. If everything worked out, she would have the baby in the late spring, two months before he began filming a thriller in New York City. Quinn would close down her practice temporarily, and she, the baby and Doug would go with him and stay at his apartment in Manhattan.

"You're at twelve weeks. I've heard that's the magic number. Have you told anyone yet?"

"Just Mom." Nora had always felt left out, so Quinn had wanted her to know before the St. Clairs. Her mother had agreed to keep the news secret until Carter's family was told. Nora still could be difficult, but it seemed she was trying. She was seeing Emily regularly and was planning a trip in a few weeks to Tennessee to visit the Pickwells and Kents.

"What does Nora think?"

"Well, she's excited about another grandchild—"

"But she thinks we should be married." Tucking several strands of her hair behind her ear, Carter looked into her eyes. "Did you tell her that's what *I* think, too?"

"We've had a reason for waiting," she rationalized. "We only found out a few weeks before you left for Vancouver."

"I'm back *now*." He touched her face, his voice soft. "I know what you're thinking, Quinn. You're afraid marriage will jinx us. Your parents' marriage didn't last, and whatever it was you had with Medero was a disaster." He pressed his forehead briefly to hers, then looked into her eyes again. "That's *not* going to be you and me. And we've talked about this. It might be the Hollywood thing to do, but I don't want to have a child and just live together." His voice grew rough with emotion. "I want our baby to have a perfect life. I want *us* to have a perfect life."

He stood so close she could feel the movement of his breathing. Carter had come to know her so well. She didn't speak for several long moments.

"If we do this…I want to keep it small and private. And I don't want to walk down some aisle in front of everyone, looking like a whale."

"We'll have it as soon as you want. *Tomorrow's* fine with me."

Quinn laughed softly. "That might be a little *too* soon, but I appreciate the enthusiasm."

"Seriously, whenever you want it, Quinn." His fingers tangled with hers. "I'll marry you anytime and anywhere. We can have it in a church or at the hotel, or even right here on the beach like Mark and Samantha did. We'll swear everyone to secrecy so the media doesn't find out."

Her pulse quickened at the decision they seemed to have made. Looking up at him, Quinn could hardly believe this was her life. That she could love someone as much as she loved him. She had concerns about a child growing up in the spotlight, but Carter had promised they would do everything to keep their lives as private and as grounded as possible.

"I think it's time we told everyone while we're all together," he pressed gently.

"What about Olivia and Anders?"

"We'll call them and put them on speaker. It's their own

fault for lazing around Europe. I'm going to explode if I have to hold this in much longer."

Her heart bumping inside her chest, Quinn finally nodded.

"That's my girl."

His smile was infectious, chasing away any lingering anxiety. Quinn felt hope and anticipation for their future. Wrapping his arm around her shoulders, Carter kissed her temple. The roar and crash of the ocean behind them, they walked back to the bungalow to share their news.

ACKNOWLEDGMENTS

Thank you sincerely for reading LOW TIDE. As always, my readers are the reason I write, and I'm so appreciative of your ongoing enthusiasm and support.

There are several people I would like to thank for their assistance with this book. They include Kimberly Melvan, DPT, SCS, CSCS, CKTP, who readily answered endless questions about physical therapy to help me more accurately depict her occupation. I'd also like to thank my copy editor, Joyce Lamb; critique partner, Michelle Muto; and beta reader Katherine Knight. Kathy opened herself to many invaluable character and plot discussions on our morning walks with our dogs.

Finally, thank you to my husband, Robert, for your unending patience, love and companionship, and for always being my shelter in the storm.

ABOUT THE AUTHOR

Leslie Tentler is also the author of BEFORE THE STORM, FALLEN and the Chasing Evil Trilogy (MIDNIGHT CALLER, MIDNIGHT FEAR and EDGE OF MIDNIGHT). She was a finalist for Best First Novel at ThrillerFest 2012 and is a two-time finalist for the Daphne du Maurier Award for Excellence in Mystery and Suspense. She is also the recipient of the prestigious Maggie Award of Excellence.

Leslie is a member of Romance Writers of America, International Thriller Writers and Novelists, Inc. A native of East Tennessee, she currently resides in Atlanta.

If you enjoyed reading Leslie's work, please consider leaving an online review, however short. Of course, simply telling others you enjoyed this book is also sincerely appreciated. Word of mouth is the best promotion.

Visit Leslie and sign up for her newsletter at
www.LeslieTentler.com.

Other Works by Leslie Tentler

Before the Storm

Fallen

Midnight Caller

Midnight Fear

Edge of Midnight

Made in the USA
Middletown, DE
19 June 2017